Flutter

Flutter

Gina Linko

Random House ⌂ New York

Text copyright © 2012 by Gina Linko
Jacket art copyright © 2012 by Colleen Trusky

Visit us on the Web!
randomhouse.com/teens

Educators and librarians, for a variety of teaching tools, visit us at
RHTeachersLibrarians.com

Library of Congress Cataloging-in-Publication Data
Linko, G. J.
Flutter / Gina Linko. — 1st ed.
p. cm.
Summary: Although doctors want to treat 17-year-old Emery Land for the seizures that define her life, she runs away from the hospital in the hopes of uncovering the secret behind her "loops"—the moments during her seizures when she travels to different places and moments in time.
ISBN 978-0-375-86996-9 (trade) — ISBN 978-0-375-96996-6 (lib. bdg.) —
ISBN 978-0-375-98636-9 (ebook)
[1. Convulsions—Fiction. 2. Near-death experiences—Fiction. 3. Future life—Fiction.
4. Love—Fiction. 5. Runaways—Fiction. 6. Fathers—Fiction.] I. Title.
PZ7.L66288Flu 2012 [Fic]—dc23 2011049637

Printed in the United States of America
10 9 8 7 6 5 4 3 2 1
First Edition

For Zoe, Maia, and Jack

The Loop

It is bright. I try to shield my eyes from the sun, but my hand moves clumsily. I'm thick, awkward in the loop. Dad looks much older. What's left of his hair is silver, his bald head covered with age spots, his eyes warm and alert, yet wrinkled at the corners.

"We scientists don't like to be without the answers," he says.

"I know," I say, thinking of my pink notebook back home, with so much unverifiable data scribbled in each entry. In the back of my mind, I'm semi-aware of a thousand questions swirling around, begging to be asked, so many facts and hypotheses that I need to run by Dad, now that I'm finally with him again. But as usual when I'm here, serenity rules. I'm calm, in the moment. Zen.

I take in a deep breath of the crisp spring breeze coming off the river and smile. We sit on our favorite bench in Setina Park overlooking the water and the university buildings. The stone fountain flows on the far side of the park, and a gaggle of white geese sun themselves on the nearby lawn. The skyline looks the same as it does in my home loop. I'm sure in the years between then and now, there have been changes, buildings added or demolished, changes in the landscape of downtown Ann Arbor. But I can't pick them out. It looks the same to me.

"Things are going to happen soon," Dad says.

"What things?" I ask.

"Different things." He considers this. "I know about the boy. Your boy. You have to help him."

"I do?"

Dad nods then, and I notice the wrinkles under his chin, on his neck. The brightness of the day shadows over for a moment, as a large bird flies directly above our heads. The thwack, thwack of its wings reverberates in my eardrums. I look up and see the gray-blue heron as it lands not ten feet from us, folding its wide wings close to its body.

Dad watches the heron too, but he continues, "You will be scared."

"You're kind of freaking me out here."

Dad just smiles.

The heron stands in a regal pose, its long neck and beak pointed directly toward us. It's staring right at us, I think. Like it knows something. It watches me and walks slowly forward, now only three or four feet away. The bird seems oddly close, unnatural in how it watches me. I kind of want to reach out and poke one of its

black, beady eyes. I'm uneasy here in the loop. This is new, weird.
Usually, my loops are pleasant, good.

Dad ignores the heron now. "You will think you can't do what
you have to, but you can," he says. "Maybe not anyone else, but
you can, *Emery."*

I tear my eyes from the heron and gaze uncertainly at Dad.
"What's going to happen?"

"Soon," he says. "Just remember that you can do this."

I feel pride swelling in my chest then, competing with some-
thing else. Fear? Unworthiness?

I reach my arms toward Dad, but I feel awkward and can't
lean in exactly right. My body seems rigid, my joints stiff.

Dad hugs me. I lay my head on his shoulder for a moment. He
smells different, this older Dad. He must've changed his after-
shave. *I look over Dad's shoulder to see the heron, but it is gone,*
down near the shore. I see the colors then, a prism in my peripheral
vision, and I know I'm going.

For a split second, I raise my head to look at Dad, suddenly
aware of this lost opportunity—Do we find the answers? Do we
figure it all out? Do I get control soon?—but there isn't time.

"See ya," I say.

Dad smiles.

I'm gone.

One

"The loss of oxygen, however temporary, however minimal in the grand scheme of things, is taking its toll." Dr. Chen spoke in low tones, but she knew I was listening.

"What was the length of this episode?" Dad asked. Present-day Dad. Distant Dad. Emotionless Dad.

I turned toward the window then and tuned them out. This *episode* had been long. The loop had been long, and I knew it.

They knew it too, I think. My body was having a harder time coming out of it. I could tell. My breath was still uneven in my chest, and I had been awake and back here for over an hour. My double vision had stopped, but still I knew that it was getting worse.

When I was younger, when I was little, I barely noticed

the physical effects of looping. It was just my brain, my thoughts, left with all these odd little questions about the other places, the other people, my other lives.

Back then, I thought I was normal. I thought the loops were normal. Daydreams.

But I started to put the pieces together when I was about six:

"Her eyes flutter when she sleeps, Jonathan. We need to talk about this." Mom's lips were pressed together, and she had that fist at her hip, her elbow cocked out in that funny way, the way that always told me she meant business.

"REM," Dad quipped. "Particularly vivid dreams." He didn't look up from his newspaper.

"Seems more than that," Mom answered, watching me carefully as I drew with crayons at the kitchen counter. "And the stories she tells."

Uh-oh, I remember thinking to myself. I knew they were not dreams. Mom knew this too, I think. Part of me wanted to run and hide under the butterfly bedspread in my room, but the other part of me, the part that was on the cusp of grasping that something different, something important, was being addressed or at least circled, wanted to stay. Even then, I guess I was hungry for answers.

"Tell him how I knew about your old doggie, Mom."

"Jonathan," Mom said sternly. Dad looked up from his newspaper then.

"Tell me, Emery," Dad said. "What are you dreaming?"

"He only has three legs, and he has one black spot on his eye. He likes to play in the water. On the beach." I looked at Mom. She nodded, urging me to go on. "He goes under the water and stays for a second. You get afraid, Mom, like he's drowning. But then he pops up."

It was silent for a moment while my parents traded looks, and then Dad said, "I'm sure you told her about these memories, Veronica. She's seen the pictures."

Mom shook her head. "Emery, tell him about how Bailey lost his leg."

"Well, he got his leg caught in a squirrel trap in the woods. It had metal teeth." I made a big chomping sound, my teeth meeting with a click.

"I thought it was just a car accident," Dad said.

"So did I. That's what they told me," Mom said, eyeing Dad hard. "But I just asked my mother about it earlier. Emery's right. Bailey gnawed himself out of the trap. Limped home. My parents concocted the whole story because they thought the truth was too violent."

"Maybe your mom told her," Dad offered. But Mom just looked at him, shook her head.

Dad studied me, like he was seeing me for the first time. And I knew, even at age six, that something important was going on. That I was different somehow.

I think I scared Mom back then.

I remembered how her eyes had narrowed at me when I had been about to tell my grandmother, Nan, about the loops. From then on, I just instinctively knew it was all a secret. That had been when I was about seven, right before Mom died, before it was just Dad and me against the world.

Then, a few years later, I was fairly certain I had my episodes figured out. I chose my words very carefully, and I explained to Dad that I was jumping the space-time continuum. And I think I finally scared Dad too.

I listened to the beeps on the monitors and let my eyes unfocus in the low-lit room, all the glowing numbers and blips fading into a blurry cloud of blues and greens. I bit down on what was left of my thumbnail and closed my eyes, swallowing hard. I turned back toward Dad and Dr. Chen. I took a deep breath and summoned my courage.

"You know it's a loop, right?" I said. "Tell me you're considering it."

"Emery, of course—" Dad began, running his hand nervously through his thinning hair, his eyes avoiding mine. The gesture angered me. He was brushing me off.

"You're going to go bald," I said, wanting to hurt him. Something.

"What?"

"In the future. Someday. I saw it." I hated how childish I sounded.

"Sweetheart, really—"

"Don't *sweetheart* me." I tried to sound stern, but I was tired, and my voice was uneven, shaky.

Dr. Chen surprised me then, pulling up a chair and

sitting next to my bed. "Emery, of course we are considering it. It's just that we have to consider all the options in front of us. It's not that we don't believe you." She was younger than some of the others. And she looked at me a little more like I was a person and not just a lab chimp.

She was the one who had brought me that article from the *New England Journal of Medicine* that one time, when I had mentioned the new research on homeopathic controls for epilepsy: passionflower, skullcap. At the time, I thought she had done it to show me that she was on my side, possibly believed me, and maybe she had for a moment.

I looked at Dr. Chen now. "If you believed me, you would test my theory and quit shutting me down. I mean, what's wrong with you people?" I locked eyes with Dr. Chen. "Help me convince him," I said, gesturing to Dad.

Dr. Chen's eyes met Dad's, and I hated the understanding that passed between them, the silent agreement that I was wrong. But worse than that was the pity. A fresh wave of exhaustion washed over me. I gave in to it, let my head sink into the pillow, and let the urgency of being understood fold in on itself inside me. It was always there, an uncomfortable weight in my chest, a bitter seed.

Dad rose from his chair, signaling the end of our conversation. "You are our number one concern," he said, shaking his finger at me. The same finger that had wagged at me when he had caught me painting with nail polish on my bathroom wall or smuggling green olives under the table to Pancake.

His number one concern and a significant scientific breakthrough. I was sure Dad could already see his byline on the *Harvard Medical Review* abstract or the *Time* magazine article.

I closed my eyes then, signaling to them that I needed to rest. But I added one more thing.

"You were there again, Dad. Today."

Silence. He didn't believe me. I knew that. I heard him whisper something to Dr. Chen. The scratching of a pencil on paper.

I was exhausted from my loop and from having to keep up with the differing feelings that I had for my father. How could the future version of Dad be so supportive when the present-day Dad was everything but? It opened up too many questions. Was Dad destined to become that version of himself at Setina Park, or was that just one possible path? Too many big questions I had worried about for too many years. The truth was I just didn't know.

I glanced at the pink notebook on my bedside table. Part of me wanted to record my data before I drifted off. I usually did, almost always. I thought about the stacks of filled-up notebooks in my closet at home. Where had it all gotten me? No closer to control, no closer to understanding it, proving it, owning it. No closer to the big question. Why?

I heaved a deep sigh and let my body relax, my eyes close. I could record my information in the notebook later. I would wait to write down my encounter with Dad, his warnings, the uneasiness.

"You were there," I said again to Dad stubbornly.

I was drifting off to sleep and to whatever else, but I knew the look that had been exchanged between Dr. Chen and Dad. I had seen it many times before.

My eyes fluttered. I saw the crisp, pale blue of the hospital room wall for a moment. It looked cold. I felt cold.

I closed my eyes.

I felt the exhaustion wash over me and my body relax.

I began to seize again. In a moment, my eyes rolled back and my body stiffened. My breath came in fits and starts. Then the smell of ammonia. And I was gone, in a flash, back to the loop. Back to my other . . . my other me . . . my other places. My other times.

My Boy

Ammonia. I open my eyes, and I'm there—this time with the boy.

"Hi," I say.

He smiles back at me. He must be nine or ten, gangly, all teeth and ears. I think briefly that I should ask his name, but it doesn't seem important. I'm already feeling Zen.

I blink a few times. The colors are bright, as always. It's sunny, very sunny. Cheery. Happy. We are on Next Hill again, by the well. Clusters of clover bloom in the grass around me, and I can smell them so clearly.

I raise my head and breathe in a big gulp of fresh air, and I feel the calming buzz of the loop wash over me. A soothing, electric sensation radiates through my core, my limbs, my head. I'm content, serene.

The boy takes my hand then and pulls me up. I realize for the first time that I must have been sitting. His hand feels exactly real in mine, a small, tanned-from-the-sun hand grasping my own.

The grass is knee-deep here on the hill, and I take in the view of the farm below, the red barn, the blue-and-yellow farmhouse, the multiple outbuildings. Everything beautifully maintained. A picture postcard. I think briefly of when I first met the boy down in that red barn, where he showed me many of his treasures: the Victrola, the early windup jukebox—antiques to me, yet marvels to this young boy in this past time.

My boy yells, "Come on!" and yanks me in the opposite direction from the barn. He takes off toward the stream at a good clip, pulling me after him, and my legs feel rubbery, heavy, less coordinated than they do at home.

I trip. I stumble a bit and then find my rhythm. He laughs and pulls me faster. I'm slow, thick, as I always am in the loop.

But I am here.

We are at the stream, and he lets go of my hand and kneels down. "There!"

I crouch down, miscalculating the incline of the stream bank, and land on my butt. I laugh and then see what it is that he's showing me.

"Tadpoles!" I say.

He takes a jar from his knapsack and dips it into the stream, attempting to capture a few of the tiny fish-frogs.

I dip my hand in the water and try to swish the little tadpoles into the jar, but my movements are awkward. I watch the boy gracefully scoop the jar out of the water, and then he's sealing the top in a moment. He smiles at me.

"They'll be frogs soon," he says.

"But right now they're just happy to be swimming around, aren't they?" I say. "Look, that one is starting to grow feet!"

"Heavens to Betsy!" the boy says with a laugh.

I find this funny and giggle, watching the smile on my boy's face. We stare at the four little tadpoles swimming in the jar for a long moment.

A cool breeze catches my hair, and I watch as the boy takes his jar up the bank a few feet and settles in the tall green grass, sitting cross-legged, a serious look on his face, a look of concentration.

I turn to join him on the bank and lose my footing. I trip and land on my knees in the shallowest part of the stream. The water is cold on my skin. The bubbling and gurgling of the stream, which has been in the background, registers in my ears now. Through the clear blue water, the stones on the bottom are many shades of greens and blues and grays. A fish swims quickly by and startles me.

It is then that I stand up, and out of the corner of my eye, I see a movement in the stream, at the farthest point of my eye line. A slinking blackness on the surface of the water. A shape, a motion that seems a bit unnatural. Shadows, but not really. Instantly—oddly—I think of an old black-and-white movie being projected onto the surface of the stream.

I don't like the way the water moves on my skin now. I have

goose bumps, and I don't like how the sun has gone behind a cloud. I don't like the stillness on Next Hill or the look on my boy's face either.

I feel a bit on edge. I think briefly of Dad in the other loop and the heron.

I look again at the surface of the stream. All I see is the clear, pale blue. I think of the hospital room wall then.

I steal one more glance at the boy's face. He looks serious, almost grim. The colors come in my peripheral vision now—I see them like a prism, feel them there, and I know I'm going.

"Can you help me?" he pleads.

"What?" I say, feeling the familiar thrum begin behind my eyes.

"Please, help me," he says.

"I'll be back," I say.

"Esperanza," he says. And now he smiles.

And I am gone.

Two

The intercom clicked on, and then I heard the nurse's voice. "Did you need something, hon?"

"No, I just accidentally hit the button," I answered, rolling my eyes at myself.

The intercom clicked again. "Emery, you didn't eat any of your breakfast."

"Loretta, it smelled like pickled eyeballs."

"Do you need some chocolate?" Loretta's voice asked.

"No thanks," I answered. But then I thought better of it, pushed the button again. "Something with peanut butter." Loretta laughed her crazy, loud laugh, and I heard it in stereo, over the speaker and through the open door of my hospital room.

"I'll bring you a snack in a while." Loretta didn't know

what was wrong with me, but she was pretty sure it could be cured with chocolate.

I flicked the power button on the side of my laptop and sat myself up more comfortably in the bed. I opened up my pink notebook and recorded the date, the time of my last two loops. I described them clinically, scientifically, avoiding emotion and sentiment. But it was difficult to be that way, now that my loops were becoming something *more*. They were usually calm—mundane, really. Just my boy and me fishing in the stream behind his barn, snacking on blackberries, not talking much. Or a very old and very bald Dad teaching me how to drive a stick shift on some nameless country road, snorting with laughter while I ground the gears and swore under my breath. And sometimes it was just me. Me sitting cross-legged in the sand, staring out at the surreal turquoise water, running my fingers through the clean white sand. Me eating ice cream in my backyard. Me alone with a feeling of completeness. A feeling of calm. These were normal loops.

Requests for help, warnings from Dad, these were new developments. And even though there was no official scientific term for *freaked out*, that didn't mean I wasn't feeling it.

I stared at the last sentence in my notebook. *Esperanza.* I wasn't sure, but I thought that in Spanish it meant "hope." I grabbed my laptop, searched for the meaning. There it was.

I was right. *Esperanza* = "hope." I wrote that down in my notebook, circling and underlining the words. What did my boy want me to glean from this?

I sighed. I wasn't too familiar with hope lately. The Spanish or English version.

What did my boy mean by it? Did he *hope* that I could help him? Why the Spanish version? I remembered the fleeting panic in his eyes when he asked if I could help him.

Then I wrote down one more word: *scared.*

I closed the notebook and my computer, and shoved them onto my bedside table, my vision finally beginning to clear from the loop, the headache shrinking. I looked around my room.

Long-term patients—lifers, as some called themselves— liked to bring things from home, make their rooms more comfortable, more personal. Heather down the hall had recently gotten permission from the board to paint a mural on her wall.

I stared at the blank, pale blue of my walls. There were no knickknacks. No pictures. No signs of life.

This would not be my life. *Could* not be my life.

I had planned to leave this place many times. I made the decision constantly, on again and off again in my mind, but had never actually left. I thought that . . . that they would eventually believe me. They didn't. They wouldn't even listen.

I would give Dad and the team one more chance, and if it didn't work, if they didn't do a one-eighty and believe me wholeheartedly, well, then I was going to leave.

I pushed away my hospital blankets and climbed out of the bed, nearing the window to get a good look at the Ann Arbor sky. It was blue and sunny—clear and bright, the trees bare and vulnerable, bracing for the upcoming winter.

It had been a long time since I had felt free and young and not so exhausted. I thought about the possibility of hiking down by Brock Point or riding my bike out by the lake. I thought of last fall, how Gia and I had gone to a Halloween party near the lake with a handful of kids from school. We had carved pumpkins and toasted the seeds over an open fire. Gia's pumpkin had definitely looked a lot like Johnny Hatfield, her old next-door neighbor. It was the gap in the teeth.

I laughed at the memory.

That seemed like a lifetime ago. The loops were taking so much out of me now. Only months ago I had spent my days at Loganbridge Academy, at the ballet studio, being normal—or quasi-normal—with only my nights captive to the loops. But now I was too worn, too wiped out to even leave the hospital some days. Things were obviously getting worse, and getting worse quickly.

I had had such high hopes for figuring this all out when Dad had proposed the "team" to me, the study. I had been so happy to have someone, anyone, listen to me and even half believe me that I had jumped at the chance.

Nights at the hospital? No problem. How naive I had been.

As I pondered my looming final face-off with Dad and my team of doctors, I started to wonder which I wanted more: for them to finally believe me or for me to just pack my bags.

Maybe I could start midsemester at school.

No, that was crazy. I was in no physical shape for anything, really. I knew that.

Maybe Nan and I could finally go visit Monet's bridge, go to Giverny, paint it ourselves, like we had talked about for so long.

I decided to get some breakfast after all. *Maybe eggs,* I thought as my brush got tangled in my curls. I caught a look at myself in the mirror. I looked the same—same blue eyes and red hair, same fair skin, same long, slightly off-center nose, just like Mom's. Nan always called it elegant.

But I looked different somehow. Beaten.

I slipped on my robe, and once I was convinced I was at least hospital-type presentable, I walked out into the hallway and pressed the elevator button.

A few of the newer nurses stared a bit. I was used to it. I knew I was the freak on the grounds. I waved over to Loretta at the nurses' station.

I rode the elevator down to the cafeteria, aware that I

had my arms crossed over my chest the whole way. Everything was so squeaky-clean, so shiny. So very clinical. Even the elevator buttons looked free of smudges and smears and signs of life. I didn't want to touch a thing, as if becoming familiar with my surroundings would somehow mean I was accepting my fate here.

"Emery!" I heard the familiar squeal as soon as I stepped off the elevator.

"Gia!" I leaned in a bit and tried as always not to seem awkward when Gia gave me her requisite hug. Gia is a hugger, unlike the Land family. But she is my best friend—my only friend, really.

"I didn't know you were coming! Does Dad know you're here? How's school? How's Xander's class—"

"Emery!" She gave me another hug and pushed me out at arm's length. "You look like hell."

"Thanks," I mumbled. "You look great too."

She moved us toward the cafeteria line and hooked her arm through mine. I was instantly lighter in her presence.

"Gia," I told her, "I'm so glad you showed up. I needed a visit."

"That's what your dad said," she replied, popping an apple slice in her mouth from the salad bar. She was wearing her dark hair flatironed, stick straight. And she had the same old sequined cat's-eye glasses. She wore dark, skinny jeans and lots of silver bracelets.

I pulled my robe tighter as we grabbed our breakfasts. *I'm dressing like one of them,* I thought, wincing.

"My dad called you?" I asked. This was new . . . curious.

"Texted me, actually," Gia said, lifting her eyebrows. "Can you believe it? Dr. Land and the twenty-first century."

"Next he'll be getting hair plugs and a spray tan," I joked. We laughed and made our way over to a table near the kitchen door, and I sat down, trying to smooth my flyaway hair into some kind of shape, knowing it was useless.

"So, give me the details. What's new at school?"

"Emery, I think I'm in love."

"Not again," I answered, not even looking up from putting ketchup on my eggs.

"He's gorgeous and emo but not too emo, no guyliner or anything. Turtlenecks but no wallet chains. You know what I mean."

I nodded, smiling, glad to have the distraction. "Just no guys with hair dye, okay? All goth and moody, writing bad poetry."

Gia was already on to the next topic. "Mr. Phelps, the health teacher? Well, he's been canned because of the whole blogging thing. I'm sure you heard about that?"

I shook my head and buttered my toast, listening to Gia recount all the news. It was so good to have something close to normal to talk about. But I also felt that familiar snaky coil of envy in my stomach.

I wanted Gia to have all this fun. I wanted this for her, but I wanted it too.

"What's up with Julliard?" I asked her.

"I got the audition, Emery!" Her eyes danced, and I reached across the table.

"You do? When? I knew you would. I'm so happy for you!"

"January. The week after Christmas break."

"You rock, Gia! That is awesome, really." I could feel my eyes tearing up. I couldn't help it.

"Emery?"

"I'm sorry, Gia. I'm sorry. I'm happy for you. I am. It's just . . ."

"I know. How are you? We need to talk about it."

"It's okay."

"Emery, you don't look good."

"I know."

"And I know everything is top secret, double-oh-seven and all, but I'm here and your dad called me, and I can see that—"

"They don't believe me."

"The team? I know."

"I've been thinking of quitting it all. Leaving," I told her, not looking up from tearing the crust off my toast.

"I've heard that before."

"It feels different this time."

"How?" Gia grabbed my hand over the table and squeezed it until I looked at her.

"I'll be eighteen soon. I can go be somewhere else. . . ." And at the last instant, I added, "Or some time else."

"You can't control it," she whispered.

"Not yet."

"But you think you might?"

"It feels more physical lately."

"Yeah, it looks more physical, Emery. You look—"

"Gia, I know it's killing me."

"Emery, please! Ha!" Her attempt at a laugh sounded more like an accusation. She looked at my eyes for an instant but then looked away.

We sat in silence for a long moment.

"Emery, I wish—" Gia started.

"I don't think I want to die in a hospital bed having lived only for my scientific observers, data recorders, and data interpreters. Maybe I don't have too much time left. Maybe I just want to go . . . to be . . . normal. I mean, what did I used to do before Dad stuck me here? Before the meaning behind the loops became my whole reason for existence?"

"You worried about pimples and boys and did homework, Emery. It's not that great."

"But it's normal."

"You don't want normal."

"I don't know," I said. "I don't want to be a lab rat anymore."

"What *do* you want?"

I looked at Gia, attempted to lift my mouth in a smile. "To live. Really live."

"Emery, you—"

"I want choices."

Gia nodded.

"How did I get here?" I said, gesturing to my bathrobe and the bright white, too-clean hospital surfaces around us.

"That first crazy EEG when you were, what, twelve?" Gia said.

"That started it, I guess."

"I remember," Gia said, and began humming while she took a bite of her breakfast burrito.

And then I nearly choked on my eggs. There on the inside of her left wrist, Gia had a tattoo. Just a plain blue-and-black cluster of different-sized stars. Six or eight of them, a few dark blue, the rest a black outline with sky blue in the middle.

A tattoo.

How many times had we talked about doing that to-gether? How many designs had we drawn out together?

I put my fork down for a moment and rubbed my eyes with the heels of my hands, not wanting Gia to see that I had noticed.

I didn't know if I even wanted a damn tattoo anymore. They were kind of stupid, really. But who had Gia gone with? When did she go? Where? That place on Margaret Drive? Did it hurt?

I cleared my throat and went back to eating, tried not to make eye contact until I could calm down, not wanting to have to endure a conversation about this mini-betrayal that I felt inside. I knew to Gia it would be no big deal.

She lived in the regular world.

I tried to ignore the way my nose stung with tears that wanted so badly to break through. I rubbed the heels of my hands in my eyes again and focused on my plate of eggs.

Gia was still humming. That song from an earlier loop. The one that I had come to think of as *my* song.

Gia stopped humming and said, "I actually put that song down on some sheet music so I could play it for you on my guitar."

"Yeah?" I whispered, not trusting my voice, glancing up but trying not to look at her tattoo.

"Does it have any words?" she asked.

"All I can remember is the last line. You know, 'You're my home. You're my ho-ome.'"

Gia grabbed my hand again. "They're going to fix you, Emery. The doctors will find the answers, I think—"

"I've got my answers, Gia. I know what's going on. I just can't control it, or keep it from killing me—or making me a vegetable. But I know what it is. These past few years may not have proved it to anyone else, but I know what my loops are."

"What do you think needs to happen for them to believe you?"

"Maybe if I can demonstrate the wormhole," I said solemnly. "Or bring back a DeLorean."

"Or Marty McFly," Gia said, giggling.

For some reason, my mind flashed back to Ryan McClannis. I thought about his nervous gaze when he had asked me to the frosh-soph homecoming dance, how I had had to say no because it was being held on a yacht on Lake Michigan, with all the kids getting to stay overnight with chaperones on the boat. But I couldn't, of course. Because nights were off-limits. Nights meant sleep, which meant possible loops, which meant doctors, hospitals, and the little liquidy gel-probes stuck to my forehead.

I remembered that I had tugged at the cuffs of my long sleeves while I was talking to Ryan, rejecting him, trying so hard not to hurt his feelings because he was so nice and his left eye had this little nervous twitch, and I just couldn't bear for him to think it was because of him. Tugging at my sleeves had been my habit, to cover the IV marks on my arms.

I was fifteen then.

Gia took the last bite of her breakfast burrito, gave me a smile. Thank God for Gia. She believed because she couldn't *not* believe and still look me in the eye, she said.

It was so human and real in the land of the statistic, in the land of the report, the medical journal, the unyielding, all-powerful *beep, beep, beep* of the monitors and their untruth.

Gia checked her cell phone. I tried to hide my disappointment that she would be leaving so soon. But what did I expect? She had a life.

"It's eight-forty," she said, taking one last swig of her orange juice. "I gotta motor."

I looked at the clock on the cafeteria wall, behind Gia's head. "I think your cell is messed up. It's nine-ten."

Gia craned her neck around. "Heavens to Betsy! I'm late."

She got up with her tray, but I stayed at the table, kind of in shock.

Gia came back and gave me a quick hug. "Why did you say that?" I asked.

"What?"

"Heavens to Betsy." I was used to my boy saying things like that—"Heavens to Betsy" or "For the love of Pete." He had all kinds of old-fashioned sayings. But Gia? I was used to "OMG." "It's weird that you would say that."

"You're pale."

"I'm always pale. Why did you say that, though? You don't usually say that."

"I don't know."

I got up and emptied my tray, shaking my head. I walked with Gia to the door. "That's weird," I said.

"Okay, but not *that* weird. You look like you've seen a ghost." Gia squeezed my hand then and looked at her cell phone again. "I'll call later."

"Okay," I answered.

I stood there, in the sky-blue hallway, tying and untying

my bathrobe, thinking of my boy, remembering his plea for help. And all of a sudden I didn't care about the damn tattoo, or school, or being normal. I knew that something important was going on. My boy. I wished more than ever that I could control this damn looping, so I could go there right now and figure out what he needed from me.

It scared me to think he was in some kind of danger.

Three

That morning, after my breakfast with Gia, I came back to my room and found two Reese's Peanut Butter Cups on my pillow. I smiled and shoved these in my backpack, along with my laptop. I called down to the nurses' station, to let them know I was leaving. I needed a break. I changed into some jeans and a T-shirt, pulled my hair into a ponytail. Then Dad showed up. Unscheduled. Looking all kinds of worried, running his hand through his hair.

He didn't say anything at first, just sort of stood in the doorway. "Did I forget about some test or consultation?" I asked, shoving my feet into my boots.

"No," he said, but he sounded weird. Worried.

Something hit me then. Was there a breach? "I'm not

going public?" I whispered, seeing flashes of government agencies, E.T.-type secrecy, and me living in a bubble.

"No, nothing like that," Dad said, rubbing his temple in his uncertain way. "You shouldn't leave."

I got it then. Was he going to stop me from leaving? I actually laughed. "Dad!"

But it didn't feel funny. It was a breach after all, of our trust, or what was left of it, what hung so loosely between us, the last threads of what used to be so impenetrable.

"Dad, you . . ." I didn't finish.

"You don't know what the episodes are doing to you, Emery. I see the data."

"I live the data, Dad. I do know."

"We don't have time." Dad shook his head then. He had said too much, although he wasn't surprising me. He wasn't shocking me. I knew it all on some level.

This infuriated me. This whole situation was nuts. I needed out. A break.

Dad stood there for a while, scarlet burning on his high cheekbones. I caught a glimpse of him out of the corner of my eye as I found my favorite gray sweatshirt. I grabbed my iPod, my notebook. Dad looked the same, tall and reed-thin, but different too. He looked beaten a bit, shell-shocked.

The difference between him and me was that he hadn't accepted that the loops were probably going to kill me before we figured this out.

I had accepted this long ago. Once you are no longer

afraid, once you are no longer prisoner to the what-ifs and the if-onlys, there's a pocket of calm in the middle of the craziness. As if you can see things as they really are instead of just how you wish them to be, or how they could be, if this place—this life—wasn't so messed up, so contrary.

I needed to leave, and so that was what I did. I left. My shoulder brushed Dad's arm as I went past him, and I think I might have seen a bit of remorse there in his expression, a certain line to his lip. I wanted to believe that I was still his daughter more than his scientific conquest. I wiped a few tears away before they had a chance to fall, thinking of my future-dad in the loop, yearning for him to hurry up and learn his life lessons and turn into that man—the man who knew compassion, who knew empathy, who knew how to be more than clinical.

I asked the taxi to wait as I went up to the apartment and grabbed my pink gym bag, my shoes. Then I gave the driver the address of the studio. It was early in the afternoon, and I knew it wouldn't be busy until later, after school got out and little girls in tutus came twirling in for their lessons.

I sighed as we pulled up to the studio. Had it been so long since I had spent my days at an actual high school, my evenings teaching at the studio? It seemed like a lifetime.

Lucinda was out, so I had to use my key to let myself in. I changed quickly in the dressing room into a leotard and tights. I kept the studio lights low, and I sat on the hard oak floors and laced up my toe shoes, humming softly under my breath—Beethoven's Fifth.

Mom had taught me ballet, before she had gotten sick, before she died. I could remember the black see-through skirt she would wear over her leotard. I remembered running my fingers over it as a young girl, looking up at my mom, who could move so beautifully to the music.

I caught a glimpse of myself in the mirrored wall. An actual gasp escaped my lips. I looked like a ghost, like a shell of myself. I stood up straight and tall, and I put my feet in first position, arms at second. *I can almost see through myself,* I thought, and then rolled my eyes at the ridiculous idea.

My eyes were drawn, with gray-and-red rims. My skin impossibly pale, my flyaway red curls wispier than usual. My whole body seemed less solid, less opaque, less *here*.

I bent in a demi-plié, my hand on the barre. I began to stretch and feel the stress of the past few weeks dissipate from my muscles as I extended each limb. I was feeling a bit better already. This had been a calming ritual for me. A place where I always felt like myself. Ballet kept me in the moment, in the here and now.

I sat on the ground and spread my legs in a V. After stretching my glutes and my hamstrings, I sprang up quickly and did an arabesque, giving myself a confident smile in the mirror. I stuck my tongue out at my reflection.

And then it happened. The first time ever when I was completely and utterly awake.

My eyes rolled back for a millisecond; my leg muscles tightened. I fell to the floor, thunking my head hard against the barre on the way down. I saw a slow-motion version of my fall reflected in the mirrors, and the look on my face was startling. I didn't look scared. I didn't even look that surprised. I looked beaten. I looked—

I was gone again. Back to the other side, the loop:

Kaleidoscope

The cathedral is beautiful. It has a cavernous, domed ceiling painted with a blue sky and white, fluffy clouds. The stained-glass windows on either side of the mahogany altar are floor-to-ceiling, gorgeous, impressive artistic panels, not showing any biblical scenes but rather just a kaleidoscope of colors and patterns. I sit in a pew toward the front of the church, along with many other people, and stare at the stained glass, the many shades of greens and blues, some yellows. The colors and textures play with my eyes, giving the windows a 3-D effect. I raise my hand to shield the brightness of it all and feel out of sync with my body.

I want to see the stained glass. I'm agitated again, which is unusual in the loop. I take a deep breath and can smell the flowers from the altar. Lilacs. Just like the ones in the little boy's yard, on his farm.

I turn my head then to look for the boy. My eyes move slower in their sockets than I command them to, making me feel a little dizzy. I strain my neck and stand up on my tiptoes, still wearing my pointe shoes from the studio. I scan the faces around me as they sing along to a hymn I don't know, but I don't see the boy, not this time. And I really want to.

A young man in a dark suit plays the piano as the church-goers sing, and the song seems a bit familiar now but I can't place it.

The music fades, and I turn toward the middle-aged woman next to me. She has golden hair, a wide smile, a beauty mark just below her left eye. "Esperanza Beach," she says. I repeat it. "Esperanza Beach?" It's the same as what my boy said, but more. The woman nods. And I sense, feel the colors coming to the edges of my vision. And there they are, like a kaleidoscope themselves.

And I am gone.

Four

Lucinda found me seizing in the middle of the ballet studio floor at approximately three-thirty in the afternoon.

I was rushed to the hospital, given many drugs, including a shitload of adrenaline, and that saved me, I guess, because the nurses were all talking about it. Loretta had come in to check on me with a tearstained face, her rosary still in hand.

The first thing Dad said to me when I regained consciousness was that he had been able to get a short EEG reading while I was still in the loop. He hadn't missed any data.

God forbid we miss any data, I thought. My face crumpled, and I felt like crying, but I turned toward the window so he couldn't see me.

"This thing is getting too big, honey." Dad was talking

quickly and too loudly, like he always did when he got nervous. "Your EEG has changed drastically. We have got to keep you here. It's getting too big, Emery."

"This new variable is troublesome," Dr. Chen began as soon as she swept in. "Beginning from an awake state changes the entire flow of the study." She spoke more to Dad than me.

"Sleep apnea, clairvoyance, the blood pooling in her abdomen, are just not—"

I strained to sit up. "Excuse me here!"

A third doctor who I did not know joined them then. I felt the after-loop headache swell between my eyes. The doctors continued to speak to each other, and I was ignored. I let my head flop back upon the pillow and took in a deep breath. I could still smell the lilacs from my loop.

I had to leave. I was *never* getting out of here unless I did.

I sighed. I thought about the first time I had met the little boy a few years ago. And I remembered the book light.

I always brought my physical self, my physical being exactly as it was, through to the other time. I once had one of those little book lights that clip onto your book in my hand when I fell asleep, and it came with me. But I didn't bring it back.

He still has it, the little boy. He shows it to me sometimes, and we laugh about it. While I'm here with Dad and Dr. Chen—on my home loop, as I think of it—I realize that it would be fabulous, life-altering, and extremely pertinent for me to do something like just bring back that damn book light, just bring it back out of the loop.

But once I get over there, it's like I don't really understand the importance, the urgency. I change. I'm just . . . happy.

Of course, I've tried to bring other items with me over there—to do that at least for Dad, for Dr. Chen, to bring an object with me. But I haven't been able to. I didn't have all the particulars figured out.

Gia nearly fell out of her chair when I told her about the book light, about my loops.

It was during the National Honor Society blood drive at Loganbridge, at the start of the school year, right before I had to give up going to school altogether.

I had dislocated my shoulder for the third time in as many months, and Gia wasn't buying the I-did-it-dancing excuse again.

She was donating blood, lying in a big beige recliner in the school gymnasium, and I sat next to her, just keeping her company during our free period.

"Tell me, Emery," she demanded.

"Okay, it wasn't ballet," I said, keeping my voice low, my eyes flashing toward the rows of students in identical recliners around us. I scooted my chair closer. Gia leaned forward, enrapt. "Okay," I told her, taking a dramatic breath. "I'm having a rather physical affair with Mr. Lankey."

Gia threw her head back and laughed. "You dork," she

said, slapping me on the arm. And we both fell into another fit of laughter as Mr. Lankey, his comb-over, and his totally huge beer gut appeared down the row from us.

"Okay, Emery," Gia said, still not letting me off the hook. "Spill it. The truth this time."

I swallowed hard, measured what hung in the balance here. "When I'm sleeping, I sometimes . . . seize. Lately, the seizures are so violent, they've been dislocating my shoulder, and when I broke my wrist—"

"I can tell this is definitely closer to the truth," Gia said, sitting up straight, twirling her then-curly hair around her finger. "Does this have to do with why you can't ever do stuff at night? No sleepovers? No all-night cramming sessions? No nothing?"

"Yes," I answered, averting my eyes.

"So if it's just seizures, don't you take medicine?"

"They haven't found a seizure medication that helps me yet." *Because they aren't really seizures,* I added in my head.

Gia squinted at me. "Emery, you've got to trust me," she pleaded. "We've been friends since fifth grade. I deserve to know."

"Shhh," I hissed. "Keep your voice down." I adjusted the line of her IV, retaped it on her hand so it wouldn't bother her, wouldn't leave a bruise.

"And this," Gia continued. "You know way too much about this stuff." She gestured toward the IV.

"I spend my nights at the hospital, Gia. I'm sure you've figured that out," I whispered, feeling the sweat break out on my brow.

"Because of your seizures." Gia put air quotes around the word *seizures* when she spoke, and I chewed my thumbnail. She shook her head and turned away from me.

I sat there for a long time, knowing I shouldn't tell her, knowing she would never believe me, knowing that I had to heed Dad's warnings about telling anyone.

But something in me wanted to tell her. Something in me saw this as a chance to keep from being completely isolated. Completely alone.

And Gia knew what it meant to be alone, to be the one on the outside. I thought back to when she had moved here, when those kids in the fifth grade had designated her the odd man out, the geek, the outcast. Back before Gia had become Gia the Cool, Gia of the Cat's-Eye Glasses, Gia of the Razor-Sharp Wit, she had been the chubby new girl with no friends.

And I had stuck up for her. I had made the difference for her then, all those years ago.

I made a decision that day of the blood drive, staring at the back of Gia's head so obstinately turned away from me. A big decision. I decided to trust her, to let her come to my aid. To keep me from being all alone—falling too far down this hole by myself.

"I time-travel. I travel to the past, the future. That's what the seizures are," I blurted out. And I immediately regretted it. But I just bit my thumbnail and watched Gia's face as she turned toward me.

"Time travel?" she whispered.

I braced myself for her laugh, for her to squeal into giggles, but she didn't do anything. She just looked at me for a long while, squinting behind her glasses.

"No one believes me, not Dad, not anyone. But I *know*."

"What does your dad think it is, then?"

"Once I hit thirteen, I started having these . . . episodes . . . like crazy. And I started to have these bouts afterward when I couldn't remember stuff—"

"Like amnesia?" Gia offered.

"No, I would forget how to do these sort of automatic things—tie my shoes, stuff like that—after an episode. And then they started getting more violent, like with my shoulder, when I broke my collarbone a couple of years ago. Dad got interested then. My EEG showed completely unorganized, uncoordinated firings of impulses in my brain while I'm in the loop—when I time-travel. When Dad looked more closely at these EEGs, he found there was a pattern, just a new, more intricate pattern of chaos. Whatever that means. He thinks that my EEG in the loop demonstrates a higher kind of intelligence, a way to harness or capture a larger percentage of the brain's power . . . extrasensory power."

Gia nodded. She just looked at me and nodded.

I had opened the door to Gia. I had let someone other

than my team in on my secret, and the world had not stopped rotating on its axis.

"So what's it like?"

"It's . . . the same, but different. Brighter. Slower. Dreamlike."

"Couldn't it all just be dreams?"

"No." I shook my head.

"Why not?"

"I just know, Gia. I'm there. Physically in the loop."

The nurse started working her way down the line of students, and I knew she would soon be near us. I was nervous and exhilarated, but I half expected Dad to pop up from behind a curtain and steal Gia away and erase her memory like some crazy spy movie.

Gia sat up and leaned close to me. "So you can tell what's real—in your loop—and what's just a regular dream?"

"Yes, they are very different. The loop is as real as you and me sitting here," I said. "It could be *here* . . . just a different *time*."

Gia eyed me. "So do you see people you know? Me?"

"No. But Dad. I know him in the future."

"You're kidding."

"No, he's balder, grayer . . . nicer."

"Really? Do you ever see your mom?"

"No. I wish I did. . . . I go forward and back, past and future. There are people, places, that I go to more often than others, but not always. It's all very random and crazy. I can't control it. Yet."

Gia sat deep in thought. I knew she would have many questions, but the nurse was coming.

"So at night, much like a superhero-vampire, you don't have epilepsy, but you seize into another dimension?" Gia smiled, but I could tell she was teasing me, not judging.

I smiled back at her, and the nurse appeared to take out her IV. Gia got her Band-Aid, the requisite I DONATED sticker, and her free cookies, and we exited the cafeteria in silence.

"That's some freaky shit," Gia said finally on our way to physics class.

Nothing changed with Gia and me after that. Except that I trusted her with my secret and she kept it.

And I had a confidante. It was a total relief.

I rolled over in my hospital bed and shut my eyes tight against that memory, of a time when I had hopes of anything good. I kept my eyes shut against the reality of where I was, what I was doing here. Gia was probably off with emo-boy getting another tattoo. She was probably practicing her piano recital for Juilliard. She was most definitely *living.*

I reluctantly opened my eyes and saw Dr. Chen, Dad, and this new doctor planning my next steps, my next hours, my next days, the rest of my life.

"We can remove a fraction of skull and manually try

to reproduce these episodes by stimulating the temporal lobe. . . ."

"Her organs are aging. We could induce a coma state for thirty to ninety days in order to . . ."

Dad turned and looked at me for a moment. I let my stare bore into him. He turned his back to me then, whispering to Dr. Chen something that I couldn't catch. They whispered like that for a few moments, all serious and exclusive.

"Hello? I'm right here!" I said. I was trying for sarcastic, but all it came out like was pathetic, lonely.

Dad held up a finger toward me, indicating to wait. But I had done enough waiting.

If I was going to run, if I was going to be able to get my thoughts together and really figure out what I wanted to do with whatever time I had left, then I had to make a plan.

What did I want to do?

It was such a gloriously open-ended question, one that I hadn't let myself entertain for so long.

What did I want to do?

For starters, I was going to Google "Esperanza Beach."

Five

For me to escape—because that was what this was now, an escape—I knew I'd have to plan it and keep it absolutely top secret. No one could know anything. This was difficult because the newfound resolve that I had to escape was making me crazy optimistic.

It took me only like three seconds to find Esperanza Beach online. It was a town with less than five thousand people in the Upper Peninsula of Michigan, a mountain of snow in the winter, cold and gray, nestled into the freezing and unwelcoming shore of Lake Michigan, recording subzero temperatures all winter long, with a couple of ski mountains and several snowmobile trails. There was a lot of information about the UP, but not much about Esperanza itself. It was just a blip of nothing on the radar; even the Internet didn't care about this town.

But I did. And it felt good to have a purpose, outside of myself and my hospital room's walls.

The boy wanted me to go there. My loops were pushing me there. And I was anxious to go back to my loop and figure out exactly why, although I was all too aware that when I went to the loop, I often lost my resolve to do, well, anything, and I would just spend my time dancing, braiding weeping willow leaves, or eating a particularly well-made piece of blueberry pie in the meadow with my boy.

Esperanza Beach. I had to leave, I knew this. Now I had a destination as well.

The next day, I quickly got myself together. I researched the bus routes. I slipped out to the bank and withdrew a big chunk of my college account, forging my dad's signature. I flirted mercilessly with the young teller, batting my eyelashes, feeling like a moron, hoping he wouldn't study the withdrawal slip too closely.

In the end, I gave him a fake phone number, and he gave me my money. I stuffed the cash in my backpack and headed back to the hospital. I reminded myself that I would have to toss my cell phone and my bank card. I wouldn't want to be tempted to use them, because, of course, I knew they could be tracked. I bought a new notebook, a purple one, in the hospital gift shop, my pink one nearing full capacity. I threw a few magazines on the counter too, for the ride.

I was leaving—and soon.

The following morning, I found myself in a nondescript conference room within a nondescript medical research wing, facing my new research team: three new doctors plus Dad and Dr. Chen.

It was a briefing, complete with a PowerPoint presentation and red file folders marked for levels of clearance. Me, my loops, my total existence, were boiled down to bar graphs, statistics, and percentages. A recap for the old team and a summary for the new doctors.

They sat across from me at a long table. The lights were low and eerie in the conference room, and that really put me in a black mood. I also found it interesting that Dad chose to sit on the side with the doctors rather than next to me.

My case was confidential to almost everyone involved at the hospital. No one was allowed to know all that was going on, not nurses, med techs, orderlies. Only the core team knew everything.

"The variables have changed," Dad said as I took my seat.

"Yes, good morning to you too," I said blackly.

Dad ignored me and introduced the new members of the team.

"The fact that we have had one episode from a completely wakeful state, with little to no warning, means that we are going to approach things a bit differently, more aggressively," this new doctor with the impossibly shaggy mustache was telling me. Dr. Curne or Curtin, something. It didn't matter. I was leaving. I was escaping.

But I nodded and pursed my lips, knit my eyebrows, and feigned interest.

Dad watched me closely. I let myself imagine that he might sense something was off with me.

The tiny blond doctor now took over. "How are you, Emery?" she asked in a tiny voice.

This level of humanity took me by surprise. "Fine, thank you," I answered automatically.

"I've read much about you. You are a very bright young lady. I see here in this report that you are actually the one who brought the idea of time travel to the core unit here. That you are the one who explained the wormhole idea—the loop, you call it?—to the original team." She paused here and looked at me with a smile.

"Yes, ma'am," I answered. "There is a lot to the new theoretical physics of time travel."

"Of which you understand?" Dr. Mustache chimed in.

I glared at him. "I had plans to go to Yale next year, sir. If any of you had done your job, I'd be getting ready for that instead of sitting here. I think I can grasp the gist of a scientific abstract."

Blondie kept going. "Your physical state is suffering, of course, from the many episodes of low oxidation to the brain, to your temporal lobe in particular. We are especially wary of brain damage. Several organs are showing early signs of imminent failure. Your optic nerve has aged. You know all this, of course. However, your heart rate remains calm and normal throughout all of your recorded episodes, which leads us to have hope that cardiac arrest is not imminent. Although in most situations that closely resemble this one, the patient does have that risk at all times. . . ."

I nodded and bit my lip. I didn't want to tell them, but this bit of data, that my heart rate never changed dramatically, this information that so comforted the doctors, well, I think that had changed this last time. When I woke after the ballet studio, I felt my heart racing. But I wasn't going to tell them; I knew to them it would be a harbinger of death.

Dad caught me biting my thumbnail down to the quick. "Emery, tell us what you are thinking."

I threw them a bone. "The time that I left from the awake state, at the ballet studio, I didn't have my physical warning signs."

"What are these signs?" asked Dr. Mustache.

"The fluttering eyelids," Dad answered, his eyes still on me.

"We've recorded this each and every episode while she's been monitored," Dr. Chen added.

"I had no warning at the studio. And I didn't have the smell either."

Dr. Chen was writing madly on her paper, and she shoved this over to Dad.

"What is the smell?" asked Dr. Blonde.

"Emery says she usually smells ammonia as soon as she begins to loop," Dad answered.

I was comforted by the fact that he used the terminology *loop*, since mostly the doctors refrained from accepting anything that had to do with my theories.

I smelled lilacs, though, I almost told them. But then Dad added to the rest of the group, "The subject may be encouraging the sense-inducing behavior in order to have some stability."

I laughed under my breath—because Dad and Dr. Chen were writing back and forth madly on their legal pads, and I was reminded of why I needed to leave. Dad had just referred to me as "the subject."

"I'm time-traveling," I said. "Why can't we discuss this, research it, accept it?" My voice trembled, betraying me.

There was silence at the table. They were not taking me seriously. I knew this. I just had to give them one more chance. I had to give Dad one more chance to do right by me.

I watched the team shift around in their seats, averting their eyes. Dad shook his head then, and I saw him rub his temple nervously.

I could feel the tears coming to my eyes. But I willed them back.

And then I felt my eyelids flutter. A funny thought hit me the moment before I looped. I smelled the ammonia, and I wondered, when I did die, what Dad would miss more, me or my data.

The Dala Horses

I'm standing inside a tiny, one-room house . . . no, a cabin. The boy sits at the small kitchen table, tracing his little fingers over the cracks in the red Formica of the table. He smiles and motions around the room.

The first thing I notice are the horses. Dala horses, I think they are called.

I stumble a few steps over to the gigantic limestone fireplace and pick a horse off the mantel. It is cherry red with a flowery saddle painted on its back, all in primary colors. It is Nordic or Scandinavian, this I know. I think they are for good luck, good fortune.

The cabin is stark and clean, yet has a homey feel. A full bed in one corner has a handmade red-and-white quilt on top of it. The kitchen is tiny, with a sink, a small refrigerator, but no stove.

The focal point of the cabin is the fireplace. I sit down slowly and clumsily on the worn yellow love seat facing the hearth, taking in the room. Its one extravagance is the collection of Dala horses on all its surfaces, the windowsills, the mantel, the bookshelf. There are mostly small ones, only a few inches high, but there are also a couple of larger ones standing on the hearth, at least eight inches tall. They are all painted in blues and greens, reds and yellows. Their colors are bright, happy.

I decide I like the cabin.

"Hi," I say to the boy.

For a flicker of a moment, I want to ask the boy a million questions. For just a split second, I feel this utter urgency to ask him if there's something he wants, something he needs from me. But then the moment passes, and I feel serene, calm, enjoying the rustic-firewood and clean-sheet scent of the cabin.

The boy gets up and opens the cabin door. A freezing wind blows in. I shiver and the hair stands up on the back of my neck.

"You have to leave now. Before it's too late," he says.

"What's going on? Too late for you? How?"

"No." He shakes his head. "Too late for you."

He's gesturing outside. I see the snow, and then I realize the edges of the snow, the edges of my vision, are turning a rainbow of colors, and I am going.

My boy looks at me again. "I won't be there, but you'll find nine."

"Nine what?" I say.

Another gust of wind pushes a great swirl of snow into the cabin with us, and then I leave.

Six

I woke up much later in my hospital bed, the dark room glowing blue and green from the various monitors. I struggled to orient myself in the dark. My vision blurred, and my head throbbed. I vaguely remembered coming to, waking from my loop in the conference room. I remembered Dad offering me a drink of water, lots of hushed voices. I remembered sheer exhaustion. I must've been sleeping for hours.

Now I heard the unmistakable squeak of rubber soles on the scrubbed-clean hospital tiles.

My breath felt a bit ragged in my throat.

"Shhh, don't turn the light on," said a familiar voice as a figure appeared at the foot of my bed. Gia's face leaned into the light, toward me. "I'm breaking you out tonight. Get changed."

I smiled, felt lighter. She threw a pile of clothes at me and went and stood guard at the door. I slowed my breathing and called to the nurses' station, even as I was pulling the jeans on under my hospital gown. "Yes?" came a familiar voice.

"Sandy?" I said, yanking the electrodes from my scalp.

"Emery, do you want us to call your father?"

"No!" I answered a bit too quickly. "I'm awake now. I . . . I can't . . . um . . . sleep. I'm going downstairs for a . . . some . . . some milk and cookies."

Gia rolled her eyes at that one. "Okay," Sandy answered, probably flipping to the next page in her bodice ripper. Thank God Loretta wasn't on tonight. She would've seen right through me.

"Hurry up!" Gia hissed. I pulled the T-shirt on, slipped into some shoes, and grabbed a hair tie. "You can use my makeup in the car," Gia said. "We are going *out*."

We slid past the security desk, hiding my telltale hair under a cap on the way out, albeit a feather-covered newsboy cap from Gia's thrift-store days, but a hat nonetheless.

When we reached Gia's yellow VW bug, I was giddy with excitement.

"Where are we going?" I said, smiling at myself while I used the mirror to put on lip gloss.

"Look here," Gia said, and when I turned toward her, she brushed some blush onto my cheeks. She pulled out a mascara wand and expertly did my eyes.

"Did I tell you that Chaney is a *fraternity* emo-boy?"

"Oh, really," I said. "I didn't know they existed." I gave her a smirk, then stole a brush from her purse and worked it through my hair.

Gia took off toward the university neighborhoods. I switched on the radio. It had been such a long time since I had done any of this. Gia unrolled her window and started singing along with the music, as she always did. The clock said 12:45 a.m.

I felt alive. I unrolled my window too, letting the wind hit my face, blow through my hair. I leaned out the window, took a big breath of the chilly December air.

I began bopping to the beat along with Gia, and I saw the house party from a distance. It was unmistakable: kids on the lawn, the *thud-thump* of the bass music from the house resonating in my teeth as we got closer.

I felt a sharp pang in my chest when I thought about leaving Ann Arbor, about going to Esperanza, knowing Gia would care. I had gone back and forth, back and forth, over whether I should tell her.

Now I wondered if I could ever really leave her. She would be so mad. Boiling.

I looked over at Gia, who smiled back at me. She was my friend. A good friend. But she could never understand the many, layered reasons I had to leave. I decided I would keep Esperanza a secret.

We circled the block twice before we found a parking space, and once we entered the party, it was a smash of people, lots of supposedly manly cologne, college T-shirts, and the unmistakable smell of stale beer. I tried not to feel like a fish out of water. But although it was invigorating to be where I so wanted to be, with normal college kids—my peers, as Dad would call them—doing what normal kids do, I felt like all eyes were on me. And everyone was too close, everything was too loud, too intense.

I bit my lip hard, steadied myself against the stimulation overload, and tried instead to enjoy it.

Gia and I wound up on an old tattered plaid couch, each with a Coke. Emo-boy turned out to be handsome and dressed in all black, a striped scarf expertly placed around his neck, and a guitar hanging off his left shoulder. Everything I expected he would be. Gia was smitten, and I could see why.

"Hey" was all he said to me, raising his plastic beer glass in a greeting.

"Hey," I answered, but when car headlights poured through the front window, for a second, I saw his face in the bright light, and I thought maybe . . . maybe . . . I could see some eyeliner around his eyes. Emo-boy. I would tease Gia later.

Gia was chitchatting as usual, but it was hard to hear. I thought I heard emo-boy ask if I was *the one*. Then Gia shot him a look of the "shut up already" variety.

I caught a glimpse of Chaney's wrist as he took a swig of beer. Did emo-boy have a matching tattoo? I blinked and looked again. But his sleeve had slipped down and covered his wrist.

I was nervous. My palms began to sweat, and I had the overwhelming urge to leave. The party, packed with boys and girls my age, didn't seem so cool anymore. The girls with their too-tight T-shirts, their flatironed side parts, the boys with their combed-forward shags. Everyone was trying so hard.

This was not my crowd, would never be my crowd. Too much noise, too much motion, too many pairs of eyes peering at me, the lab rat.

I knew I could trust Gia. *Right?* She wouldn't sell my secrets out to some guy, even if he did have perfectly placed shaggy forehead hair, right?

I excused myself from the couch and went to the bathroom. I locked the door then, and I could still feel the *bang-thud* of the bass music in my fillings as I splashed some water on my face and my flyaway hair.

These were not my peers. Who was I trying to kid?

I was starting to feel . . . heightened. I knew. I was going to loop right in the middle of this party if I didn't leave.

I found Gia and dragged her out on the front lawn. "I gotta go," I told her.

"Are you okay?" she asked.

"No," I said. "No, I'm not. I'm going to loop right—"

"Emery, you're not. Just relax."

"I have to go, Gia. Take me home."

"Emery, it's good for you to get out. You said so yourself. You need—"

"To go home. Now."

"Emery, you need to—"

The thrum began behind my eyes then. "Gia, I'm going to seize and time-travel right on this fucking lawn if you don't get me out of here." I started for the car.

Gia muttered under her breath, "Your dad thinks that is an utter impossibility, you know."

I stopped and turned back, walking toward Gia. "What?" I said. I was sure I hadn't heard her correctly.

"Emery, please, you don't *really* think you are time-traveling."

I stopped dead in my tracks then. There it was.

She didn't really believe me.

I slowly turned around and walked toward her bug, my legs shuddering with adrenaline, anger. I grabbed the door handle and let myself in. I couldn't believe it. I shook my head against the tears. I couldn't believe Gia. But, of course, I could.

Gia followed to her side of the car. The drive back to the hospital was silent, the small space of the car feeling cramped and taut with what had now unraveled between us. "I'm sorry" was all she said as I got out of the car. I slammed the door without replying.

How could I have thought anyone cared enough to believe something so ludicrous? But the worst thing was that she had pretended. She had acted like . . . like I wasn't crazy. Like she had believed me.

And, really, as mad as I was at Gia, I was more mad at myself, at the world, at my loops. Why couldn't I just be normal?

As I rode alone in the elevator back up to my hospital room, I silently counted my blessings that I hadn't told Gia about Esperanza, that I hadn't ruined my getaway. I told myself to focus on that. To think of the adventure I was about to begin. It hit me that this might have been what the boy was talking about in my loop. Maybe I had to leave for Esperanza *now*.

Just as the elevator settled at my floor, I became conscious of the music playing over the speaker. I could hear the song clearly. I would have known it anywhere, although this was the first time I had ever heard it in my home loop, here, in this time.

I steadied myself, grabbing the door of the elevator as it opened to my floor. I held my hand against the door to keep it from closing, and stood there, staring up at the ceiling, up at the everyday, gray-metal elevator speaker, transfixed. I listened for a good thirty seconds or so as the song came to a close. The same lilting, graceful chords of an acoustic guitar, playing those same four notes as the song ended, the sad—yet somehow hopeful—voice of a male country singer finishing with the words I knew so well. "You're my home."

"My song," I said to myself.

In a few hurried moments, I was back in my room, clicking on iTunes, looking up my song.

Deep down, I think I had known somehow.

Even though I had been humming it, whistling it, and singing it since probably 2008, James Eugene Sawyer wrote it in 2012, recorded it in 2012, copyrighted it in 2012, and it was brand-new to iTunes this month.

I gasped, covering my mouth with my hand.

"How's that for time travel?" I said aloud to myself. My voice rang against the hospital room walls, a hollow, lonely sound.

Seven

I left unceremoniously early in the morning, the first Wednesday in December. I called a cab from the hospital, and I simply slipped into our apartment, with my dad gone to work, and packed my duffel bag and backpack with the necessities— some warm clothes, my painting supplies, my new purple notebook—and I left.

I was completely alone on this new adventure, probably my last, and you know what?

It didn't feel that different than usual.

The hum of the Greyhound bus lulled me toward sleep, but I fought it so as to hopefully keep from looping. We drove along Route 31 north, up to the Upper Peninsula, up toward my impending freedom. I pulled out my new notebook and turned to the first page. I dated it and wrote two words: *Esperanza* and *freedom*. Then I wrote it all down. I listed everything I knew about Esperanza, all the facts, and then I listed everything that seemed to be pointing me here from my loops, anything that might be construed as a clue, everything that had happened since my future version of Dad had told me that things were going to scare me, things were going to happen.

"Nine," I said out loud. "Nine what?"

I thought of the heron then for some reason, and I watched the scenery pass outside the bus window. Every now and then the bells in the Christmas wreath that the driver had fastened onto his steering wheel would jingle and jerk me from my thoughts, and I would catch a snippet of conversation here and there from the passengers around me. I tried not to eye everyone suspiciously, but I felt so close to being free. And I kept picturing a neatly dressed and blank-faced orderly suddenly appearing and toting me back to Dad.

I knew I was being overly dramatic. I shook my head and stared out the window, leaning my forehead on the cold, icy glass. I sensed the dip in the temperature, not only by the feel on my skin but by the way the wind whipped around us as we drove, making whistling and groaning noises, passing through various crevices and slats in the bus.

We drove over the Mackinac Bridge, and I figured we were getting close. The Lake Michigan waters were gray and unfriendly beneath us. Excitement swirled in my belly as we crossed that bridge, like I was entering a new world. I kind of was.

It took us about eight hours total to reach Esperanza, with all the other passengers having gotten off at their stops, save for myself and a little, blue-haired old lady. She offered to give me a ride to where I was going when we both got off at the small bus station. I politely declined, feeling like I wanted to do it all on my own. Plus, it was hard to find the words for what exactly I was doing here.

Yes, I was running. But it was more than that. I was being beckoned, called here. Of this I was absolutely sure. The boy wanted me to come here. So, yes, Little Old Lady, I'm running away from my mad scientist father, and I was told by a small boy in another time to hop aboard a bus and find this town. Want to help me out?

In the end, I asked the lady if she could give me directions to the town square I had read about. She happily complied, and I dutifully followed Savoya Avenue through a small residential neighborhood. It was only a quick two-minute walk, lined with modest homes—brick bungalows, larger trilevels. Lawns were clutter-free, the shrubs trimmed even in this cold season. And there were no paint-chipped houses, no screen doors with holes. This was a place that people took pride in. I liked it.

I found a stone bench on the edge of the town square,

and I dropped my duffel and my backpack. I took a deep breath. It was cold. But not scary, ridiculous cold like I had read about on the Internet. And there wasn't even much snow, just enough to make that homey crunching sound underfoot. But it was only December. If I was here in January, in February, I might then know what the term *cold* really meant in the Upper Peninsula. Would I still be here in January or February? Would I even still be alive?

I bit my lip hard and made myself think about the here, the now, what I was doing in Esperanza.

I looked around. The town square was picturesque, and, not for the first time in my life, I was reminded of the film *Back to the Future.* There was even a clock tower across the square from the bus station, atop what looked to be the post office.

A woman walked by in a yellow beret and yellow scarf, pushing a stroller. Two young children, boys, followed her, holding each other's mittened hands.

"Hello," the lady said as they passed.

"Hi," I answered.

I laughed to myself quietly as I realized that I was searching out the faces of each of the children, hoping that one might be my boy, that he might just skip up to me here in the square and tell me exactly what I should be doing.

A bakery sat across from the clock tower. HEAVEN AT BETSY'S, the sign read. FRESH EVERY MORNING.

My hand went to my mouth. I gasped. Blinked a few times to make sure I was reading it correctly.

"Holy crow," I said out loud, another one of my boy's sayings. I could not take this in. I mean, was this how it was going to be now? My home loop and my other loops crossing, intersecting, freaking me out? This would take some getting used to.

I stared at the bakery sign for a long time in disbelief. Finally, my stomach rolled over and got me moving, made me snap out of it. I started toward the bakery, deciding on a cup of hot chocolate and a donut, and I would ask there about a nearby motel, or maybe a bed-and-breakfast. Esperanza really did seem like bed-and-breakfast material.

Betsy's was warm and softly lit, the smells every bit as welcoming as I had hoped they would be. The bakery was small, mostly taken up by a large glass display counter, showing off cookies, éclairs, donuts, scones, cakes, and pastries of all kinds. I sat down at a little bistro table in the corner, next to a small Christmas tree complete with a pink satin ribbon garland. I smiled as I realized that each ornament on the tree was a miniature cake, cup of coffee, or something to do with the bakery. Elvis's Christmas album played over the speakers.

My pink frosted donut tasted light and sugary, melting in my mouth with each sip of hot chocolate. Two college girls sat at the table nearest to mine, their heads leaning toward each other, deep in discussion. I sighed then, trying to resist the feeling of betrayal that was washing over me.

Gia.

The woman behind the counter came over and asked if I needed anything else. "You should try a pasty," she told me. "We yoopers are famous for them, potatoes and vegetables, all wrapped up in a yummy crust," she said with a smile.

"Yoopers?"

"That's what we call ourselves," she said. "We live in the UP—so we are yoopers."

"Oh," I said, getting it finally. Duh. "Um, no thanks," I said, feeling her eyes upon me, feeling that sudden raising of my hackles, as if everyone was in on things with Dad and I had a tattoo across my forehead that read RUNAWAY.

"You're not from around here, eh?" she asked.

"No, ma'am," I answered, my eyes stealing a glance at the woman. She was tiny and round, with shiny, dark hair cut at her chin. JEANNETTE, her name tag said.

I felt my ears burn scarlet. Did I look like I was running away? I frantically searched my mind for some clue that I could have possibly overlooked, some sliver of information that might lead Dad to Esperanza Beach.

My hand shook as I reached for my hot chocolate, and the cup clanked against the saucer. The waitress gave me a concerned look, and then she patted my shoulder and let me be.

Get ahold of yourself, Emery, I told myself. *No one knows you. Dad's reach is not so long. There is no GPS chip surgically implanted in your hip.* The thought actually made me stop for a moment, but I pushed it away.

No one knew where I was. I was here on a mission, with a mystery to solve. And I was here to figure out what to do with myself, with my time . . . with my life, no matter how little might be left.

Jeannette looked like a mom, a charming, cherubic, smiley-faced mom. She wore a pink Christmas sweater, one with a large embroidered Christmas tree bedazzled with sequins and beads, as well as a white partridge perched at the top.

I steeled my nerves and lifted my face to the counter. "Ma'am?" I asked.

"Yes?" she replied, coming around to my table again.

"I'm new around here, and I really could use some help finding a place to stay. Something out of the way, or . . ."

"We don't have any motels, but over the Mackinac Bridge there's—" She tapped her chin. "Let me just give you the address of the Realtor down the street. He'll be able to get you something, I'm sure. How long are you staying?"

She was already writing down directions on her waitress pad as she bent her head over the counter.

"I don't know for how long. Maybe a month or two," I answered.

"I heard Roy Genk at the diner saying just yesterday how

no one's stayed at Dala Cabin in winter for months. Can't rent that thing—"

"What? What did you say?"

"Roy at the diner."

"No, the cabin . . . What kind of cabin?"

"Dala Cabin. It's a little place out by the lake, lonely. . . . Nearest neighbor is the lighthouse."

I felt goose bumps break out all over my arms now. This was weird. Beyond weird. "Dala? Like the little Dala horses?"

"Yes." Jeannette nodded.

Of course. The boy had showed me. "I want to stay there," I said.

Jeannette looked a little confused. "Well, I—"

"Will this Roy be able to rent that to me or—"

"I'm not sure, but—"

"I have to stay there," I said, feeling a rush of excitement, a thrill that, yes, these loops were real. Confirmation. I was right about all this, my loops, about coming to Esperanza, about being needed by this boy.

Jeannette gave me a quizzical look. "Well, sweetheart, sure. I'm sure Roy'd be glad to help you out if he can."

I realized I probably sounded a little crazy. But I smiled, and Jeannette smiled back at me.

I felt my heart beating a bit faster. Now I just needed to find the nine . . . the nine what? I was getting closer. The cabin was the first step.

* * *

I found the cabin easily, although Roy's map turned out to be quite useless. I felt all Nancy Drew, paying Roy in cash and giving him a false name. In the end, all I could think of was Emery Smith instead of Emery Land. I nearly laughed out loud as it came out of my mouth. I was sure Gia would've come up with something much more romantic—Emery St. Claire, Emery Monalisa.

I ended up asking for directions at the post office, and I got a quizzical stare from the gray-haired guy manning the counter. He had an underbite and the bushiest eyebrows I'd ever seen. I tried not to stare as he offered me a few simple directions to "catch" a footpath that would cut right out toward the lake. I just had to find Red Rock Creek, behind Winging Stables.

"Welcome to these parts, miss," he said. "Although I just don't know why a young girl wants to stay all alone out at Dala Cabin, eh?"

"Right by the lighthouse," I said, ignoring his question.

The man nodded and offered to give me a ride. I declined.

"We got a bowling alley here in town," he told me with a very serious expression.

"Okay," I said, unsure of the appropriate response.

"A nice one with electronic scoring."

I still didn't know what to say. "Okay . . ." We just stared at each other. "Thanks," I told him quickly, turning for the door, happy to be on my way.

The short trek through the woods was beautiful. Thick pines lined the footpath, a light dusting of snow beginning to fall as I walked. The moment I stepped into the forest, onto the path, a hush seemed to come over the place. The noise from the town square, the stables—traffic and voices—seemed to dissipate more quickly than it should have, and there I was under this canopy of pine and falling snow.

I heard the lake first, before I saw it. As I followed the path's easy-to-miss curve toward the east, I saw the lake and the lighthouse, just like I had expected, just like I had imagined it. It was gorgeous. I would have to paint it.

And there was the cabin. It was nothing special, a gray clapboard square with flaking white-painted shutters. But the location, the circumstance of this little cabin, it was extraordinary in that it was even here still, built too close to the bare, rocky shore, the Michigan winters having beaten the paint off three-quarters of the place with winds and water and life. If it stood here too much longer, I would be surprised.

Its little window looked at me, peered right back at me, as if it was waiting for me. It instantly welcomed me. I dropped my duffel and backpack in the clearing and ran up to the cabin, smiling. DALA CABIN, the sign said in blue letters, with little red and yellow flowers on either side of it. I traced the letters with my finger. I took a big breath of the brisk air and enjoyed how it burned in my throat. It was all mine.

I pulled my long scarf, hand-knit by Gia, up over my

ears and walked around the perimeter of Dala Cabin. I saw that there was a huge pile of firewood chopped and neatly stacked near the west wall, and I began to feel a bit nervous that possibly Roy had been wrong about the cabin, that someone else was already here. I could see footprints in the snow too, around the cabin, the woodpile.

I tried the door and it was unlocked. As I pushed the door open gently, peering inside, I held my breath and half expected an orderly to jump into my view and cart me back to the hospital. I took a step forward on the threshold of the cabin, and a small pile of icy snow dislodged from the DALA CABIN sign and fell right onto the back of my neck.

"Aaahh!" I screamed, unnerved. I wiped the snow off and stepped into the cabin, taking a deep breath. The place looked unused, lonely even. But it was just like I remembered it. Just like the last time I had been here. In the loop. In that instant, so much of my existence, my theories, my life, felt validated.

The air in the cabin seemed to let out a sigh, as if it had been expecting me.

The one room really was impeccable. Clean and well lit—homey, yet stark.

I laughed, a loud and startling noise, as I saw the red Dala horse on the mantel that I had picked up and looked at in my loop. I noticed a photograph too on the mantel, a photograph that truly looked like an advertisement for Michigan summers. The lake in summer, blue and glistening, with the cabin in the background, everything green and blooming.

I went back out to the clearing for my things. And then I dropped my backpack and my duffel right onto the hearth of the monstrous and beautiful fireplace and tiptoed around the little room. It smelled of coffee and earth, firewood and clean sheets. I was here, out of place, and stealing away a piece of this tranquility, but I so drank it up. Everything about the cabin calmed me instantly.

Everything about it told me I had done the right thing. *This is where I need to be right now,* I thought. At this time, this place was the right one.

I didn't know much about how things were going to go, about what exactly was in store for me, but I knew that being here, sitting down on this red-and-white-checked bedspread, felt right.

I let my head flop back on the pillow and smelled a clean, soapy scent from the pillowcase. I inhaled deeply, and that was when I saw the tiny drawings, on paper no bigger than index cards, all lined up on the west windowsill—seven of them. Each one better than the last.

I had to sit up and get a good look. They were each done in pen and ink, with many sharp angles and deep strokes: a sketch of the cabin itself, a blue heron—which I chalked up to coincidence—an empty bottle, a Dala horse, the heron again, and a portrait. It was a handsome young man, with a shock of dark hair and sad eyes. The last one, I couldn't quite figure out what it was supposed to be.

The most recent tenant must have been an artist, I told myself. If I had only known.

I took the last drawing back to the bed with me. I lay down and stared deeply into it. It was something very close up. There were lots of lines, scratching, the whole paper almost black with ink. I couldn't tell what it was supposed to be.

I turned it around for a fresh perspective. And then I saw it: a woman's face, agony, a scream. For a moment, it felt like the sound echoed in my ears.

It was unsettling. I folded the drawing in half and shoved it in my pocket. I didn't want to look at it again.

I spent the afternoon sleeping. I have always been one to need things perfectly perfect in order to fall asleep—a hard mattress, darkness—but not today. My sleep was oddly deep, undisturbed by loops or dreams or otherwise. I counted back. It had been at least seven days since I had slept a whole night without looping. This peaceful nap seemed like a good omen to me, a good start. Could stress have been triggering the onslaught of loops at the hospital lately? I thought about it. Maybe. Maybe the cabin would help me to decompress, give me some time to think and figure all this out.

After my nap, I walked back to town. I spent some time in Hansen's General Store, picking out just enough groceries that I could comfortably carry in my backpack, and I bought two Duraflame logs, knowing I had never paid enough attention in Girl Scouts to count on only the firewood at the cabin. I stopped in at The Stacks, a cool used bookstore. I realized while I was flipping through old vintage comics that my cheeks were hurting from smiling. I was smiling too much.

The walk back to the cabin was gorgeous. The amber-gray twilight gave the snow a magical glow. It surrounded me, not too cold, feeling like insulation, like a cushion against all things bad.

But I could feel just how much my physical self had been deteriorating. I was winded, tired, light-headed by the time I reached the cabin.

I fumbled a bit with my keys at the door, sucking on some Lemonheads that I'd bought at the market. But by the time I reached up with my keys toward the doorknob, the door was open.

I looked up, startled, dropping my Lemonheads all over the ground. Someone was standing in my threshold, just inside my cabin. A man. *Dad?* I thought immediately. But no, it wasn't him. Cowboy hat, jeans, his arms up in an "I surrender" position.

All of this registered in an instant, and I felt the whoosh and hum behind my eyes. I felt my eyes flutter, my body stiffen.

I was gone.

The Key

I'm trying to run, but I stumble over my feet. I fall onto my knees and push myself up on the heels of my hands, deciding to walk. I'm alone in a cornfield. I remember for only an instant that I should be terrified of the man in my cabin, but I'm in the loop, so serenity rules. I calmly walk through the corn rows, the stalks all taller than I am. I can't see where I'm going exactly. But I think I know.

Sure enough, I turn a corner then, right where I picture that I should, and I see him. My boy.

"You found me," he says.

"I did," I answer.

"Don't lose this," he tells me, and hands me a silver key.

I reach for it clumsily, my hands uncoordinated and heavy. "I won't lose it," I tell him. I don't think to ask what it is or why I shouldn't lose it.

I pocket the key, and the boy grabs my hand. We walk slowly toward the creek.

"They're frogs now," he says. I squint, and I can see two tiny frogs swimming in the shallow water near the edge. One hops onto the bank of the stream for a moment, and the boy bends down and catches it, watches it jump from one of his hands to the other. I marvel at how tiny it is. He lets it go, back into the water.

We walk down the hill toward the farm then, and we settle on a big blue plaid blanket under an oak tree.

He has a picnic lunch, in a real hamper with cloth napkins, with the most fantastic egg-salad sandwiches, tied up in brown paper and string.

I love the old-fashionedness of it all, and I sit down on the picnic blanket and smile. I like it here.

We eat our lunch together, talk about the go-cart he is building in his barn, and play tic-tac-toe. He beats me more than I beat him. After a dessert of fresh whipped cream and strawberries, I lie back on the picnic blanket.

I start to count the leaves on the closest branch of the hanging oak, feeling so content, but then the leaves blur. They begin to have fuzzy, oddly colored edges, rainbow colors, a prism in my peripheral vision.

I realize only then that I should ask what the key is for. I want to look at the boy and decipher exactly what period his clothes are from. I want to ask him about Dala Cabin, about the nine something. I want to ask him about Esperanza. I want to—

I'm gone again.

Eight

I came back abruptly and opened my eyes. I was lying on the bed, in what I had already begun to think of as my cabin. I suppressed the urge to scream, reliving the moment before the loop, seeing this man in my cabin.

I swallowed hard and looked to my left. And there he was—all large and broad-shouldered.

He sat in a chair at the kitchen table, his head bent over a small sketchbook. He was drawing intently. He hadn't yet realized that I was awake. I again swallowed back the urge to scream.

I watched him for a second, his large hand gracefully shading his picture. I looked at the line of his profile, his shock of blue-black hair. He was younger than I had first thought, not too much older than me. And somehow he didn't seem quite as menacing now. But I was still scared. I glanced at the door. I could be there in six steps if I had to, out the door. Had Dad tracked me already?

I swung my legs onto the floor, cleared my throat. Part of me wanted to yell at him to get out. Part of me knew I needed to thank him for . . . what? "Um . . ." I stood up from the bed, eyeing the door again. "I don't know you."

I startled him. He stood up immediately, his hands in the air in surrender. "I'm sorry. I'm not going to hurt you. I—"

"It's okay," I said, relaxing a bit, shaking my head. I rubbed at my temples and between my brows. My knees shook. "I figure if you had wanted to kill me or worse, I'm sure . . ." I let my voice trail off. I was so exhausted from the loop, from my trip. My knees buckled, and he crossed the room in a beat to steady me.

"I'm okay," I said, resisting his hand, his help.

"Clearly," he mumbled.

He turned and reached for his hat on the table. I was relieved that he was going to leave. "Mr. Genk gave me the keys this morning," I explained to him. "Did you just have the wrong cabin or . . . ?"

He looked at me then. Our eyes met for the first time. He started to say something, but then thought better of it.

He shook his head and hid his eyes once again under the brim of his hat.

He turned toward the door, then turned back one more

time. "I reckon you had some sort of seizure. Are you epileptic? I—" He shoved his notebook and pencil in his pocket. "Are you okay?"

"I'm fine," I answered. "You don't know my father, do you?"

He cocked his head to the right a bit. "I just had to make sure you were okay before I left. I—"

"Thank you," I said. "It happens sometimes. I'm fine, really."

"You almost cracked your head on the threshold."

"I'm really fine," I said, and averted my eyes. "I wasn't expect—"

"I apologize that I used your cabin," he began. His voice was surprisingly low, gruff. "No one was here, and I—"

So he was a squatter. I knit my brow then, began to bite my thumbnail. "Huh," I said, giving up and sitting back down on the bed. I was exhausted.

"I'm sorry, miss," he said. "I'll get out of your way here." He took a few steps and grabbed the doorknob.

"So you are the artist?" I asked, putting some pieces together.

"I am," he said, glancing at the drawings on the windowsill.

He turned the knob and left then.

I settled back onto the bed, pulling my knees to my chest. I let out a sigh, a lonely and quiet sound in the now-empty cabin. The air settled down without my visitor.

I closed my eyes against the headache swelling behind

them. I waited a few seconds and then got out of bed and turned the dead bolt on the lock. I pulled one of the kitchen chairs over and secured it under the knob, just like they do in the movies. I didn't really think it would be much of a deterrent, but at least I would hear someone who tried to get in. At least it would wake me.

So this guy was not a cowboy–bounty hunter sent by Dad, or so it seemed. But I wasn't taking any chances.

No more surprises today.

I flopped back onto the bed and thought of my loop. I shoved my hand into my jeans pocket and touched something cold, metal.

"Holy shit!" I pulled the key from my pocket as I sat up in the bed. I laid the key in the palm of my hand and stared at it. I rolled it around in my palm. I held it up to the light. There it was. Proof. It was silver and shiny and tangible. Real.

What Dr. Chen and Dad would give for that.

"I'm right," I said to the empty room around me. "I'm right about it all." I let out a sad, lonely laugh.

The first day of my last great adventure.

Nine

Morning broke with the sun streaming through the eastern window, glittering and glowing off the frigid-looking waves of Lake Michigan. I stretched and surveyed the landscape out my window. It was truly gorgeous. The lighthouse sat maybe a half mile down the rocky shore, the cabin's nearest neighbor. I watched for a while, listening to my iPod, as seagulls glided and dove for their morning breakfast.

I caught a glimpse of my reflection in the window, all crazy hair and sleepy eyes. But I was smiling, rested and ready to recapture the feeling that I was here, and this was a new start.

I put some water in the teakettle to boil and opened my notebook at the kitchen table, recording the events of my loop from last night, flipping the key over in my hand the whole time as I wrote. When I finished, I walked toward the west window, absentmindedly surveying the forest of evergreens across the clearing. And then I nearly dropped my iPod.

"What in the world?" I said.

He was out there. My cabin squatter. Folding a sleeping bag of some sort into his backpack. Turning his work-coat collar up against the wind. It was unmistakably the same guy. He stood up and put on his cowboy hat, and his silhouette against the early-morning sky, it was almost too much. Like a movie star on a set. But when he looked up for a second, I saw the serious clench in his jaw, and I reminded myself that I didn't know this guy. At all.

"Stalk much?" I let out a laugh, but it sounded nervous, out of place.

The fire pit glowed with now-dying embers. Had he stayed out there all night? And more importantly, why? Wouldn't he have just about frozen to death?

I was totally annoyed. Why did he think it was okay to stay out in the clearing? A prickly sensation of fear slithered up my spine. Who was he?

I watched him as he started for the evergreens. He took one look back at the cabin, and I shrank away from the window, the breath catching in my throat.

This is my cabin, I told myself. *I don't have to hide from him.*

I stood staring out the window after him. There was something . . . familiar about this cowboy, though. Something I couldn't quite put my finger on.

I shook my head and forced myself to forget about him, to focus on why I was here. I was here to figure out what to do with myself, how to help my boy, before Dad found me and I had no more choices.

I stepped away from the window and thought of Dad. He would've realized what had happened by now. He would be trying to find me.

Could I really do this?

"We can remove a section of skull. . . ."

The teakettle began to whistle then, and it startled me. I turned the hot plate off.

I gathered my clothes, deciding to take a shower and get started on figuring things out around here. I would begin my day by going into town, maybe to the library. I was determined to find out what this little boy wanted me to know about Esperanza Beach, what he needed from me. I could ask a few questions here and there. I knew that it was a small town. I knew that I would raise some eyebrows, and the last thing I wanted to do was draw attention to myself, but I had to start somewhere.

I made my way to the world's tiniest bathroom, off to the left of the kitchen. My bare feet crunched onto something on the bathroom floor, little pebbles, gravel almost. I looked down, squatted to see what it was, little and black, almost like bird poop. I scraped my foot clean on the metal edge of the shower, dropped my clothes onto the sink, and as I reached to turn the water on, I saw something I hadn't noticed the day before. I drew my hand back and screeched, "Ahh!"

The little creature didn't stir—it was hairy and chubby, balanced upside down, with leather-looking wings, hanging from the shower curtain rod. I didn't wait around to wake him up. I had never seen a real live bat before, and I was freaked.

I shut the bathroom accordion door between us and stood there staring at the faux wood, breathing quickly. *Okay, Emery, you are a big girl. You can do this. Just shoo it into an old pillowcase like they would in the movies.*

I pictured those beady rodent eyes flapping open, me flipping out, looping, and waking up to my new friend nesting in my hair.

"Eww!" I said, creeped out, but with a resolve to do this on my own.

"I can do this," I said, shaking out my arms and taking a deep breath. I looked around the cabin for something, anything that I might use to shoo it out the door. There was an old push broom with an orange handle in the corner of the kitchen.

I considered using a garbage bag to try to sneak up on it, but I decided that would require much too much hand-to-hand combat. I opened the front door to the cabin so the bat could make a quick exit, and I grabbed the broom.

I swung the door of the bathroom open and took one

last deep breath. I let out a little war cry, "Aaah!" and I beat the green shower curtain three quick times with the broom.

With his wings spread, he was much bigger than I had given him credit for. And with his eyes open, he was much creepier too.

And he chittered, this weird little insect sound. I gave up then—that sealed the deal. One swoop at my head, and I was out the front door. I shut the door to Dala Cabin behind me.

"Yuck!" I screamed.

I took a few deep breaths, then shivered and shook off the heebie-jeebies. I was standing out on the front step, still in my jeans and T-shirt from yesterday, no shoes or socks.

"Great," I said, ticked that I couldn't handle this, not wanting to have to be the damsel in distress the moment I arrived here.

After a few minutes, I couldn't hear any flapping bat wings, no chittering or other horror movie noises, so I opened the door slowly, checked for any flying/flapping/stalking behaviors, then ran in and grabbed my coat, boots, and backpack.

I would have to get some help in town, try to find Roy Genk. My Nancy Drew library detective plan would have to wait.

Ten

Sam's Broken Egg stood on the far northwest corner of the town square. My stomach rumbled the whole walk to town, so I decided I would start my morning there, and as I swung open the glass door to the diner and the little bell gave off its requisite "clang," I realized that most of the town must have had the same idea. And all their eyes were peering straight at me. Only a few hushed whispers here and there. The girl at Dala Cabin. And there I was: crazy hair, no shower, fresh from a bat attack.

I took a few hesitant steps toward the PLEASE WAIT TO BE SEATED sign and found myself staring at my snow boots.

"Hi," I said as a young, blond waitress came up to me, a pot of coffee in her hand, a pencil behind her ear.

"Morning. Want to sit at the counter, hon?" She smacked her gum noisily. "I'm Daisy. I'll be with you in a minute."

I nodded and sat down at one of the few open stools at the counter. I tried to ignore the eyeballs on me, and soon enough the diner made its way back to a friendly, noisy hum. I stared blankly at the menu for a while, convincing myself that no one knew any of my secrets. I was just the new person, a curiosity.

When I did look up, I took in the place. Silver chrome stools, a long blue Formica counter on one side, blue-and-white booths on the other. A jukebox at the far end of the room. It was very bright, with a griddle behind the counter in plain view. The cooks wore white paper hats and aprons, the waitresses, old-fashioned pink dresses.

"Hello there, dear," the woman next to me said.

When I turned to the left, I registered her round, smiley face, but it took me a few moments before I could place her. It was the nice woman from the bakery yesterday. Jean. No, Jeannette.

"Hello," I said brightly.

"How is the cabin?"

"Actually, I need to find Roy this morning. You'll never believe what was in my shower."

"A raccoon?"

"Jeez, no. Probably worse, though. A bat."

"A bat?" Daisy was back, filling my coffee cup, although she hadn't asked. "Do you know what you want?"

"I'll have two eggs and toast. Scrambled."

"I can walk you down to Roy's office, and he'll have to get rid of that bat for you, dear," said Jeannette. "I'm so sorry about that. Not a very nice welcome."

"You should just ask Ash to get it, or Julian, somebody from your stables," Daisy offered, still smacking her gum. "Roy'll keep her waiting till July." She was young, probably only a few years older than me. She had the most beautiful bronzed skin. In December.

"That's a good idea," Jeannette agreed. "My husband, Jimmy, runs an animal shelter at our farm," she explained.

"Okay," I said.

"We don't usually do bats, but anyone would be quicker at things than Roy. I'll have my husband send somebody over to get rid of the bat for you," she finished.

"Thank you, Mrs. . . . ?"

"Winging. Jeannette Winging. You can call me Jeannette." The din of the breakfast rush went on around us.

Jeannette introduced me to Lily, her ten-year-old daughter, who sat at the counter with her, and who was already late for the school bus.

"Nice to meet you," Lily said before she left, all shy, averting her eyes, yet just as smiley-faced as her mom.

A few townspeople came up to Jeannette, who promptly introduced me to them. The first was Mr. McGarry, the underbiter from the post office.

"Nice to properly meet you," I said to him, shaking his hand.

"You too," he offered, then quickly went back to his booth, his coffee.

"He might not be *all there,*" Jeannette whispered, pointing at her head, squishing up her nose, in a knowing look. I nodded. "He is nice enough, though, eh? Harmless."

Next up was Eva Richards, a beautiful young woman with auburn hair. She had some urgent question for Jeannette about a bakery order, one that seemed like a ruse, just so she could eye me up and down from a close distance.

"Nice to meet you," Eva said, looking down her nose at me.

"You too," I said, thinking no such thing.

"She's the town gossip," Jeannette told me quietly with a wink when she left. *Great,* I thought. I didn't want to have the whole town gossiping, trying to find out who . . . or what I was. But it was too late for that.

When the place had quieted some, Daisy came back with my breakfast. I peppered my eggs, gave them a bit of ketchup.

"Jeannette, I'm also looking for a church. Do you have any churches in Esperanza with big, tall stained-glass windows?" I gestured with my arms, indicating floor to ceiling.

Jeannette considered this. "I don't think so. We have the Catholic church out on Hickory, but it's just a redbrick building, no stained glass. And the Lutheran church is behind the post office. We do have stained glass. But nothing like you're describing." She pursed her lips for a moment, taking a sip of her coffee. She gave me a motherly look. "Are you okay, dear?"

"Yes, ma'am," I told her, trying not to look disappointed.

Jeannette counted some bills from her big patchwork purse and laid them on the counter, turning to me. "If you need anything, you can usually find me at Betsy's," she said, giving me a pat on the shoulder.

"Thank you," I told her, hoping I hadn't drawn too much attention to myself. Jeannette left then, and I finished my breakfast, loving the warm food in my empty belly.

I made my way back to the cabin, in hopes that the person from the animal shelter would be there soon to get rid of my bat. I was winded and worn, realizing I might have to wait to make another trip to town to go to the library. My stamina had really taken a hit.

Once I was back at the cabin, I took a deep breath and risked one more trip inside with the bat so that I could grab my laptop.

I sat on a large rock in the clearing, near my handsome stranger's fire pit, and powered up my laptop. I got all the way to clicking on my Internet icon before I realized that I wouldn't have any Wi-Fi out here. I felt like a dope then. What was I thinking? That was why I had wanted to go to the library.

I shook my head in frustration. It was then that I heard

the unmistakable crunch of boots on snow. I turned toward the evergreen path. I hoped it would be my bat helper, but instead, as I shut my laptop and stood up, I saw that it was the cowboy from last night.

Every muscle in me instantly tensed. Ugh. I clenched my fists and scowled. I had thought I was rid of him. But now here he was, raising his hand in a wave, swaggering over here. And was that a little smirk on his face?

"Hello again," he said as he reached the fire pit.

"Hi," I said grumpily. "I'm waiting for—"

"I'm Ash," he said. "Asher Clarke."

"Oh." Of course. That was the kind of day I was having. "I'm Emery," I told him.

"Jeannette sent me," he said, shoving his hands in his jacket. "I hear you have a bat in your belfry."

He smiled a little crooked smile, but I just rolled my eyes. "Very funny," I said. "I tried to get it myself. But I have to admit that I'm a little out of my element here. I don't usually have bats in my shower."

"No problem," he answered. His smirk was gone, his demeanor businesslike. "I'll have it out in just a minute."

As he walked toward the cabin, I thought of something. "Hey, when you were staying here, before I came, was the bat here?"

"Yeah," he answered, turning back to me. "I didn't think of it, or I would've warned you."

"And didn't you . . ."

"Yes, I took a shower. I just didn't disturb him."

"And you slept with him in there with you?"

He just shrugged and let himself in the cabin.

Well, isn't he smug, I thought. Oh, how I wished that I could've just gotten rid of the bat myself. *I could've stuck it down the back of his shirt. That would've served him right. Bat in my belfry. Ha-ha.*

I sat there, miffed, but realized that when I thought of "bat in my belfry," I started smiling.

All of a sudden, I heard a racket from the cabin. Loud clanks of something, maybe the broom against furniture. Then I heard a yell. I stifled a laugh.

He wasn't such a brave cowboy now, was he?

The door flew open, and out ran a disheveled Ash, swinging at the air around his head with his cowboy hat in his hand, the bat flying right behind him. I thought I heard it chitter a bit, and then it was gone, to the forest.

"Quick, close the door!" he barked at me. And I ran up to the cabin and obeyed.

"Holy shit!" Ash yelled, laughing, bending over to catch his breath, hands on his knees.

I sauntered back toward him, trying to bite my tongue so I wouldn't have to say any I-told-you-sos.

When he looked up at me, laughing, his cheeks flushed from the bat chase, the breath caught in my throat for a moment. His dark eyes, the line of his crooked smile. It was familiar.

Ash, I said to myself. And it was like I knew him. Déjà vu. But not déjà vu. Worse than that. Stronger. Better.

I found myself tongue-tied as Ash composed himself. My mind searched for some lost connection, some way I could know him, something. . . .

I realized he was saying his goodbyes now. He tipped his hat at me, gave me a bit of a quizzical look. "You okay?" he asked.

"Yeah, yeah," I said, quickly coming back to the real world. "Let me pay you. I have cash."

"No," he answered. "Consider it part payment for yesterday, scaring the daylights out of you."

I nodded, still trying to find my bearings. I tried to smile. "You sure you're okay?"

"Yeah."

And he left.

Eleven

With the morning's activities, I was exhausted. And after my visit to the diner, I felt exposed. So I decided to lay low, painting the cabin's Dala horses in watercolors, snacking on popcorn. Just hanging out. I curled up on the love seat, a cup of tea in my hand, watching through the eastern window as the sky darkened against the white of the falling snow. My eyelids felt heavier and heavier, and eventually I just set my teacup down and gave in, even though it was probably no later than seven.

I awoke with a start in the early hours of the morning. It was still dark out. For a moment, I didn't know why I had woken up. But I was scared, and my muscles were tense, at the ready. I was holding my breath.

For a second, I thought I might be about to loop. But

then I heard it again, and I realized it wasn't part of my sleep, part of my dream, or part of a loop. It was a yelp, a man's voice. Surprise. Fear.

I looked around as I threw off the red-and-white quilt, and I put the pieces back together, where I was, what I was doing here. Who could be making noise out there?

In the few steps that it took me to get to the door, I had an idea.

I threw the cabin door open and hurried outside toward him, adjusting my eyes to the dark, to what little light was given off by the waning fire. I realized I was only wearing socks and yoga pants and my U of M T-shirt. I curled my arms around myself instinctively. That was when he turned to me—Ash.

I could see that the arm of his coat was smoldering, blackened and curling. I gasped and took a few more steps toward him. He reached for a handful of snow and patted down his sleeve with it. His eyes were wide.

"The fire. I slept too close. I'm fine. . . . I didn't mean to wake you."

I took a few steps closer and could see that he really was fine. His jacket was burned, certainly, but I didn't think that it had gotten any farther down. His sleeping bag had some black edges to it too, but all in all, it could have been much worse.

"I'm fine." He looked up at me this time, squarely turning his head, and I gasped.

He had a thick glob of blood running down his left brow, over his eye. "You're bleeding!" I exclaimed.

"I know," he said, touching his hand to his brow. He grabbed some more snow and wiped it off. The blood did not stop. It kept seeping.

"When I awoke, I jumped up and must have had my feet tangled. I fell right over and thunked my head on that rock." He gestured toward the rock about the size of a truck tire near the fire.

I stood there, mouth agape, rubbing my arms, shifting my weight from one foot to another, lifting one sloppy sock out of the snow at a time. I was freezing.

The firelight danced in his eyes. He had a broad and long nose, a strong jaw, full lips, and uncannily straight teeth, save for one eyetooth that twisted to the side a bit. *God, he is so handsome.* I didn't want to notice it. But there it was.

"It's bleeding a lot" was all I could muster.

"I know." He grinned then, for the first time, and my knees almost buckled. Because the way he looked at me was new and full of expectation, but even more than that, there was that sense of déjà vu.

We stood there in the cold, in the firelight, for a few moments. Him grinning, me staring. A drop of blood fell from his brow to the snow between us. Red and thick on the whitest white.

"Why are you out here, anyway?" I finally asked.

He considered this for a second, brushing the black bits of burned cloth off his coat. "I can leave . . . ," he began.

And for a split second, a fleeting moment, I was scared. I saw myself from outside myself, standing here, in this clearing, in this little remote pocket of a little remote nowhere. Me standing here in my sopping socks, and Ash, twice my size. Here. Stalking me.

An icy sensation swirled its way up my spine and sat at the base of my neck, and I just wanted to run back into the cabin, wait for daylight, trek back into Esperanza, and call my dad for a ride back home.

Safety.

Routine.

All that in an instant, and then Ash cleared his throat. He finished his sentence. "I was going to leave, but I wanted to make sure you were okay out here by yourself."

He looked at me and his gaze didn't falter, like he was telling the truth.

"That sounds kind of crazy," I said.

"Does it?" he said, apologizing with his eyes.

Although part of me wanted to tell him off, roll my eyes at him, I didn't.

"Come in," I said instead. "I'll fix you up." I turned on one heel and went toward the cabin, not giving him a chance to say no.

He didn't say anything, to his credit. But I could feel

his hesitation. I could sense it in the way that his footsteps began behind me, but more than that, I saw it in how his grin had disappeared when I glanced back at him.

Once we were in the cabin, I turned on my lantern and placed it on the mantel so that I could see what I was doing. I sopped up the blood on his brow first with a damp washcloth and then put some water on to boil, dropping some chamomile tea into the pot as well—Nan's old home remedy for swelling.

I quickly changed my socks and threw on a sweatshirt while I waited for the water because I was beginning to feel my teeth chatter from the wet, frozen feel of my feet.

"You are freezing," he said. He shook his head at the lousy fire in the fireplace, sputtering out its last embers. He ripped up some newspaper from the pile next to the hearth and used the metal poker to get the fire going, the orange-red flames growing higher and higher, the warmth reaching me all the way in the small kitchen. He added two logs and seemed satisfied with the blaze.

I motioned for him to sit in the kitchen chair. He obeyed, sat down, and glanced up at me. I turned back toward the hot plate, not wanting him to see my cheeks redden. This act of chivalry—building the fire—was just so nice, friendly.

For a second I felt light-headed. I steadied myself with one hand on the edge of the sink and tried to control the pattern of my breathing, so as not to give away my incredible dorkery. I stood there for a solid minute, trying to get my breath back.

Then I dipped another washcloth in the chamomile water, when it had cooled enough, and walked over toward him.

Neither of us spoke as I cleaned off the cut. It was about two inches long and just above his left eyebrow. Even his wound was perfectly handsome and rough-and-tumble.

"You should get stitches in the morning," I told him.

"Have you had any more seizures?" He didn't look up.

"I'm fine." I was aware of the cloth shaking a bit in my hand. I was aware of his skin, his hands, his smell. I caught my breath in my throat and tried to calm myself. I was only inches from his face, which was almost level with my petite self standing. His scent—soap and hay, fire and snow—wafted toward me.

"You're fine?" he asked as he looked up.

I couldn't answer. I just stared at him. At his eyes. What was it I saw in his eyes? Concern?

"You're sure you're fine?" he repeated after a few moments. I knew he had to be speaking only about the seizure, but standing in front of him, breathing him in, seeing his eyes locked on mine, it seemed like he was asking more.

Like he knew somehow.

That was when I remembered the drawing that I had stuffed in my pocket. The woman. To draw that pain, he had to know that pain.

And it broke my heart for this guy. I couldn't take it. Him asking me if I was fine. Me knowing this about him, this drawing. It was too much.

I guess the past few days—the past few years—caught up with me. Because all of a sudden, I couldn't take it anymore. The curse of these loops. The utter isolation that was my life. Devoid of hope. Only pokes and probes and monitors and data. Me as a subject, a lab rat, an anomaly.

And what I had been missing for so long, so many years, here it was staring at me. Concern.

I shook my head and turned away then, covering my eyes with my hands. I cried silently for a few moments, trying to hold it in. But then it just came in a couple of blubbery sobs.

He stood up behind me and took my left elbow, led me over to the couch, and sat me down. He sat beside me for a minute. I quieted myself a bit, wiping my tears with the back of my hand.

He got up from the couch, brought me a paper towel from the kitchen, and settled back next to me.

He didn't leave. He didn't demand any answers.

He just sat there and let me finish crying. When I was done, I kept my head down and stared at my hands in my lap. "Sorry. I'm a moron, obviously."

"Can I draw you?" he asked.

I looked up. I didn't want him to. I didn't want to be a subject, not again. I opened my mouth to protest. But I didn't.

He pulled out a pad of paper from his pocket, a small

one, and started to sketch. "I began this the other night . . . when you were out. I'm sorry I did it without asking."

If he was confessing, so was I. "I kept one of your drawings. It was—"

"I know which one it was."

"I'll give it back. I—"

"No." He didn't look up from his drawing. "I'm sorry that you had to see that—"

"It was beautiful in its pain."

He looked up then but stared past me. "It was my mom. She died."

"I'm sorry." I could think of nothing else to say to this, my mind conjuring up the awful, hollow scream in the drawing. I tried to push it away. I almost confided that my mom was also dead, but it felt strange to bond over such a thing. Plus, the look on his face showed that this loss was much more fresh, more alive than mine.

Ash returned to his work, and we sat in silence for a while. I watched him as he moved the pen across the paper, deftly, quickly, confidently. I scratched my nose, self-aware, inadequate, a bit annoyed with myself for being thrilled to be here with him.

"This isn't your family's cabin." It was a statement.

"No," I answered anyway.

"You were in the hospital." Another statement.

"Yes, how . . . ?"

"I saw the IV marks on your arm."

Through the east window, the first glimmer of the rising sun began to sift into the cabin. I watched his hand working the ink on the paper. He wore a red flannel shirt, his cuffs turned back at the wrists, revealing thick, strong forearms, but his hands were graceful, worked the pen and paper with ease.

"I'm finished. And I should be going." He stood up quickly. He took a few steps and deposited my sketch on the windowsill.

His footsteps were loud. He grabbed for the doorknob. "You're fine?"

"I am."

He held on to the doorknob, his head down. "I shouldn't have . . . I'm not . . ." He just turned around then and looked at me, his eyes pleading with me. He had secrets. I did too.

"I understand," I willed myself to say, but I wanted him to stay. I was surprised at how much I wanted him to stay.

He shut the door quietly behind him. I watched him head west into the woods. Then I realized that he had left his hat on the table.

I called to him, "Ash!" I slipped on my boots and headed out the door after him.

"Your hat!" I called. I ran toward him and handed it to him. Our hands touched for the briefest of moments and our eyes locked. I immediately found it impossible to catch my breath. The clearing, the air between us felt charged, electric.

"Emery," he said.

He held my gaze, and the way the corner of his mouth turned up, I began to feel self-conscious. I broke the gaze. "You need stitches."

"I'll get them at the shelter." He nodded and left.

I trudged back to the cabin, my head spinning. I put on some water for tea. I flitted about the cabin, picking up Dala horses and giving them a look. I pirouetted over to the east window and looked out at the cold lake, so crisp and gray-blue. "Ash," I said aloud to myself, and smiled. I quickly rolled my eyes at myself, and shook my head.

And then I remembered the picture—my portrait. I smiled as I retrieved it from the windowsill.

It was strikingly good. I knew enough about art to know that he had talent, that he was no hack. The hard angles of his lines, the abandon of perspective, it was modern. Clean and new.

That was when I saw it, the way that he had drawn the curls in my hair.

"No!" I whispered.

The two parallel lines, the one line meandering away from the other into a loop, just like I had drawn over and over for each new doctor, for each new member of my team, for each nonbeliever. My loops. Here they were in black and white. My secret, laid out for everyone to see. How did he know? Who was he?

Who sent him?

I quickly sat down on the bed before I could faint for the second time in as many days inside this cabin.

My breath felt ragged in my throat. Then, a hint of ammonia. Not now! But my eyelids fluttered. I gripped the bedspread in both my fists, and I fought it. I fought back against that thrum behind my eyes.

But I didn't win.

Scared

I'm instantly knee-deep in the stream, all alone. I know something is wrong. I feel goose bumps break out over my skin, and I look around, hoping to see my boy, someone, anyone. But no one is there. It is dusk, that moment in between the night and the day, when the air takes on that eerie, smoky quality. It is oddly quiet. No wind blowing. No gurgling from the stream.

And I don't like it.

A frog croaks in the distance, and I jump a bit in the water. A mosquito buzzes past my ear. I try to swat it, but my hand doesn't move quickly enough.

For the first time ever, I wonder if I can be physically harmed in the loop. I can't imagine why not. I just have never had to think about it before.

I see movement out of the corner of my left eye, and I turn and it is gone. Again, in a moment, the same movement, like a shadow, dark and slithery, moving across the surface tension of the now-still water.

I don't turn this time, afraid it will go, yet wanting it to. I move my eyes only a bit so that I can get a better look at it—just out of the corner of my vision. My heart beats heavy, fast, hard in my chest.

I watch as the shadows play out on the top of the stream, and a picture forms. Shadow pictures. I see a face in a moment, but then it is gone. The black shadows, moving, swirling, and then in an instant, I see it again. I recognize it.

The picture Ash drew. His mom. It is there.

I gasp. The shadows move, and the picture is gone.

I flail back a few steps out of the water. I turn and see him then. My boy, all rosy-cheeked, dark disheveled hair, his eyes serious. "Emery," he says. He smiles.

I reach for him, but then I see the prism of light, not just in my peripheral vision this time. It's surrounding the boy, in waves of color, around the edges of his body, his arms, his head . . . almost like a halo. He shakes his head, and in that instant I have so many questions on the tip of my tongue.

But they will have to wait for another time.

Twelve

I awoke in my cabin, exhausted, wrung. The sun was higher in the sky.

Was my little boy trying to warn me about Ash?

It certainly seemed like it. I shook my head and tried to clear away the in-the-loop cloudiness, but I couldn't get a hold on what was going on here. There were too many pieces. My head throbbed behind my eyes, and I couldn't think straight.

I realized my pants and socks were damp and mud-caked from my time in the stream. My loop. How exactly would Dad and Dr. Chen have explained that? I changed into a clean sweatshirt and pair of jeans, marveling at the physicality of my loops.

I saw Ash's picture of me sitting on the kitchen table. I

threw on my boots and coat. He would have some kind of answers for me. He knew too much about me. It was all laid out as plain as day in that picture.

I walked toward the portrait, grabbed it without looking at it, and shoved it in my pocket, heading out into the cold, fading afternoon, determined to get some kind of answers about what was going on.

I trudged toward Winging Stables, crabby and disappointed. Disappointed that I might have to leave Dala Cabin and the little bit of refuge this place had offered me. Crabby that Ash had wormed himself into my situation. Why couldn't I have just come here and had some peace and quiet? Hadn't I earned that?

And maybe I was a little disappointed that Ash . . . well, that he wasn't just a happy coincidence, that he wasn't just a handsome stranger with a kind smile.

He was obviously something. Sent by Dad. Something.

I was winded and ridiculously worn out by the time I got to the stables. My endurance was shot to hell. Dad and Dr. Chen would not like this.

A fatherly-looking man stood smoking a pipe on the porch of the nearest outbuilding on the Winging Stables property. The farm buildings were clean and well kept; the horses in the pens were impeccably groomed. People took pride in their work here.

"Hello, sir," I said, and waved as I came nearer. The man wore his silver hair in a ponytail and had wire-rimmed spectacles at the end of his nose. He didn't smile when I walked up, but he didn't look unfriendly.

"Hello, I'm—"

"You must be Emery," he said. "Jeannette, my wife, has told me all about you."

I flushed. Of course. Small town. I grimaced at the thought of how everyone by this time tomorrow would know that I had come here to see Ash. "Yes, sir," I answered. "I'm looking for a boy that works for you. Ash. Is he here?"

"Yes, he is. Check in the round barn. He was mucking stalls there."

"Thanks," I said, heading toward the stables nearest to the round pen.

"And welcome to Esperanza," he said, eyeing me quizzically.

"Some welcome," I muttered under my breath.

I stepped into the viewing room attached to the indoor arena. A large picture window opened up to the arena, and there were two young girls taking a riding lesson. I could hear the muted sounds of a teacher yelling out commands to the girls, their horses. On the walls hung awards—ribbons, trophies, certificates. Ash sat at a desk in the far corner of the room, his head bent over something, reading intently.

I almost lost my nerve, turned on my heel, and walked right back out the door. The way he sat there, so . . . unsuspecting. He looked so unthreatening.

But he glanced up then, and I saw his expression change. He smiled at me, but caught himself, studying my most certainly venomous expression. He looked taken aback. I pulled out the portrait quickly. I took another look at it and felt the sting of utter betrayal fresh and whole. How could he know?

Well, he did.

I walked over and slapped the portrait onto the desk in front of him.

"This. How do you know? Who sent you already?" I spit out every word between clenched teeth.

He looked at the paper. "What? How do I know about what?" he ventured.

I pointed right at the way he had drawn my curls, my hand shaking. "This!"

My voice broke over the word *this*, and I watched his expression change. He still looked confused, but also . . . concerned.

He stood up next to me. "I'm not sure what you think I know," he said. "But I don't know it. I promise."

For a moment, my anger fell away a bit. I looked around, unsure what I was doing here, how I had gotten to this point.

"No! What is going on here?" I said.

"I don't know," he said.

I gave him my most ferocious look. "You know too much about me. And you are stalking me. I should call the police."

"I don't know what you think I do," he said.

I clenched my hands at my sides. "Can't you just leave me alone!" I yelled at him, like a child.

He considered this. His eyes locked on mine.

I shook my head, put my face in my hands. "You don't know my father?" I asked.

"No," he answered.

And when I looked at his eyes again, I saw something there. Loneliness? Empathy? Or just me reflected?

"I'm sorry," I said, getting that stingy feeling in my nose. I was going to lose it. Everything was getting away from me, everything seemed upside down.

He clenched his jaw, and again his face looked familiar. Did I know him?

I should have been afraid. But I stood there.

He took a step closer to me then. The air between us still and exploding at the same time.

I sniffled once. But I didn't let the tears come. I willed them back. Ash reached one hand up and placed it gently on my shoulder.

"I'm leaving," I said, because I couldn't think of anything else to say.

I turned around and headed for the door. I looked back just for a moment, and he looked like how I felt. Not hurt, not defensive, not agitated. No, it was more than that. His mouth was parted like he wanted to say something, but didn't know what. He held his right hand out after me, beckoning me, but not really.

He looked confused. Unnerved. Baffled.

"I don't know what's going on," he said.

I stopped for a moment, sighed. I reached and left my hand on the door handle for a moment, then shook my head.

We said nothing. Only the ticking of the large clock above the windows to the arena made noise.

"Emery," he said finally.

I didn't move. "Yes?" I said, but didn't turn around.

"I don't know your secrets."

"I know. . . . I'm sorry."

"Don't be."

I opened the door then finally. I mustered all the courage, all the resolve that I had in me, because what I was about to say felt so wrong in such an inexplicable way, so odd, even eerie. But I knew I couldn't involve *this* boy with my plans, with my life, with anything.

"Please leave me alone, okay?" I said quietly, staring intently at my hand on the brass door handle.

"Okay," he answered. I didn't turn around and look at him. I couldn't.

"Stop camping out, stop showing up, stop being nice," I forced myself to spit out. I stepped out of the viewing room then. I let the door slam closed before I had time to hear a response, my mouth twisted into a frown, the cold, chilling wind whipping my hair into my face.

Thirteen

The Esperanza Library was easy to find, tucked in a residential neighborhood, away from the commerce of the square but just a few blocks north of the Broken Egg. It was a short, squat building. Lots of cement, barely any windows. I was happy to finally get there and find some leads.

I spent the afternoon there holed up at a computer station, in the far back corner of the library, searching fruitlessly on the Internet, trying to find something, anything, that might point me toward what I was supposed to be doing for my boy in the loop, what it was he needed help with. I looked through dozens of pages on the Web, desperately trying to find the church with the windows or anything about a farm called Next Hill. I added the words *silver* and *key* to my searches, the word *nine,* but found nothing that made much sense.

Although I was trying to be invisible, I did force myself to ask the nerdy young librarian if he knew about Next Hill. He apologized that, no, he did not.

"I'm Rob, by the way," he said. "Is there something else I can help you with?" And I realized in that moment that I would have to come up with some kind of cover story. Something. And I would have to be careful how much asking around I did. I couldn't leave too obvious a trail.

I shook my head, told Rob thanks, and left for the day, feeling exposed, watching over my shoulder the whole way to the cabin.

On my second morning at the library, I found a book that I hoped would lead me somewhere—a large, heavy volume on keys throughout history. Apparently, people collected keys, all sorts of keys, antiques and automotive, decorative and utilitarian.

I sat down at a table, opened the book, and saw that it contained photo after photo of keys: skeleton keys and diary keys, ancient golden pirate-looking keys, silver keys, all with some kind of obvious physical significance. There were written histories to accompany each of these keys and more pictures, sketches, tables of monetary values.

It was interesting to someone, I'm sure. But not helpful to me. I turned my key around in my fingers as I sat at the library table, the fluorescent lights reflecting off its surface.

It was just a normal, everyday silver key, to someone's house, to someone's car, to someone's something. There were no markings, no telltale engravings. Just a plain silver key.

I sat down at the computer station again, trying to talk myself out of checking my email. I didn't want to do it, was scared, didn't know if I could bear to face what I had done to Dad. How I had left him. And Gia.

I had been gone a few days now, and at that moment, it got the best of me. I clicked on the Internet icon. I logged on to my email account and found only a handful of emails so far. I opened the most recent one from Dad. *Where are you?*

I thought about emailing Gia. Part of me wanted to tell her to look up my song, to prove it all to her. But you couldn't make someone believe you, even if sometimes it was all laid out right in front of them. I didn't know much. But I did know that.

Instead, I sent her a one-sentence email. "I'm okay." That was all I wrote. I felt that I owed this to everyone. They couldn't have me back, couldn't know where I was, but when I thought of Dad, Gia . . . They had failed me—yes—but they loved me.

And Gia would tell Dad I was okay.

Late in the afternoon, as I walked back from the library, the wind snaked down my coat collar, and I realized that it was getting colder. I could see my breath in front of me, and I was aware of every part of my body that was exposed to the frigid air—my face, my neck, my hands. I put my hood up and wound my scarf around my face, my mouth. I slipped my mittens from my pockets and tugged them on. And I thought about Ash, just as I had a zillion times since I'd seen him at the stables. I struggled not to feel guilty about how I had treated him.

How I had blown him off.

Last night, I had checked out the window before I went to bed, and again when I woke in the morning. But he wasn't camping out. I wanted to feel relief about that.

But I also felt a pang of . . . what? Guilt. Curiosity.

I wasn't sure.

But this morning, I had woken extra early, and I had struck out for Betsy's and the library at an early hour, probably not much after seven. And when I walked past the fire pit in the clearing, the wind picked up a bit. The breeze wafted the scent of slow-dying embers over toward me, and it got my attention.

When I took a few steps closer to the fire pit, a scattering of embers were still smoldering. Could Ash have been here last night?

No.

Maybe he just came later, left earlier.

I didn't know for sure.

But as I walked back to the cabin from the library that evening, trudging through the evergreens, I made a plan.

Tonight I would stay out here until it got too cold, until I couldn't take it, so that I could tell Ash to leave if he showed up. Tell him that I meant what I said. Tell him to stay away from me.

After my dinner of Cup-a-Soup and a stack of Ritz crackers, I dumped my art supplies into an empty crate from the bookshelf. I took it out to the clearing, sat down on the big flat rock near the fire pit, and opened my sketchbook. I sharpened my favorite pencil with a small pocketknife and began to sketch Dala Cabin, in the hope that I would get around to painting it.

I glanced at the pepper spray I had put in my crate with my art supplies. I knew I would threaten to use it if I had to.

I was slightly sick to my stomach, thinking that I would have to be so mean to him. But I had always been a logical girl, a careful girl, and I couldn't afford to get embroiled in something else. Anything else.

I did not want Ash sleeping out here. Hovering.

Plus, I kept reminding myself, *I don't know anything about him.*

I hoped that if I kept saying it to myself, maybe it would ring more true. I kept reminding myself that I should be scared of him.

I got up and moved, choosing instead a spot on the eastern side of the cabin, close to the lakeshore, so I would be somewhat hidden from Ash's view when he came through the forest path. If.

I piled a few pieces of firewood to use as a stool. I sat and sketched my little cabin, carefully, slowly. Its large limestone chimney, its shabby roof, and its beautiful view of the lake. The sun moved lower in the sky, and I was grateful for the light of my lantern, which I had left on in the cabin window. I shaded the lake in the background of my drawing. I wiggled my toes in my boots, realizing they were beginning to sting, tingle. I considered building a fire in the clearing. *Should I stay out here and wait longer?*

That was when I heard motion in the evergreens, right at the opening of the path.

He was coming here, all right. I couldn't believe it, after I had specifically told him not to. Indignation swelled right in the center of my chest. I set my jaw hard and steeled myself for this confrontation. *This is my cabin,* I told myself. *I have things to do here.* I didn't need a knight in shining armor. Plus, did I really know that he was the good guy and not some crazy ax murderer? I mean, in the loop, wasn't my boy warning me about Ash?

I got up and placed my sketchbook and pencils in the art crate.

I waited for a few moments, trying to stay hidden from view, shoving my hands in my pockets, scowling, but Ash did not appear from the pathway. I walked toward the clearing. I heard the scuffling of feet on the snow, the ice, the forest underbrush, but I couldn't see anything. The pathway was only about a hundred yards away, but dusk had really fallen then in all its gloom, giving the air that twilight glow. I couldn't get a good look at the edge of the forest, the path.

My hackles rose, the prickly sensation of fear running through my veins.

"Ash?" I called.

He didn't answer. Just more shuffling, ice scratching beneath feet.

"Answer me! Come out here."

Still nothing.

"I don't want you to camp here. Just stop freaking me out."

I saw something then, a shape. It was large, white, moving just beyond the evergreens that lined the pathway toward the creek, the stables.

I considered running back to the cabin, locking the door, and was about to do just that when I realized there was a familiar shape to the movement, a familiar outline, stepping bashfully into the opening of the pathway.

"Well, hello," I said quietly.

It was a beautiful white horse, looking majestic and a bit surreal against the frozen white of the ground and the twinkling of the snowy evergreen branches.

I clicked my tongue toward the animal, approached him slowly, my hands out. I was not familiar with horses. Did they sniff your hand like dogs? I didn't know. But the horse took a step closer. So I did too. I figured this one must have gotten away from the nearby stables. He was beautifully groomed, well fed, completely clean.

After we spent a few moments dancing around each

other, the horse let me get close enough to pet him, to touch his velvety nose, stroke his gorgeous and freshly brushed mane.

"Someone must be sick with worry over you," I told him, and grabbed the bridle and led him toward the path. He nuzzled next to me, his nose right against my neck. But when I moved ahead on the path, he didn't follow. My mind flashed to a movie about horses I had seen with Gia when we were younger. In it, a horse followed a little boy around for peppermints. I remembered the lemon drops in my pocket and decided to give it a try.

"You can have these if you let me take you home," I told him. I held the lemon drops out in my open palm a few feet in front of his nose, and sure enough, he followed me onto the path.

"Okay," I told him as we took a few steps in the right direction. I let him have one of the candies, and he whinnied slightly in thanks.

"Mr. Winging will be glad to see you." We walked quietly through the woods, and darkness slowly leaked in around us. I considered going back to the cabin for a flashlight, but I decided against it, just picking up our pace a bit.

The horse whinnied twice as the light faded in the sky, my insides slippery. *Stay calm*, I told myself. All I needed was to loop out here with the horse.

The woods were silent. I told myself everything was fine, not to worry, I knew where I was going.

It only took five or ten minutes to get the horse back to Winging Stables, but when I saw the floodlights from the outdoor round pen, I was relieved. I opened my palm and gave the horse another lemon drop.

As we emerged from the pathway by the creek, I noticed the flurries of the afternoon had left the farm and all its buildings covered in a soft, cottony pillow of snow. I looked around at the many outbuildings. This was quite an operation here, six buildings in all. I scanned the place and found a swirl of smoke coming from the porch of the old Victorian farmhouse.

We took a few steps toward the farmhouse, and I realized it was Jimmy Winging, smoking his pipe. He raised his arms high in greeting and surprise.

"I found him just out by the lake, by the cabin," I explained. Jimmy jogged toward us, the sweet smell of his pipe smoke filling the air.

"Ghost! What were you doing out there!" Jimmy grumbled at the horse, taking the bridle from me. "He does this once in a while," he explained, talking around his pipe. "Thank you, young lady. Thank you."

"No problem," I said, shoving my hands in my pockets.

Mr. Winging led the horse back toward the round barn. I waited there for a second, in front of the house, unsure if I was ready to trek back through the woods in the dark. I quickly decided I would wait for Mr. Winging to return and ask to borrow a flashlight.

He appeared from the barn in less than a minute, and I waved at him. "I was wondering—"

"Want some dinner?" He cut me off, beckoning me over to the house. "Jeannette would love it if you would, eh?"

"Um." I considered. "I don't think so. But I would like a flashlight."

"Nonsense," he said, shaking his head, his silver ponytail wagging. "I'll take you back. I really appreciate you finding Ghost."

"No, sir. I don't want to be a bother. I—"

But I was following him even before I could finish protesting. Mr. Winging led me up to the front porch, and I could hear voices laughing in the kitchen, children talking. It heartened me, in a way that I wasn't used to.

"Go on," Mr. Winging said, motioning for me to go ahead of him. I put my hand on the screen door then, and in that second, someone—a small blond boy—came slamming through the door from the other side.

"Daddy!" he yelled excitedly. The door swung with a mighty force, and I wasn't expecting it. It thumped me hard, square in the nose. It sent a sharp, stinging pain right into my head. My hands instantly flew up to my face.

There was blood. Lots of blood.

"Oh, Jesus, Mary, and Joseph!" Mr. Winging yelled. "Cody, you knucklehead. Jeannette!" he called. "Can you bring us a dishrag?"

Jeannette appeared and shoved a kitchen towel into my hands, and I held my head back, hoping the bleeding would stop. Blood was everywhere, thick red streams on my hands, my shirt.

"I'm sowwy," I heard myself saying.

"Sit down, sit down," Jeannette said, pulling me into the house, into the front hallway. "Emery, put your head forward," she said, pushing me onto a bench. "You don't want the blood to go down your throat."

I was instantly surrounded by the whole family, several children, all eyes and chatter.

"Okay," I said. This was not a big deal. I was not squeamish about blood. I could handle this. "I'm fine," I told them.

"Should we take her to the Quick Clinic?" Jeannette asked.

"I don't think so, Jeannette," Jimmy said. "It's just a bloody nose."

"But, Jimmy, she's so pale, and Cody—"

"No! I'm fine!" I protested. This couldn't happen. I could *not* get checked into any doctor's office, any emergency room, anywhere. Who knew what these new doctors might find and question. . . .

I got up quickly from the bench then and felt myself get light-headed. *I cannot loop. No!* But I steadied my breathing and didn't feel the thrum. I wasn't going anywhere. No loop. Just a bad blow to the nose. "I can't go to the doctor," I said. "I mean, I don't need to."

"I don't know," Jeannette said.

The front door opened then, and Ash walked in.

"Hello," he said, his eyes registering my presence, then quickly looking away.

"Great," I mumbled to myself.

"What happened?" he asked.

"I hit her with the door," Cody said. "Sorry, girl." Cody, who couldn't have been more than four or five, looked up at me then. And he burst into tears.

Ash didn't hesitate. "Oh, buddy, it was an accident. It happens," he told him. He swooped the little boy up over his head and began flying him like an airplane.

"It's okay," I told Cody, taking the opportunity to show everyone I was fine. I took the towel from my nose and tried to smile, but Jeannette's hand went quickly to her mouth.

"Oh!" she said.

"Ouch!" said Jeannette's daughter.

"You may have a black eye or two," Jimmy said.

"Sir," Ash said, ignoring me, putting Cody down, giving him a stick of gum from his pocket, then giving another to his brother. "The mare is going to foal soon. I just thought I would let you know before I left."

"Jeannette, I'll be in the gray barn," Mr. Winging said. "Thanks again," he said to me, tipping his pipe toward me. "And sorry about the nose."

Jeannette pushed a bit of hair out of my eyes and tucked it behind my ear in a very motherly fashion. She took my elbow. "Now, I'm not going to take no for an answer. Let's just go to the doctor, make sure it's not brok—"

"No," I told her. "I'm fine. I can take care of it." I tried to pull my arm from her, to extricate myself without being rude.

I saw Ash looking at me then, and I pleaded with him with my eyes. Maybe he could help me.

"Emery's tough, Jeannette. She's the one who bandaged this up," he said, lying for me, pointing to his eyebrow, a butterfly bandage. He reached over then and took Jeannette's arm gently from my elbow. "If she says she doesn't need to go, she doesn't."

He did this all with a smile and an easy charm.

"Oh, well, you sure, Emery?" Jeannette asked.

"Yes, ma'am," I said. "It's feeling better already." I bit my lip and nodded at Ash, trying to convey my thanks.

"Well, Ash, why don't you walk her home—it's kind of on your way to your place," Jeannette said. "It's supposed to storm. You want to take the truck?"

"No, I'm fine. That's unnecessary," I said, wanting to get Ash off the hook.

"We can walk," Ash said, not meeting my gaze. He nodded at Jeannette. "I mean . . . if it's okay with you, Emery?"

"That would be great. Thank you," I said, agreeing quickly, so relieved that I wouldn't have to face a doctor's office. I took a deep breath then and hustled myself toward the door.

"Call me if you don't feel well!" Jeannette hollered to me from the porch.

"Sorry, girl!" Cody called.

"Thank you," I told Ash, holding the dish towel to my nose again. It was still bleeding, and, boy, was it starting to throb.

"Thank you," I said again.

"You're welcome," he said, but didn't look at me.

We entered the pathway, and it was nearly pitch black. Night had completely fallen, and I almost asked Ash if we should go back for a flashlight. But I didn't.

He walked like he was doing a chore, getting something over with. It didn't seem so scary to be in the woods, in the dark, as long as Ash was with me.

As we walked, side by side, I tried to think of something to say to him that might lighten what was wound tightly between us. But I couldn't.

He wasn't talking to me. And he wasn't looking at me. The other day, after his drawing of me, I had asked him to leave me alone. *Told* him to leave me alone. He was doing just that.

In the few minutes that passed since we'd left the Wingings' house, the wind had picked up, and the snow began to fall. The snowflakes came down in fluffy clusters at first, nonthreatening little cottony flakes, but then the wind came charging out of the east, bearing down on both of us. I had to push my legs against it with each step in order to keep myself from being bowled over. I bent my head down and forced my whole body forward, into the gale.

As we trudged against the wind toward the lake, toward the cabin, Ash did turn my way, but the wind made conversation impossible. When a sudden and ridiculously strong gust of wind caught me off guard, Ash reached his gloved hand back toward me, and I grabbed it. He pulled me behind him down the path.

The wind roared into our faces as we rounded off to the right toward the clearing. The force of the wind blew me back unexpectedly. I lost my footing in the snow, and even with Ash's hand gripping my mittened hand, I fell back onto my butt with a thud, letting out a surprised shout.

Visibility was now at about zero, with the snow seeming to push every which way. The wind was swirling, and I quickly felt disoriented. I immediately understood the dangers in not giving the weather the respect it deserved, especially somewhere like here in the UP. This blizzard was like nothing I had ever experienced. The term *whiteout* now truly made sense to me.

Ash stepped from the swirling white nothingness into my vision while I struggled to get up from the snowbank, and I saw the tight-lipped expression on his face.

"Sorry," I mumbled.

Ash helped me up with one gloved hand and curled his

arm around me, and we hurried against the wind toward the cabin. I fiddled with the keys in the door, felt the click, and the door ripped open against its hinges, with the wind blowing us both into the tiny cabin.

"Just till this dies down," Ash muttered, stomping his boots on the welcome mat.

I took my coat and boots off and rubbed my hands together. Ash kept his boots and coat on, staring out the west window, the white swirling snow obscuring any kind of view. "It just came up so quick." His face was tight, annoyed.

"Yeah," I answered. I walked toward the hearth. I stacked a few pieces of kindling first, then put a Duraflame log on top, feeling a bit city-slickerish in Ash's presence.

"I can help you—"

"I don't need help," I said, sounding more defensive than I'd meant to.

When I looked up, ready to apologize, he had turned toward the window again, his shoulders squared exactly away from me. "I know you can do it on your own," he said. "You can do everything on your own, I'm sure."

"What's that supposed to mean?" I said indignantly.

"Not a thing."

"I'm not a damsel in distress, you know."

"I never said you were."

"Well, you certainly act like it." I tried my third match, which would still not light, and bit my lip, trying to calm myself down, telling myself not to get mad at him, not to waste my breath.

"Hold the match nearer toward the head."

Trying to position myself so he wouldn't see me take his advice, I tried the match once again, holding it closer to the head. Nothing.

"If you—"

"You do it," I cut him off, throwing the matches at him. "You constantly need to save me—the bat, this fire, camping out there. You know, maybe I might want to figure things out on my own. I might want to do it all myself. I would be just fine if it weren't for you here, you know."

"Clearly," Ash said, picking the matches up off the floor. He very calmly and slowly walked toward the fire then. He rearranged the logs in the fireplace with his jaw set hard. He replaced the Duraflame log with a few logs and kindling from the hearth, crumpled some newspaper, and put it under the grate. Then he selected a match and lit it on the first try, threw it onto the newspaper, a little smirk on his face. The fire immediately began to burn, great big orange flames licking up the sides of the kindling.

Of course.

He turned toward me and crossed his arms on his chest. "You're stubborn."

"W-well, you . . . ," I stammered, "you are *smug*." I squinted and folded my arms right back at him.

The wind ripped under the door then, howling and taking us both by surprise. "And don't just leave now in a big manly huff either," I said. "It's too damn windy."

"Fine," he said, and he threw his coat over the back of the chair and sat down cross-legged on the hearth, ignoring me.

I walked into the bathroom then and checked out my nose. It was swollen a bit over the bridge, but not as bad as I expected. My face was red and my eyes wide from fighting with Ash, and my hair made me look like a crazy woman.

I walked quietly back into the kitchen after washing my face, shook two ibuprofen from the bottle for my nose, and gulped them down with a glass of water. Ash was lying on his back on the hearth, his cowboy hat over his face, probably pretending to be asleep.

I grabbed my lantern and tiptoed over to the bed, resisting the urge to give Ash a little kick in the ribs as I walked by. I sat cross-legged on the bedspread and stared at him, sprawled out on the floor. There was no way I could relax with him in here with me, the two of us cramped in this tiny space. The sheer size of him was enough reason for me to be uneasy.

I should be scared of him, I thought. I was annoyed, yes. But not scared.

I looked through the few books on the cabin's tiny bookshelf and selected one, *Pride and Prejudice,* although I had read it many times.

I settled back onto the bed. The cabin had an orange

glow to it now, with a toasty warmth radiating from the ever-so-perfect fire. Had I been caught in this cabin with Mr. Darcy, I would have found it extremely romantic. I let out a laugh at the thought.

"What's so funny?" Ash asked from beneath his cowboy hat.

"Nothing," I said. I cleared my throat. "Thank you for helping me out with Jeannette tonight. I really didn't want to go to the doctor."

"I could tell."

There was an unanswered question between us, an expectation that I would explain why. But I didn't. Couldn't.

We sat for a long while in silence, him with his cowboy hat over his face and me reading and rereading the same three sentences, my eyes flitting toward him every few seconds, his large folded hands on his chest, the dirt under his fingernails, the calm rise and fall of his chest.

"I don't do anything in a *manly huff*," he said out of nowhere.

This caught me off guard. I laughed. "Right."

He turned onto his side, took the hat off his face, and propped himself on his elbow. I watched him, his face in a slight smirk. I expected him to fill the empty space between us with conversation, with something, but he didn't.

And I didn't either. We sat together in silence, him watching the fire, me now actually reading, and the snow falling silently outside all around us.

After a long while, he got up, walked to the window. I couldn't hear the wind anymore. "It's dying down," he said.

"Oh," I said, relieved that he would be leaving the cabin, but surprised that in some small way, I wished he wouldn't. His company seemed . . . comfortable.

I watched as the firelight hit his jawline then. His eyes flicked toward me apologetically for just a moment. I saw something there, something familiar again.

Then we both spoke at the same time:

"I'll leave—"

"I'm sorry," I said, getting up from the bed and walking toward him.

He took a few steps toward me, closing the space between us, and suddenly I couldn't find my words, couldn't remember what it was I had wanted to say. It felt like there was a tether between us now, pulling me closer. He bent down over me and scanned my face. I held my breath. He peered at my nose closely. "It looks okay," he said.

And in that moment, breathing in his soap-and-hay-and-skin smell, it was hard to remember, to recall all those many dangerous and realistic reasons that I had listed to myself, that I had used to convince myself to stay away from him.

"Come to the cabin for dinner tomorrow, Ash. I have to make this up to you," I said, before I even knew what I was saying.

He looked away then. "No," he answered. "I shouldn't."

"Please?" I asked. Because I knew in a few seconds he

would walk out of this cabin, and the spell between us would be broken, and at this moment, all I wanted, all I needed, was to make sure, make absolutely certain, that this would not be the last time I felt this. The last time I saw him look at me.

I saw him considering, weighing it. "I'm sorry," he said. Before I could argue, he opened the door of the cabin. "Good night."

Once I was alone, I stood in the little cabin for a long moment, completely still. What had just happened?

I walked to the sink, gulped down a glass of water, waited for my head to clear.

With this distance between us, when I wasn't next to him, breathing in his smell, wondering at his character, desperately trying to avoid staring, well, this distance gave me the opportunity to think logically. I could think like the normal Emery, the sane Emery, the cautious Emery.

Why had I just invited him to dinner? Why did I want to further complicate my existence with this boy? What was I doing?

This was not the normal Emery, the thoughtful, suspicious Emery, who took precautions, played it close, trusted nearly no one.

Now, as I stoked the fire, looking for that perfect blue center—I did remember that much from Girl Scout books—I touched my throbbing nose. I looked in the bathroom mirror and saw a smudge of bruising beginning to appear under each eye.

I thought about what my boy in the loop might think of my black eyes if I saw him soon. My boy, my last loop. The stream, the drawing on the surface of the water, the slithery sensation of fear up my spine.

I should be scared of Ash.

I told myself that it was good that he had declined to come to dinner. I made myself a grilled cheese, changed into my pajamas, and tried to rid my mind of Asher Clarke.

But after I ate, I looked out the window and saw that he had returned, with a tent, no less. He sat on the rock near the fire pit tearing up newspaper to start a fire. He was going to sleep out there again. "Ass," I mumbled under my breath.

I wanted to hate him. I pretended I did. I promised myself over and over that I was done with Ash, this little dance between us. I didn't have time for this. I needed to find out how he fit into my mystery, what information he might have. But that was it.

I'm here because I'm dying. I made myself repeat that sentence in my mind a few times. I even said it out loud.

But inside, deep inside, I was comforted as I brushed my teeth, then climbed under my red-and-white-checked quilt, knowing Ash was out there, knowing that he was lying in his tent less than a hundred feet away. Ash.

And although there was a part of me that wanted to tsk-tsk myself and tell me I was stupid, I knew. Deep down, where I felt that feeling . . . that flutter.

I knew this was just the beginning.

Fourteen

At the library the next morning, I approached Nerdy Rob at the desk, clearing my throat, rehearsing my cover story in my mind. I knew it would draw attention to me, but I had to get some help. I couldn't just search the Internet forever. I'd come here with a purpose.

"I'm doing a research paper for a college class," I said, hoping Rob wouldn't see right through my lie. "I was wondering if you might be able to help me find a church." I explained the stained-glass windows to him, and he listened carefully, asking questions, taking notes. He searched with me for over an hour, some online, but mostly in the stacks. We looked through the library's reference and history sections, locating as many area church photos as he could find, from several volumes on local architecture, from filed building plans, and from local newspapers. Rob's pants were an inch too short and he was constantly pushing his glasses up his nose, but he was friendly and helpful, and didn't seem too suspicious. He did ask about my semi-black eyes, though.

"Clumsy," I offered. "A friend opened a door right into my face." It felt good not to have to lie about that at least.

After a disappointing few hours, Rob suggested the Esperanza Historical Society. "Let me give them a call," he said. And I nodded, happy to have something, anything, that might be considered a lead. Rob explained the windows to the person on the other end of the phone and began nodding. "Much appreciated." He hung up quickly. "Tomorrow morning. Ten a.m."

"Thank you, Rob," I told him.

"Happy to help," he said, blushing, pushing up his glasses. "They have a lot of local history and documentation. Older information that we don't have."

I gathered my stuff for the cabin, a tiny kernel of hope sprouting deep within. *This could get me somewhere.* Maybe I was on the cusp of something.

And that evening I felt restless, cooped up. I danced around the cabin, listening to my iPod, dusting all the Dala horses, trying desperately to keep myself from looking out into the clearing. At sunset, I still hadn't checked, but by full dark, I looked out the west window. And, yes, he was there. He tipped his hat to me, and I turned away, feeling spurned, rejected over dinner. But feeling that rush of something—that flutter deep in my chest.

The next morning, I awoke from my second full night of undisturbed sleep in God knew how long. I could explain away one night, but two in a row? I rubbed at my eyes, stretched my well-rested muscles, and swallowed hard. I wanted to think that this hiatus from my loops was caused by getting away. By relieving the stress of the hospital. I wanted to believe that. I wanted to hope that maybe I was even getting better. But I couldn't believe it. Something in me knew better. I couldn't shake the feeling that my body was just gearing up for something, building up to something even bigger. I didn't know why exactly I felt like that. But there it was. The fear that I was experiencing the calm before the storm.

I hiked over to the Esperanza Historical Society, which was really just a room in the back of the town VFW, full of file boxes, a couple of bookshelves, and the stale smell of cigarette smoke. I looked carefully through several photo albums that cataloged area stained-glass windows, their artists, their histories, et cetera. It turned out that stained glass had quite a tradition in the UP, and the historical society had a lot of information, beginning from the turn of the last century. But I found nothing that looked like the church in my loop.

The pair of older ladies, sisters, running the Historical

Society were friendly enough, but they hovered over me the whole time, asked me questions I didn't want to answer. They gave me more facts about the town of Esperanza than I ever would've cared to know. Did I know that Esperanza was the third city in Michigan to be granted a charter for a bank? Did I know that Charlie Chaplin's uncle once shot a movie in the town square? They finished each other's sentences and giggled at each other's jokes. It made me miss Gia.

They did, however, give me one nugget of useful information. They told me I should visit the Northern Michigan Historical Society in Charlevoix, which might have what I was looking for.

"It's a lovely town. The bus goes right there," the taller sister told me.

"Make a day of it," the other sister agreed. "They're open to the public only on certain Fridays. You could even make it a weekend."

"They have more of this, more stained-glass information," the tall one said. "And Charlevoix is the U.S. leader in imported herring."

"Sardines too," the other one added.

In my notebook, I wrote down the name of a volunteer they knew and thanked the ladies for their time. The sisters let me use their telephone to call the Lutheran church and set up a visit with the pastor.

When I arrived, I could tell from the outside that it probably was not the church from my loop. I knew this already from Jeannette. But I figured it couldn't hurt to talk to the pastor, see if he knew anything, knew any other churches in the area with stained glass.

"Reverend Sandberg?" I asked, knocking lightly on the office door.

"Yes?" He was young, maybe in his thirties, with short military-cropped hair, black glasses.

"I'm Emery Land," I said, realizing too late that I hadn't used my alias but figuring I was talking to a minister. "I just wanted to ask you a few questions about a church that I think is in the area."

"Sure," he said, finishing up what he was doing, taking notes in some sort of ledger, counting out boxes of what looked like communion wafers.

He walked with me then toward the sanctuary, sitting in the first pew, gesturing for me to sit also. I looked around as I followed him. It had been a very long time since I had been in a church, if you didn't count my loop. This space had a nice, quiet feel to it, light and airy. Not serious and threatening like so many old churches. The sanctuary was enormous, modern, with lots of natural-looking woodwork in knotty pine. Gorgeous, really, but not the church I was looking for. There were several panes of stained glass in back of the altar, each depicting a scene for one of the twelve apostles. No abstract kaleidoscope of colors here.

I sat down next to Reverend Sandberg and asked him, "I don't know anything about the church, really, except that it has very tall stained-glass windows. They are abstract, colorful. Floor to ceiling behind the altar." I fidgeted nervously, crossing and uncrossing my legs.

He didn't answer right away, considered my question. A couple of parishioners were hanging red and green garlands from the balcony. Several large natural pine wreaths had already been hung above the doorways. I could smell the Christmas tree scent hovering in the air around us.

Reverend Sandberg scratched the crown of his head. "Hmmm, miss, I don't think I recall any churches in this area that fit that description."

"Oh," I said. "You don't happen to know of a farm called Next Hill, do you?"

"I don't think so, no." Seeing I was disappointed, he offered, "But let me take your name. I'll see if I can track anything down about that church."

"Oh, um, I'll check back in with you, if that's okay," I answered.

As luck would have it, Jeannette Winging came clamoring into the sanctuary, wheeling a cart full of boxes, carrying more boxes in her arms, looking flushed and harried.

"Reverend?" she called in her happy, singsong voice.

I ran to hold the sanctuary door open. "Oh!" she exclaimed. "Emery! We are bumping into each other a rather lot, aren't we, eh? And your nose! How is it? The bruises aren't so bad, eh?"

"I'm fine, Mrs. Winging." I took some boxes from her arms. "Let me help you," I offered.

"You know, that would be lovely, Emery. Reverend, I'm sure you don't mind if Emery helps me load up these lights for the Cranes' golden anniversary party?"

"No, no, of course not," he answered. "And I will ask around for you, Emery. Jeannette, you wouldn't know anything about a church with floor-to-ceiling stained glass?"

I followed Jeannette to the back door, at the rear of the sanctuary. We both had armloads of boxes. "No, I don't think so," she answered.

Reverend Sandberg held the door open for us, and I followed Jeannette down the stone steps of the church to her minivan.

"We'll have these back for you right after the party, Reverend, so we can decorate that tree," Jeannette called to him.

We loaded up the boxes of lights and then turned back to the church to get the rest, the reverend gone on with his own business.

"I don't think you've met the Cranes yet," Jeannette said. "He and his wife have been married for fifty years. They had always planned to have quite a big to-do for their wedding anniversary. Sally had cancer—*has* cancer. No one knew if they would make it, but anyway, here they are, by golly.

"These are the white Christmas lights, from the big tree

here at the church," Jeannette continued. "Reverend said we could use them."

"Where is the party?" I asked.

"Jimmy and I are going to put it on at our round barn. Clean the place up, cater the dinner. I'm going to make the cake. We really want to do it up."

"That sounds wonderful," I said.

"It's going to be quite an event. Especially now. Last week, the reverend handed me an envelope. Two hundred dollars—anonymously, can you believe it? Someone donated it to the Cranes' party."

Jeannette looked at me. "You'll have to come, Emery, eh? The whole town will be there. Surely, you came here hoping for a little vacation, a little fun. . . ."

"Oh, I don't know," I said, self-conscious, realizing there were probably a lot of questions floating around about me in Esperanza, my reasons for being here. "I'm not much of a party person."

We finished putting the last of the boxes in the back of Jeannette's minivan, and Jeannette turned to me, hands on her hips, squinting a bit.

"Emery, is there anything else I can help you with?" She shut the back door and dusted her hands off in a quaint motion.

"I don't think so, ma'am."

"Well, of course, being new in town, you need a hot meal. Come over for dinner tonight?"

"I don't know, Mrs. Winging," I said, not wanting to get myself intertwined with anything else.

"We'll see if Ash is free too." She gave me a little wink then, as if she knew she was sweetening the deal.

This was even more reason not to go. I didn't want to see Ash, didn't want to be tempted to fall into the spell that he cast, didn't want to care about him.

"I'm a very good cook," Jeannette said. "But that's okay."

I bit my lip and thought about it. Maybe Ash had some kind of information I needed. He was tied to the loops somehow. "Okay, sure. Why not," I said. "I'd actually love to come to dinner." I couldn't leave this stone unturned. I had to find out what Ash knew that could help my boy.

"Wonderful," Jeannette said, giving me a pat on the shoulder. "See you tonight, then."

"So, Ash," I said, averting my eyes, knowing I sounded like a lovesick dork, "is he from around here?"

"No, he isn't," Jeannette said, looking for her keys in her enormous patchwork handbag. "His mom and I, well, we went way, way back, and had a falling out of sorts. We hadn't been in touch in a long time. But Ash just showed up, and I knew, of course, about what happened to her."

Jeannette stopped what she was doing, pursed her lips. "I shouldn't go on." She turned and looked at me. "He doesn't talk much, our Ash."

"I see," I answered, understanding that she felt like she was breaking a trust. But I needed more information on him.

"I know about his mom," I said, which was technically not a complete lie. I wanted to encourage her to keep talking.

"I think he's having a crisis, Emery. He needs a safe place. That's just what I think," she finished quickly.

"I understand, Mrs. Winging," I said. Because I did. I really did.

I stopped in that afternoon at Sam's Broken Egg on my way back to the cabin. I wasn't that hungry, but I needed a place to stop and rest. I sat down on one of the stools at the counter. There were only a few people in the diner with me, none I recognized.

"What'll it be?" the waitress, Daisy, asked as I took off my coat, my mittens.

"I'd like a hot chocolate."

Christmas music played over the speakers in the diner, and I heaved a big sigh. I was tired, so tired. My shoulders hunched forward, and I nervously tapped on the countertop as I waited.

"You should go bowling," a voice said, and then I saw a large, hulking shape sit down next to me. He smelled of alcohol, cigarettes. His flannel shirt had a large orange stain on the front of it.

He leaned over to me, too closely, too intensely. "Want to go bowling?"

It was Mr. McGarry from the post office.

"No thanks. I don't really like bowling." I noticed now the abnormalities in his features that I hadn't that first day, the thickness in his speech, the wide-set eyes.

"You haven't bowled here yet."

His hair was greasy and his breath sour, and he scooted much too close to me. His eyes had a funny, dilated look to them, and I didn't like it.

I tried to smile and just ignore him politely, but he leaned way too far into my personal space, and he tapped me on the shoulder.

"They play rock-and-roll music there too."

"Okay," I said. "I just want to have my hot chocolate, though." He settled back in his seat a bit.

The diner door opened and the bell clanged several times, as it was now working toward the dinner hour. The place filled up quickly. I was thankful for the crowd, hoping, wishing my hot chocolate would just hurry up so I could get out of here.

I stole a glance at Mr. McGarry, and he was still staring at me. He was obviously a little off, a sad case. I thought of how Jeannette said he was harmless. I was just getting worked up over nothing, right? Not everyone in this world was out to get me.

I looked over and smiled at the poor guy and instantly regretted it. He grabbed my hand, which I immediately drew back. "Let's just go now. Let's just bowl one game," he said.

"No," I said.

"I used to be the pinsetter," he said proudly.

"Yeah?" I said, trying to be polite, craning my neck for the waitress. The diner was bustling and busy. I looked for someone to save me from this conversation. The young mom at the door with her little girls, she couldn't have been less interested. The fry cook behind the counter, oblivious. The diner was full, humming with noise, conversation, and no one was paying any attention to us.

Mr. McGarry stood up then and said, "Let's go!" and he grabbed my arm. In retrospect, it was probably just the exuberance of a man with a childlike mind, but at that moment, panic swirled in my belly. I tried to pull my arm away, but he had a good grip on me.

Suddenly a man broke in between us, wrenching Mr. McGarry's hand off my arm. "Let go," he growled.

The force in Ash's voice startled me, made me take a step back. Mr. McGarry jumped backward and looked up at Ash in confusion. Ash's shoulders were set squarely, and the muscles in his jaw flexed angrily.

I watched the recognition of Mr. McGarry's innocent intentions register on Ash's face. Ash's features softened. He let go of Mr. McGarry's arm then. "Burke, she doesn't want to go bowling," he said flatly. "And won't Father Morgan be missing you right about now?" Ash threw a friendly arm around Mr. McGarry, avoiding my eyes.

"I s'pose, Ash," Mr. McGarry said. Ash walked him toward the door then, ignoring me altogether.

I settled back into my seat, unsure what I had been more scared of—Mr. McGarry's grip on my arm or Ash's violent reaction.

I watched through the picture window as Ash walked Mr. McGarry out onto the sidewalk. My breathing was shallow, nervous. Ash stood there talking with him for a long while, Mr. McGarry getting all kinds of excited with his conversation, no doubt about bowling, his hands flailing, a big simple smile on his face. And Ash just stood there nodding, adding a word here and there. I watched Mr. McGarry from this distance, and he seemed sympathetic, feeble even. I shook my head. Maybe all he needed was someone to lend him an ear, and Ash was certainly giving him that.

My hot chocolate came, and I drank it quickly, noticing that my hands were shaking. The hint of a smell crept up on me. Ammonia. I took a deep breath and braced myself, waited for the flutter. But something changed then. It died down inside me, my breath coming in slow, uneven spurts. It gradually disappeared, leaving me spent but here. Why? How? I had no idea.

I concentrated on steadying my breathing. In. Out.

When I glanced back toward the diner window, Mr. McGarry was gone. Ash was inside again, walking toward the counter, giving me an icy stare.

"Thanks," I said as he approached.

I expected him to sit down by me at the counter, but he just slowed his gait a moment. "I . . . um." He didn't finish. He looked at me hard, turned on his heel.

He walked to the other end of the diner, with me gaping after him. He sat down in the corner booth all alone. He unfolded his menu with a dark look on his face.

I stared at him for a moment, incredulously, then rolled my eyes. I drank the rest of my hot chocolate, squinting at Ash and trying to think of something to say to him, some cutting remark. He was so infuriating. I was so over this. This ridiculous seesaw, this crazy dance between us.

I paid the bill and left, making sure not to look over at Ash. It wasn't until I was halfway back to the cabin that I thought of a good comeback. And even then, it wasn't that good, but it made me laugh. I figured there might be another time I could use it: "Want to go bowling?"

Fifteen

Although I told myself I was simply trying to gather information, to figure out why my boy had shown me Ash's drawing in the stream, I changed my outfit approximately forty-three times before I left for the Wingings' that night. I settled on jeans and a pink turtleneck sweater, my hair piled up on my head. I rolled my eyes at myself in the mirror even as I swiped on some lip gloss.

I noticed quickly that I looked better. I looked substantial, whole, less transparent. I hadn't looped in a couple of days, not counting the near miss at the diner, and I didn't look as ragged.

As relieved as I was not to loop, I *wanted* to loop too. For my boy. To get some more clues. I was worried about him. The past few days had given me next to nothing to record in my notebook, nothing new to help solve my mystery, but I was hoping tonight might change that.

Jeannette let me in her front door with a quick kiss on the cheek and a boisterous hello. I looked around the foyer and wiped my boots on the mat, noticing the bench I had sat on the other night, the night of the bloody nose. And I noticed now the details of the place. The gingham wallpaper, a framed American flag hanging alongside many, many framed photos of the Wingings, their children, all candids. Lily skiing, Jimmy wearing a red clown nose and kissing Jeannette, the boys with matching soccer uniforms.

Looking at these photos, I realized how much I already liked this family. How welcoming they were, how normal and . . . happy.

The Winging kitchen was alive with chatter and movement, life. It was a cheery yellow-and-white deal with a white farmhouse table, complete with a long bench on each side. The aroma of the kitchen was like nothing I had ever smelled before; my mouth watered, and I was instantly ravenous. The Wingings' daughter Lily, whom I had met already, was setting the table, smiling at me. Cody and his look-alike brother were busy sweeping up some kind of mess that must have occurred moments before I came in. Dog food? No, it looked like cereal. They were sweeping up cereal.

The boys looked up at me saucer-eyed when I came in. Jeannette hustled me to a place at the table with her chirp-chirp, happy-voiced small talk, and Jimmy gave me a welcoming smile as he poured milk in each of the boys' glasses.

I sat down on one of the benches, and Lily instantly sidled up to me. I thought of my own mom and dad, and a knot formed in my stomach. I averted my eyes, unsure how to take part in this family's day-to-day happiness.

"Ash bought me a bike," Lily said.

"Ash taught me how to shoot a slingshot," said Cody, taking a seat across from me with his brother.

"I know how to do a cartwheel one-handed," said the other boy.

I didn't know who to answer first. So I just smiled at each of the kids, but they didn't seem to care. "What's your name?" I asked Cody's brother.

"I'm four," Cody continued.

"Dad says I can get my own fishing pole when I'm seven," said the other boy.

"He's Garrett," Lily answered me. And the boys kept talking.

"Ash says he can make me a fishing pole," Cody countered.

"I have my own slingshot," Garrett offered.

Jeannette brought a bowl of salad and some homemade bread to the table. "Let me help," I offered, getting up from the bench.

"No, no," said Jeannette. "You are our guest."

At that moment, the screen door in the back of the kitchen opened, and Ash appeared. He looked as if he had just come from washing up, his hands and face scrubbed clean, hair smoothed back.

"Ma'am," he said to Jeannette, and hung his cowboy hat on a hook. He had obviously been here before for many meals, although Lord knows where they thought he spent his nights.

He turned toward the table, and the boys were out of their seats in an instant, jumping on him, hanging on him, giving him five. I held my breath. Ash's eyes caught mine, and he faltered, just for the briefest of moments. But I caught it. "Hello," he said.

"Hi," I answered.

"Sit by me," Lily piped up.

"Sure, Lil," he said, picking up a boy in each arm and plopping them in their seats before he took his own.

Ash's jaw clenched hard on the sides as he passed me to sit down next to Lily. I smelled that soap-fresh scent, the same scent from my pillows at the cabin, and my stomach jumped toward my throat. *I'm here on business, nothing more,* I told myself.

Jeannette came to the table, sat down, and passed around a pan of lasagna. Everyone simultaneously started serving themselves, and I found myself in an unfamiliar clatter of silverware and happy chitchat. Ash reached out and stole the boys' Brussels sprouts from their plates and popped them in his mouth, and the boys grinned ear to ear, giving him the "shh" sign.

I reached for a piece of bread the same time that Ash did,

and our hands touched for an instant, our eyes met. There it was, that tether. He gave me a dark look.

"Emery, do you have a guinea pig?" Lily asked.

"No." I shook my head.

"We want Dad to let us get three guinea pigs," Cody explained. "One for each of us."

"I always wanted a cat," I told them. "But my parents never let me."

"I could use a lizard too," Garrett piped up.

"So, Emery," Jimmy began, "what brought you to our neck of the woods?"

"Well, I'm just working on something for school—college. I needed a quiet space." My cover story was thin. I hoped I wouldn't have to make up too many details. I didn't like to lie, didn't want to lie, but I had become sort of accustomed to it over the years.

"And how are you liking Dala Cabin?"

"It has its charms," I said, and smiled.

"Aren't you a little lonely out there?" Jimmy asked. *So he doesn't know about Ash's sleeping arrangements.*

"You would think," I answered, shooting Ash a look. "But actually, no."

"And where are you from?" Lily asked. "Mom guessed Chicago. I guessed Hawaii."

Jeannette shushed her, turning a bright pink. "You'll have to forgive us. We get so few travelers this time of year. We ladies at Betsy's can't help ourselves."

"Ann Arbor," I answered. "The university, you know." This lie was at least partially true.

"Yes, a college student," Jimmy said through a mouthful of lasagna.

"Ash is in college," Lily said.

I sat up straighter. "Yeah? Where?"

"Was. University of Illinois," he answered, avoiding my eyes.

I saw this as my opening. "What did you study?"

"Veterinary med."

Jimmy Winging cleared his throat then. "He saved a gelding last week. He found an infection in its hindquarter. Really something." Jimmy nodded over to Ash.

I saw the color rise to Ash's cheeks. He stared at his plate. He didn't like this attention. But I had to find out more.

"Why'd you leave school?" I asked.

A silence fell over the table.

"Ash bought me the bike," Lily whispered, "but I'm not supposed to know it was him. I'm not supposed to say."

I smiled.

"Then stop telling all of creation about it, Lily!" Jimmy interrupted. "You're making Ash uncomfortable."

I stole a look at Ash. He had patches of scarlet on his cheekbones, and his jaw worked hard on his French bread. His eyes looked nowhere in particular.

"So, what brought you here, Ash?" I asked, knowing I

was skating on thin ice, knowing I shouldn't, but knowing I had to.

I saw Jeannette and Jimmy exchange a glance.

"Could you pass the milk, Garrett?" Ash asked, ignoring my question.

I couldn't give up, though. I couldn't. "Do any of you know about a farm called Next Hill?"

With that, Ash spilled the decanter of milk all over the table. He stood up. "I'm sorry. I'm sorry," he said, wiping up the milk with his napkin. I could see he looked stricken, his eyes wide, surprised. And my heart broke into a zillion pieces. Because this question had hurt him somehow, and I wasn't prepared for how bad it felt to hurt him.

"Excuse me," he said, breathless, giving me a hard look and heading for the door, grabbing his coat. The soft clank of the screen door filled the silence behind him.

Jeannette was mopping up the milk now, Jimmy and the rest of the table staring after Ash.

"I'm sorry. Did I say something . . . ?"

"I don't know," Jimmy answered.

"I don't know either," Jeannette answered.

"Excuse me," I said, getting up. "I'm so sorry. I didn't mean to come here and make a scene. I just . . ." I threw on my coat and followed Ash out the screen door.

My legs shook, my knees knocking, as I chased Ash down the porch steps. He was taking long strides, walking past the creek, toward the path that led to Dala Cabin. I could see the anger in each step he took. He stopped abruptly, turned toward me.

"Who are you? How do you know about me?"

"I don't. I don't know about you." His brow was dark. I shrank away from him a bit, too aware of his size.

He opened his mouth like he was about to accuse me, about to really lay into me. There was that crazed look in his eye, the same one I had seen at the diner. But Ash shook his head, pushed it away. His face softened. "You look scared. I don't want to be someone that scares. I'm not a monster," he said, looking at the ground.

I bit my lip for a moment. "I'm not scared," I said, trying to sound convincing.

I watched him hold back his anger at me. "What's going on?"

"I can't really explain it all," I told him. *Not without giving away all my secrets, not without sounding semi-loony.* "But just like with your drawing of me . . . what you think I know . . . I don't."

We stood looking at each other for a long time in the moonlight, near the path to Dala Cabin. The evergreens were sagging and weighted down, thick with heavy, wet snow from the earlier flurries. The moonlight glistened and glowed off the frozen surface of the evergreens. It twinkled, really.

Ash reached out slowly and touched my cheek only for

an instant with the pad of his thumb. Then he moved his hand away from me abruptly.

"Emery," he said.

I took a sharp intake of air. *Business,* I tried to tell myself.

"I can't. . . ." He shook his head. "I didn't want to turn you down for dinner . . . the other day. . . . I just can't."

I nodded, wanting him to go on, wanting him to touch me again. His touch was electric on my skin.

"I'm not . . ." He took a step back from me. "I'm not someone you can know, not . . ."

"I understand," I said, although I didn't.

He took another step back from me. I moved forward without thinking, feeling pulled toward him, closing the space between us. His eyes met mine, and the breath caught in my throat, every molecule in my body feeling pulled toward him, leaning me into his space, into his energy. It was a heady feeling, disorienting.

Although I barely knew him, I didn't know if I could pretend even one more second that this thing between us—whatever it was—wasn't wonderful.

"I have to go," he said, only leaning in closer to me, our faces inches apart. I could feel the warmth from his breath.

"No," I whispered. "Where are you going?"

He shook his head then, looked down, saying something under his breath. I couldn't be too sure what it was, but it sounded like "Penance." But suddenly, watching him, with his eyes cast down, his lashes shadowing his cheekbones, the way he held himself, both leaning toward me but also restraining himself, filling the space between us with his heady, soapy scent, I just couldn't take it anymore.

So when he looked up, I closed the small distance between us. I stood on my tiptoes and pressed my lips to his. In my hurry, I missed a little bit, landing my lips more on the corner of his mouth, and for a second he didn't react, but then he turned his face toward me, pressing his lips against mine, a full kiss, a real kiss. And the fireworks exploded deep inside me, sending ribbons of heat from my center out to my limbs, a gorgeous, surprising feeling, like a warm breeze beneath my skin.

Both his hands went to my face, gently. And just when I thought he was going to pull away, he leaned into the kiss, longer, deeper. The heat inside me surged again. I smiled behind the kiss without meaning to, and I brushed my fingertips on his stubble, loving its feel.

He pulled away, and we just looked at each other. Should I apologize? Make a joke? Do it again?

"Emery," he said, my name turning to music in his voice, the quiet deepness of it. He closed his eyes for a moment, shook his head, smiled. I wanted to kiss him again. Right on that crooked eyetooth. But when he opened his eyes, his smile disappeared, and he was himself now. Measured. Cool. "Emery," he said again. A goodbye.

Then he turned on his heel and left.

Sixteen

I spent the next morning trying not to waste the whole day replaying that kiss. His hands cupped around my face. His lips on mine. The way his voice had changed the sound of my name.

I made myself focus, which was no easy task. I forced myself to read through my notes on my loops, planning exactly what I needed to ask Ash, how I could ask him about Next Hill without giving away all my secrets. I had to figure out what he might know that could help me. I knew that my little boy must be from a time roughly a hundred years ago; the Victrola, the old farm equipment, all pointed to this. What Ash might know about this, I had no idea. He was guarded. It would be difficult.

And I had to do all this without falling in love with him.

After lunch, I left for the library, with no new ideas for my search but determined to not just waste the day. As I walked down the slushy sidewalk in front of the Broken Egg, I noticed a figure ahead of me. A tall, thin girl. Glasses. The darkest hair. Wearing all black, dark against the snow.

She was here. Gia.

Oh my God. I froze. She had tracked me down. My stomach plummeted. My head spun. Who else knew I was here? I felt a zillion different things as I watched her walk down the sidewalk, eyeing the different storefronts.

She spotted me then. She dropped her silver backpack and came barreling at me, tears in her eyes. "Emery!" She wrapped her arms around me, nearly bowling me over with her hug. "Don't you ever do that to me again! Dammit! You left me!"

She pulled back and looked me in the eye. I had all this righteous indignation pent up in me. I was so ready to be mad at her, to give her the cold shoulder, but she had the gall to be mad at me.

"How could you just leave? Only a crappy email to say you're okay? You ran away, and you weren't going to call me or tell me where? Nothing?"

I took a step back then, straightened my shoulders, found my voice. "But, Gia, you didn't believe me."

Gia froze. Her face fell, and she shrank back into herself. "I know. I had a momentary lapse in judgment. So sue me."

"Gia, you—" I wasn't going to let her off that easy.

"I was pissed, okay?"

"*You* were pissed?"

"I wanted to take you out, take you to a party, give you a good time. I just wanted to see you be happy for a little while and forget what was happening to you." She looked down now. "I know it's selfish."

"But you said you didn't believe me. Do you have any idea how much it meant to me when you *did* believe me?"

Gia didn't look up. She reached beneath her glasses and rubbed one eye. She looked like she was choosing her words carefully. "I think, Emery, it's sometimes easier in the moment to decide *not* to believe you. To think that it's not true. To hope that it's all something else. 'Cause maybe then it'd be easier for them to save you."

I let out a sigh. I knew what it was like to want to ignore something. Pretend it wasn't real.

"I'm sorry, Emery." Gia finally met my gaze.

I hugged her.

"How did you find me?" We walked over toward her backpack, grabbed it, and she hooked her arm through mine. I led her to the square, and we sat on the concrete bench from the first day I'd been here.

"Your pink notebook."

My mind flashed back to that notebook, sitting atop a pile of similar notebooks in my closet. "I wrote what in there?"

"You wrote—"

"Esperanza."

"It took a few days before I could get over to your place without anybody knowing. But I took a chance. Drove up here. Prayed I could find you. Been hanging around here all day, hoping to catch a break."

"Does Dad know? Did you tell anybody or—"

"No. Of course not. Because I *do* believe you, Emery. Now. And I guess I always did. It's just, your father . . ." Gia's face darkened. "They are questioning people. Me. There were these men with badges and ridiculously stern faces and CIA haircuts. It's all totally creepy."

I considered this, feeling terror grip my belly—terror that I might be found out, that I might have to leave Esperanza before I was ready. "How'd you get into my room?"

"Your garage code."

"And you don't think Dad found that notebook first? Saw the word *Esperanza*?"

"I think even if they saw it, it might not mean anything. It just stuck out to me, though. And then I Googled it."

"They questioned people?"

"Yeah, it's kinda crazy. Loretta, everyone. They questioned me in your dad's office. It all felt very *Law and Order*."

"Oh, Gia, I'm sorry."

"No, stop it. I didn't rat you out. I didn't even have any information then."

I knew I had to ask about my father. I didn't want to. I

didn't want to think about him. "I didn't want to hurt Dad, Gia. Is he okay, or—"

"He's mad." Gia pursed her lips.

"What else? What aren't you telling me?"

"The guys. Your dad. They scared me, Emery. I think that this whole thing is bigger than you or I think it is."

I thought about this for a moment. Gia grabbed my hand, gave it a squeeze. As we sat in the snow-covered square of Esperanza Beach, the sounds of traffic and distant laughter ringing through the air, my father and his threats seemed far away, unreal. But I knew that this was a false sense of security.

"Let's get something to eat," I said. "And you are going to just love the place I'm staying."

"Four stars?" Gia asked.

"Something like that."

Gia tiptoed around Dala Cabin and shed her coat, her shoes, throwing them wherever. She flopped on the bed. "It's just when you said you wanted *choices,* I hadn't quite pictured that you would choose *this.*"

"I know you'd probably go for more of the room service, facials, and massage territory. But my boy in the loops, he told me to come here. Showed me to this place."

Gia sat up then, her eyes on me.

I unwrapped the "pasties" we had bought from Heaven

at Betsy's, and I got out a couple of cans of Coke, some plates and napkins, setting everything on the table. I kept my eyes from Gia's. I was nervous. Because here it was again. Did she really believe me?

"Tell me all of it, Emery."

"You don't want to know."

"Emery, I do."

"I don't know, Gia," I said, considering. Was she going to run back and tell Dad? I didn't think so. But . . .

"Please? I'll spit-shake, just like when we were little. I'm so sorry, Emery." She spit into her palm all businesslike, just the way we used to, then reached her hand out to me.

I considered for a long moment, still unsure. But I spit into my palm, shook her hand. "That's really kind of disgusting."

"Yeah," she laughed.

I wiped my hand on my jeans. "Gia, it's all so weird. It's like I was being called here."

"A quest. Very *Lord of the Rings*. Go on."

I nodded. There was an edge, a sliver of doubt in me, wondering if I could or should trust Gia. She came and sat with me at the table, and we both took a big bite of our pasties. Gia raised her eyebrows. "This is good!"

"It is!" I said. "Like a handheld chicken potpie."

"All it needs is a stick."

"Not this again," I said, rolling my eyes. "Not every food would be improved should it be on a stick."

"We agree to disagree. Portability. Yumminess."

"Cheesecake on a stick. Lasagna on a stick."

"Exactly." We laughed then, and I took another bite of my pasty. We talked for a while, about home, about Chaney, school. And I decided to trust her. We sat in the dim afternoon light of my cabin, and I told her about my boy, about the key, about the church, about it all. Everything except Ash. I told myself I kept him a secret because he wasn't that big a piece of the puzzle, that he was no big deal. But truthfully, even as I was talking, I wondered if I was just keeping it, keeping him close, well, because I didn't want to put words to Ash, to us. Like this connection between us was too important, too fragile to dissect in a conversation. And I couldn't bear the idea of losing any of the hope that seemed wrapped up between Ash and me.

"Well, you've certainly done it," Gia said, wiping her mouth and taking a swig of her Coke.

"What's that?"

"You've made your own choices, Emery. You're here."

"You think I'm crazy."

"No, just brave. Braver than I could ever be. I'm proud of you."

I flushed a little. "Gia, that's not true."

"I wish I could help you. I mean, what do you think you're going to find? Do you think your boy is out there right now, needing you, or—"

"I don't know." My voice sounded flat, worried. "I really hope he's okay."

"Come on," Gia said, pulling me off the chair. "We gotta get you a phone."

"A phone? Why?"

"'Cause I have to leave, like, soon, get back home, and I'm gonna be a mental case if I have to think about you living up here in this cabin and I can't get in touch with you and vice versa. I mean, what if I have a boyfriend emergency?" Gia smirked, and I knew that she was just making light of the situation. She was worried about leaving me, my loops, my life being on the line.

"Okay." Because I could think of no way to make Gia feel better about this. My life *was* on the line.

At Hansen's General, we ran into Rob from the library, who gave me a shy hello. Gia introduced herself and pretended to grab his butt as he walked away. I rolled my eyes and quickly headed toward the cell phones I had seen the other day. Gia picked out this yellow utilitarian-looking cell phone that looked like it could survive deep-sea diving and a trip through a volcano. "It's disposable, ya know. One of those kind of ready-to-go, three-hundred-minute deals."

"Whatever you say, boss."

"But it has texting included," she said, flipping over the box. "'Cause God knows I gotta text you."

I took out my money to pay at the register, but Gia wouldn't hear of it. And on the way out of the store, she shoved a wad of bills from her wallet into my coat pocket. "I know you're not using cards, you don't want a trail. You gotta take my money. I withdrew a bunch, knowing I was coming here. I don't know how else to help."

"Gia, really, I have enough—"

"Live the high life out here in Esperanza. Buy yourself two pasties instead of one. A pair of designer snowshoes."

Gia's VW traversed the snowy road toward the cabin better than I thought it would. "Thanks for coming here, Gia," I said, my voice sounding more serious than I'd intended.

"Emery, of course. Don't say another word about it."

"I don't want to sound all dramatic or—"

"Don't. 'Cause it just sounds like you're saying goodbye to me. Don't do it. You're going to be fine somehow. Okay?"

"I will," I told her, because she needed to hear it. She looked so fragile then, her pale skin against her dark lashes, so young, compared to the weathered reflection I saw in the mirror lately. And I knew instantly that I had to do this for Gia. She needed me to do this. "Gia, I really think this is all going to turn out okay. I just need some time to—"

"Really?" She brightened. "You think you might figure all this out, come back and—"

"Yeah," I lied. "Come back home with some proof, something, get the doctors to see my point."

"Yeah?" Gia squealed. "You'll be home in no time!" And I envied her there in that moment, that she could still talk herself into this, still lie to herself, still hope in this way.

It felt good to keep her from the worst of it.

As we pulled in near the cabin, my shoulders tensed. Ash was sitting by the fire pit, like he was waiting for us, for me.

Gia slowed the car, and I could feel her eyes on my face. "Spill it, Emery. You know this guy. Your ears are red."

"Oops. I think I left out a little something." Ash stood up then, tipping his hat toward us.

"Yes, a very handsome cowboy something."

Gia popped open her car door, and I followed quickly. "Exciting!" she squealed.

"Hi," I said to Ash, feeling guilty somehow.

"Hi."

"I'm Gia," she offered, shaking Ash's hand.

I bristled, knowing the conversation that I would have to have later with Gia, wishing I didn't have to explain Ash to her, not wanting to have to justify any of it.

I unlocked the cabin door as Ash introduced himself to Gia. We stepped inside. I was aware that my ears were burning with embarrassment over how transparent I must look to Gia. Ash didn't meet my eyes. He was holding something close to his chest, something wriggling inside his coat.

"I just . . . I brought you something." He was embarrassed. Surely he hadn't counted on Gia's presence. He produced a snowy white kitten, with one black paw and a black spot over her right eye and ear.

"She was a barn cat, the runt of the litter. I just thought . . . For you."

I was momentarily caught off guard. He brought me a

cat. My eyes flitted to Gia, who was trying desperately to quell her giddiness. She reached over and petted the cat.

"Th-thank you," I stammered as I grabbed the fluffball from Ash. I scratched the kitten behind her ears. "Hello!" I said. And I pushed my nose toward hers. I greeted her and snuggled her. She was no bigger than a teacup, tiny pink nose, wide green eyes. I caught a glimpse of Ash then. He smiled, beamed really, two scarlet patches high on his cheekbones, and there seemed a lightness to him that wasn't always there.

"She's gorgeous," Gia said, looking from Ash to me. "And wouldn't you know? I just have to get going. I'm sorry to rush off," she singsonged, looking from me to Ash.

"Gia, no, you can't."

"I have to. My parents will freak soon. I cut school, and I gotta get home before it's too late."

"Really?" I said.

Gia gave me a wink. "Really. Plus, I don't want to give the CIA any reason to come after me." Gia shot me a look, and I knew she was referring to Dad, his cronies.

"I've got the phone," I told her. I handed the cat to Ash. "I'm just going to walk Gia out."

Ash nodded, scratching the fluffball behind the ears.

Gia grabbed her backpack and a Coke from the fridge. On the porch steps, I closed the door behind us. "Gia, I was going to tell you about Ash, but it's a long story and it's nothing—"

Gia surprised me by hugging me tightly. "I'm so sorry about not believing you. And you don't have to explain everything to me. You don't have to explain why you might have befriended a hottie who likes to bring you kittens. No explanation needed."

"It's not like that," I said. I didn't know what it was like.

"You're safe here, though, if I go? He's okay?" Gia gestured toward the cabin. She stopped for a moment on the stoop, considering.

"Yes," I said. "And thanks for not giving me the third degree, for not—"

"Emery, I trust you."

"You do? Thanks, but he's not, we're not . . . It's nothing."

Gia just gave me a look, winking. "I'll be texting you later for the details."

I rolled my eyes. "Gia, thank you for coming. I really needed you."

"Whatever. I don't think you did. I think you've got it all under control." Gia blew me a kiss then and started toward her car. "But, Emery?" She turned back to me.

"Yeah?"

"I know you're totally focused on the loops, the mystery. And I know you'll get it all figured out. But remember what you told me in the hospital, what you told me you wanted?"

"What?" I couldn't remember. "A decent meal?"

"To live."

Even in the distance, I could see the sadness in Gia's

eyes. She knew that I had meant that I wanted to live . . .
before it all caught up to me. Before I died.

"Thank you," I said to Ash as I came back in and threw my
coat on a chair. Maybe it was Gia's goodbye, or maybe it was
just seeing this little kitten, this gesture of kindness. But I
was feeling all kinds of sentimental, blinking tears from my
eyes.

"No, no problem," he stammered. I pretended not to notice when his cheeks flushed, and I noticed he had started a
fire. I reminded myself not to fall in love with him.

Ash went out to the clearing and brought in a cardboard
box, which contained some kitten food, a water bowl, a scrap
of burlap, which I immediately knew I would replace with
one of my fluffier bath towels.

Ash took off his coat and hat, hung them on the hook
behind the door. He sat on the floor cross-legged. I sat down
across from him, and the kitten immediately went to Ash,
purring and snuggling up to his chest. Ash produced a little
red satin toy mouse, which he dangled in front of the kitten.

Ash tossed the mouse and the kitten went crazy, clawing
at it, biting it, flicking it in the air with her paws. I picked up
the mouse and threw it in the air. The kitten jumped and
caught it, stuck her proud nose high, and pranced back to
Ash, leaving the mouse in his lap. We played with the kitten
for a long while, the fire crackling behind me. We cooed and
fawned over how cute the kitten was. All the while, I stole

glances at Ash, unsure why this cowboy would do this for me, this kindness.

"You have to name her," I told Ash.

"No," he said. He held the toy mouse by the tail and jiggled it for the kitten, then shoved it up his shirtsleeve. The kitten knew exactly where it was, clawing at his wrist.

Ash chuckled and let the cat try to wrestle it out of his sleeve. The firelight danced in Ash's eyes, and I found myself drawn over and over to the gracefulness of his hands. They were large and roughened from work, but they moved with such grace, an artist's hands.

"Come here, No Name," I said, clicking my tongue. The kitten had gotten the mouse loose and was giving it quite the business. The kitten ignored me, and Ash as well, batting the mouse under the table, around the kitchen, toward the fireplace.

"Cheap entertainment," Ash said. "Emery, you have to name her. I'm sure you had a name in mind when you were a kid."

"No. You name her."

To my surprise, Ash took one look at the kitten and said, "Eyepatch."

I wrinkled my nose.

"Too weird," he said. "Socks?"

"No, too cutesy."

"How about Dala?" Ash asked.

"Dala?" I considered this.

"So, after you leave, you can have her to remember this place."

My thoughts quickly turned dark. "I may not be able to keep her and—"

"She can always go back to the barn, Emery," Ash said, eyeing me.

How could I explain that certainly this tiny kitten would outlive me? That my loops, this mystery, my odd, lonely existence, were surely coming to some sort of conclusion? Hadn't the older version of my father practically spelled it out for me? Wasn't that why I was here? To solve this last mystery? Live a little before this all finished me?

I knew this, deep down. But this kitten, brand-new and full of excitement, brought it home to me in a way that I hadn't expected.

I pushed away these morbid thoughts; they were not helpful. "Dala," I said, scratching the kitten under her chin. She flopped down in front of me flat on her back, paws raised in the air. "Oh, please may I pet your belly?"

"So Gia is a friend from home?"

"Yeah, a good friend." I cleared my throat and felt empowered by Gia's visit. "Tell me about Next Hill," I said, trying to sound casual. I stole a glance over at Ash.

He scratched the stubble on his chin, and if we were playing poker, I would bet that this was his nervous tell. "I actually have to go," he said, getting up from the floor.

"You do?"

"I do." He grabbed his coat and hat. I thanked him again, and he left us then. Dala and me.

This was going to be harder than I thought. I filled Dala's dish with water. She swirled between my feet the whole way into the kitchen, rubbing up against my ankles.

But Dala got agitated then, as I bent down to fill a bowl with the food Ash had left for her. She meowed loudly, and clawed at my feet, my ankles.

"Shh," I told her, and I set her in front of her food, but Dala wouldn't have it. She meowed more loudly now and jumped up at me, clawing at my jeans, desperately trying to get me to pick her up.

So I did, and it was then that the buzzing swelled behind my eyes. My eyelids fluttered.

I quickly sat in the kitchen chair. I tried to push back the swell, but it was too big, too forceful. The cat nuzzled her face into the crook of my elbow, hiding. "You knew," I said. Then my body stiffened.

I was gone.

Mom

I'm sitting on a hot plastic lawn chair at the public pool in Ann Arbor, in my old neighborhood. The sun beats down on the concrete pool deck, on my arms, my legs, in my eyes. I watch several small kids splashing and laughing in the water with their moms holding them. They wear bright orange floaties and crazy-happy smiles. I smell sunblock and fresh popcorn from the concession stand.

I instantly spot my own mom. She is young and pale, her dark hair pulled back from her face, a small patch of freckles dotting the bridge of her nose. I had forgotten about her freckles. Her face is tilted back in laughter, and there I am, in her arms, splashing, kicking. I'm being held by my mom. I'm small, curly-headed, in my pale green bathing suit with the blue, glittery fish print.

My four-year-old self keeps pushing away from my mom, keeps saying, "My own self!"

Mom lifts me and gently places me on the side of the pool, and I don't hesitate. I back up, take a running start, and fling myself into the water, a look of pure joy on my face. Mom catches me as I go under.

I remember this day. I remember parts of it. Refusing to wear the orange floaties. Mom's laugh, the way the water beaded on her long lashes. I remember being so happy.

"That's my girl!"

Her voice is loud, clear, rising above the clatter and splash of the swimming children. It takes a beat for me to realize that Mom is looking right at me, the grown-up me, speaking to me.

I point at my chest. She nods. I wonder briefly how I can be here—two me's at one time. But I don't care. It's Mom.

"Yes, you, Emery," she says, and nods. "I love you."

I feel then this spot of aching, this empty place inside, so familiar, so part of my everyday that I notice it now only because it changes. I feel it shrink, heal itself somewhat, fill itself up, and I smile at her. She is beautiful, just as I remember her, and she smiles back at me.

The colors fade in around my vision.

I wave goodbye.

Seventeen

I woke up smiling from my first-ever loop with Mom. My head was lying on the kitchen table, my body slack in the chair. Dala was curled up at my head, now trying to lick my cheek. It was dark in the cabin, cold. I got up to stoke the fire and could barely stand. My vision tunneled, blackness puddling around the edges. I sat back down and put my head between my knees. I stood up again after a few minutes. I was okay. Still dizzy, worn, definitely worse than my usual after-loop self. But I was happy. I felt that tingle behind my eyes, that rush in my head, and pushed back the tears. Mom. I hadn't realized how much I missed her.

How much seeing her would mean to me. How much a few words of encouragement might hearten me.

When the fire had warmed, I crept into my bed, fuzzy-headed and hollowed out from my loop. Dala nestled herself into the crook of my neck and collarbone. I sighed a deep sigh and scratched Dala's ears, my mom's face still burning brightly in my mind—and her words burning in my heart—as I drifted off to a happy sleep.

Dala bit at my hair, pulling it, tugging it. I woke up and saw that the sun was high in the sky. We had slept late. I sat up and instantly noticed a note on the floor, as if it had been slipped under my cabin door. I padded over to it. *Dinner to-night?* was all it said. The neat, elegant printing made my heart leap inside my chest.

I knew it would be hard—no, impossible—to keep things all business between us. And this scared me, but it also thrilled me. And, really, after my loop with Mom, I felt different. Like I could do anything. Like maybe I just had to dive right in.

I tried to prepare myself for any outcome. I mean, what did I think I was going to do, tell Ash my secrets over dinner and then he would explain to me exactly what was going on in my loops, figure it all out, wrap it up in a bow? Then maybe confess his odd and inexplicable attraction to me as well? It was ridiculous, and I knew that this was true on some level. But so much of my life up until this point had been ridiculous.

I trekked to Hansen's for some groceries and then spent

most of the morning trying to replicate the stained glass from my loop with my brush and acrylics. When I had finished, it was okay, good enough to show someone—like the historical society in Charlevoix—in order to ask if they'd seen it. But it wasn't perfect, so I started over with watercolors. I concentrated on my technique, forcing myself not to think only about Ash.

As the sun set, I was shaking my head against my every thought about him, cutting up tomatoes, when I heard the knock on the door. Even his knock was deliberate, forthright.

I steeled myself as I opened the door, trying to calm the ridiculous beating of my heart, telling myself to settle down and quit acting like a fool.

You just have to figure out how he fits into this puzzle, what information he has, I told myself.

"Emery," Ash said with a smile that was just a tad crooked to the left, and I could feel my resolve quickly slipping away. Dala greeted him enthusiastically, circling his legs, purring and purring.

He waited there at the door until I asked him to come in. "I can take your coat," I told him.

I savored the scent of him as I took his coat and hung it on the hook on the back of the door. We stood there together, just inside the threshold for a moment, smiling at each other. He took his hat off then, and reached past me to add it to the hook on the door. As he did this, he leaned so close to me—soap, hay, him.

I wanted to reach my hand over to him and feel the rough scrape of his stubble under my fingertips. The need to touch his face was overwhelming, but I bit my lip and got control of myself.

"Let's eat," I said cheerily, and we made our way over to the table. I put out the tossed salad and served us both a bowl of soup; then I quickly toasted the bread for the grilled cheese, tomato, and bacon sandwiches I had been preparing. "The pickings are a bit slim when you only have a hot plate," I told him as I finished up the sandwiches and joined him at the table.

"Thank you. It's good," he said, tasting his soup. He averted his eyes.

"I just wanted to apologize for ambushing you at the Wingings, and for attacking you at the stables, being ungrateful—"

"No problem." He didn't look up. I watched him break off a tiny piece of bacon and give it to a very grateful Dala.

"I acted ridiculous," I told him. "I just have been kind of under a lot of pressure, and I don't usually cry on a stranger's shoulder, or pass out upon meeting them, or need constant attention, or generally act like a lunatic. . . ." I smiled wryly, trying to lighten the mood.

He didn't look up. He didn't laugh. He took a big bite of his sandwich and licked his lips, nodding.

I stirred my soup and took a sip of lemonade. Okay . . .

"You don't need to apologize." And then he looked up. "Are you sick?" he asked.

"No," I said.

"But you were in the hospital."

"Yes. It's complicated."

"And it has to do with what you thought I knew about you."

"Yes." A part of me just wanted to spill it all to him. I was nearly positive he would believe me. But that wasn't the part that worried me. I didn't want to give him any reason to leave, to be scared of me. And given my current status in life, I knew I was acting ridiculous thinking about us together beyond this dinner. But I was. In fact, I couldn't stop thinking about it. It was a stupid thought. But there it was, stronger and more real than almost anything I'd ever felt.

We ate in silence for a bit. I picked. He ate and ate more. "You're a good cook," he told me, smiling that smile again, and my insides turned to jelly once more.

"So had you been living here in our stolen cabin long, before I came and usurped?" I asked.

"No, not long. A couple of weeks."

"And have you been in Esperanza long?"

"A few months."

"Jeannette said you have your own place."

"I did, just a one-room over the Laundromat."

"But not anymore?"

"I needed the money for other things." He didn't elaborate.

"And you didn't get stitches like I told you to."

"I just put a butterfly bandage on it. It's fine."

He sat back and pushed his plate away. He produced something from his jeans pocket then, and I immediately recognized it as the crumpled portrait of me. "What didn't you like in my picture?" He didn't talk around it. He didn't apologize for wanting to know. He just asked.

So I told him.

"The way you drew my hair, the curls."

"It gives something away? It betrays you somehow?"

I nodded.

He shook his head. "I don't get it."

"I know."

"So tell me, Emery. I want to know."

I saw something flash across his face again, remorse maybe. I didn't know him well enough yet. But I knew he wasn't without his demons.

"You tell me something first," I answered.

"Okay." His jaw set hard. He tapped his foot under the table, a nervous rhythm. "I'll tell you something." He motioned to my watercolor on the mantel of the stained glass. "That is really something."

"Does it look familiar to you?" I asked.

"No. Should it?"

I shook my head. "It's stained glass from a church."

Ash shook his head. Okay, so maybe he didn't have *all* my answers.

"You painted that?" he asked.

I nodded, not willing to let him off the hook here. He was going to answer some questions. "Why do you *still* sleep out in the clearing? I'm sure the Wingings would let you—"

"To make sure you're okay," he answered plainly.

My stomach leaped into my throat, and I felt the blush rush up to my ears and into my cheeks. It took me several seconds to regain my composure.

"A harder question," I said. "How did your mom pass away?" I thought of the picture he had drawn, the horror in the woman's face.

I watched his face and waited for him to respond, and I realized that I had already developed a habit of being completely still when he spoke so that I wouldn't miss a thing, wouldn't miss the low timbre of his voice, wouldn't miss the hint of gravelly-ness in it. It was too rich, too sparse to ignore. I wanted to memorize it.

"She was killed in a car accident. Drunk driver."

"Oh, Ash." I thought of the pain in that drawing. My heart sank for him. "I'm so sorry."

He nodded and looked away.

"Does it have anything to do with why you're running?" I asked.

"Are you so sure I'm running?"

"Hiding?" I waited and he didn't answer. "I have some

experience." I gave him a little grin then. "I've watched a few movies, read a few spy novels."

He smiled then and leaned forward. "And Next Hill is a place near where I grew up." He looked me in the eye. "How you know that, I don't know. . . ."

I offered no answer. Not yet. Some things you really couldn't get at straight on. I sensed this was one of them.

Ash rubbed the stubble on his chin, and with his other hand, he grabbed my hand across the table. "I'll probably tell you all my story, Emery, someday. Whether I should or not."

I wasn't sure what he meant by that, but with the heat of his roughened palm against my knuckles, I could think of nothing else. His touch made me feel like when I'm about to pass from the loop back to my normal self. It's a dreamy, swimmy sensation, when I *feel* all the colors around me.

It was close to that—but better.

"Your turn," he said, and took his hand back. "Tell me why you're here."

I considered lying. I opened my mouth, about to give him the college story again, but I thought of Dad then, the older version of Dad, telling me I was going to be scared. It made me change my mind somehow. I wanted to be brave, take a chance.

"I'm running away from my dad, the doctor. From a scientific course of experiments."

"So the college thing?"

"Not true."

"So you are some kind of scientist?"

"No, I'm a lab rat."

He considered this. He didn't flinch or squint his eyes in judgment. And I almost started to go on, to finish it, to tell him everything. Part of me wanted to, but I didn't. I got up to clear the dishes, unsure if I had said too much. He stood to help me, or was it to leave? I closed my eyes at the sink and steadied my breath.

He can't leave—not yet. This can't be done. I wanted him to stay. I felt my eyelids flutter a bit. Dala appeared at my feet, meowing, clawing at my legs. Ammonia stung the back of my throat.

No, not now. Not now! I fought with my consciousness. I felt my eyelids flutter once again and steeled myself, grabbing the edge of the sink, white-knuckled. No! I willed myself to stay here—to be here, with Ash.

"Scrabble?" he asked from behind me.

I pushed the flutter back. I took a big breath, then gritted my teeth. Not now! I pushed back with every muscle in my body.

Ash had gotten up to grab the dusty, unused Scrabble game off the cabin's bookshelf. I laughed a quiet laugh to myself. The thrum and swell behind my eyes diminished then, deflated like a balloon. I felt my breathing pattern slow back to normal. I had controlled it.

I had stopped myself from looping. I felt the exhaustion in every single muscle wash over me. But I had stopped it.

Holy shit! This was red-letter. I had stopped myself from looping. I stood at the sink and took a deep breath, letting my grip on the counter loosen.

So many times I had tried to do exactly this, so many failures, so many hash marks in my little pile of notebooks. I picked up Dala, nuzzled her nose.

But tonight, I had fought it and won. I had fought back the loop. I was not naive enough to think that this was the end of it, that I'd always be able to beat the loop. But it was a first. And if I could do it once—

I realized then that I had been silent for too long. Ash was saying my name.

"Are you okay? Emery?"

I turned to face him. "Scrabble?" I said. "You must be a glutton for punishment."

He studied my face for a moment, and his hand flinched at his side as if he might move forward, reach out. He didn't.

He settled himself on the floor in front of the hearth, spreading out the Scrabble board before him. He folded his large frame and sat cross-legged. "You know, I've never lost."

He gave me that smile again, and I did believe him.

"H-a-r-b-o-r," I spelled triumphantly, laying the letters down on a triple-word score, shooing Dala away from the board.

I jumped up then and celebrated with a quick pirouette.

Ash laughed. I liked how his face looked when he laughed,

and it was a deep laugh, one that came from way down in his chest.

He gave me a smirk then, and scanned over his letters. He placed them slowly, triumphantly, using his own triple-word score.

"Awry?" I said. "You are a sneaky bastard."

He let out another laugh.

"So tell me about your family," I said, hoping against hope that I wouldn't see that dark cloud come back to his face.

I watched his face carefully, the shadow briefly crossing it. But he ignored my question and the shadow went with it.

"Do you believe in God?" he said instead.

"Umm," I started, thinking this was an interesting beginning to a conversation, but I was learning that Ash was nothing short of direct. "I don't think so," I answered. I watched him carefully. "I have never been taught about God. Science, yes. Darwin, yes. Nietzsche, yes. God, not so much, except for . . ." I let my voice trail off.

"I believe in God," he said, filling in the silence. "You don't except for . . . ?"

"It's so easy to find the reasons why not. It's easy to find the reasons why he can't be. Or she!" I looked up at him then, not knowing if I should continue. "But sometimes, in the moment, sometimes it's hard to discredit an almighty being, when there is so much organized beauty in the world . . . experiences, certain people, certain feelings of the heart . . .

it's hard to credit such beauty to formulas, to science, to anything but God," I finished quietly, self-consciously.

"I know exactly what you mean," he said. My cheeks and ears flushed. He watched me in the firelight, and I could feel his eyes on my face.

I fidgeted with my Scrabble tiles, embarrassed.

He cleared his throat. "I was raised in the church, in the traditions that go with it, the rules, the stipulations, the guilt. . . ." He let his voice trail off.

"Where did you grow up?"

"Southern Illinois, near Bloomington. And you?"

So Next Hill was in Illinois. I filed this away. "Ann Arbor, mostly. My mom died when I was young. And Dad, he's a neurologist. . . . He is . . ." I considered this. "I don't know how to finish that. . . . He's my father. We used to be tight, but so much . . ."

"You don't have to tell me," Ash ventured.

I shook my head, continued. "After Mom died, it was just us against everything. But this thing that's going on with me. This thing . . ." I repeated it as if it left a bad taste in my mouth. "It's kind of come between us. Dad had always believed it was something exceptional. And for a while, I thought he was coming around to believing my theory, but . . ."

I so badly wanted to spill it all, tell him everything that had transpired, that had brought me to this place, this cabin, this moment.

But I was scared.

It startled me as I sat here in the firelight with this boy, because I wasn't sure for which reason I was hedging my bets—because I was scared I wouldn't get his help to figure out what was needed for my boy in the loop, or because I was afraid I would scare him and his crooked smile, his perfect stubble, away from this cabin.

"Some things can't be explained," Ash said.

I snapped out of my reverie then and looked at Ash. Our eyes locked. "Exactly." I waited a beat. Then, "Like how I know about Next Hill."

I knew at that moment it had gone too far. I wasn't sure why. But I knew he would leave.

"We need—I mean, *you* need firewood." He got up quickly then and grabbed his jacket. He stepped out into the clearing and headed toward the stump that he used for splitting.

I watched him out the window, my arms crossed over my chest, unsure whether he would come back, unsure how much crossing that line had cost me.

As I watched him, big fluffy flakes of snow began to fall, coating everything in a white cottony blanket.

Ash's breath came out in a heavy cloud of steam against the frigid night air. The faint light from Fischery Lighthouse began to swoop past him every few seconds, lending a rhythm to my view out the window. The thud of the ax, a heavy puff of breath, the shining funnel of light. Thud, breath, swoop of light. All the while, my mind kept returning to the look in his eyes when I had mentioned his family, the firm, hard line of his jaw, the deep, dark sadness of his eyes, the soft, gentle gracefulness with which he moved his large hands. All of these memorized with only stolen glances in the firelight.

And he had bought a bike for Lily Winging. And probably had given his hard-earned money to the Cranes' golden anniversary party. I just had a feeling.

I was so hungry to know there was still good in this world. And here he was.

He placed the ax on the ground and lifted one knee up onto the tree stump, wiping his brow with his gloved hand. There was a slump to his shoulders, a way that he carried himself in moments like these.

I was almost certain that what was bothering him was guilt. If I had to guess, it would be guilt over something with his family.

I wanted to go to him, run out there and shake him by his shoulders and make him tell me all his secrets, and, likewise, give mine up to him. But my gut told me otherwise, to let things unfold with Ash, to let him learn to trust me. And vice versa.

He didn't come back in that night. And I didn't go out after him.

The Labyrinth

I'm walking through the garden labyrinth near the aquarium in Ann Arbor. Precisely pruned green shrubs act as the walls of this intricate Michigan-famous maze. I have been here many times before in my home loop.

I walk quickly, hoping I might find Dad here. I try to run a bit, but I flail and pitch forward around a corner. I get up slowly, telling myself to settle down, although the sky is getting darker now, creepier. I walk along a pathway and hear whispering, tiny, distant voices, and I round another corner, certain that I will run into someone.

This happens once, twice. The seeds of panic begin to take root in my belly. Why can't I catch up with them? What will I do when it is completely dark?

I stand at a T-intersection in the labyrinth now. The voices are hard to hear, the darkness seeping in around me quickly. I choose left for no reason and pick up my gait.

The voices sound as if they are behind me now, and I don't like it, childlike whispers and a deep, guttural laugh. I begin to run, throwing one foot in front of the other. But my body can't handle it. I lose my footing, trip forward. I yell out as I fall.

"Slow down," a voice says. I look up from the ground, startled, then instantly calmed. It is my dad, my older dad.

Before I can answer, the colors emerge in the edges of my vision. "No, wait," I say, reaching my hands up toward him, trying to push my mind against it, but I have no success.

"Slow down," he says again.

Back home.

Eighteen

I took Dad's advice.

I slowed down.

I softened my interrogation tactics and just let Ash and me get to know each other. It became easy to fall into a pattern with Ash, to play house, together with Dala. He spent the days at work at the stables, and I went to the library or the locksmith's, trying hard to get somewhere with my key or the stained glass, finding nothing.

And then Ash and I would meet at the cabin for dinner. I made myself slow down. We played Scrabble or backgammon. We read—he read Wells's *The Time Machine,* which I secretly snickered at, and I read Austen. He was nearly as well read as I was, and we talked forever about books and movies, about lots of things. We talked about things, yes, but not yet the real things, not the things that mattered, the things that were tethering us to each other, yet holding us back. We circled around things. Circled them, coming closer each day, each night.

For whatever reason, my loops hung back as well, slowed down. I enjoyed the rest, and I forced myself not to spend too much time trying to figure out the reasons for this short break. Because, really, I knew the loops were there. Circling. I wasn't kidding myself. I could feel them building up inside me. They were coming. They were going to be strong. And I didn't have that much control.

As I drifted off to sleep that second night, a tiny idea popped into my head for the first time. Not a full-blown idea or theory, but a little kernel of possibility. Maybe my boy was not warning me against Ash, and I had gotten that wrong.

Maybe Ash was not simply a source of information in this puzzle that my boy was unfolding for me, and Ash was not a side story.

Maybe he fit in somehow in a bigger way. Did this make sense? I chewed on it for a bit. I tabled it and, over the next couple of days, plunged headfirst into getting to know Ash.

I learned Ash loved pasta with red sauce but hated capers. And he had played baseball in high school. Center field. His father had taught him to draw when he was very small. His first car was a green Pontiac, and his first girlfriend was named Melanie. And he was allergic to shellfish.

By day four, I had written many details about Ash in my

purple notebook. But I felt no closer to helping my boy. And getting to know Ash truly was unsettling in the oddest way. These pieces, these slivers of his life, of his character, were real, and a bit too inviting. I loved each new discovery more than the last.

He ate Cody's Brussels sprouts, for God's sake, and fixed sick horses, and bought bikes for little kids, and gave me a kitten, and the list went on.

And so did the texts from Gia. The first: *Did u kiss him yet?* The most recent: *Carpe diem.*

"What kind of farm did you grow up on?" I asked the next night while we were playing euchre.

"Soybean and corn."

"Lots of animals?" I asked.

"Not at first, but my little brother, Frankie, he finally wore Pop down. Frankie had this big idea that we should grow pumpkins, do a whole pumpkin patch thing in the fall, with a corn maze, a haunted house, the works. He was only four or five at the time, but he could be persuasive."

"So, did you?" I asked.

"Oh yeah. It was hard to turn down Frankie. And so, the next year, Frankie decided the pumpkin patch would be even better with animals, a petting zoo, the whole thing. He enlisted Mom too, because she always said horses would be good on our farm. She liked to ride."

"So your dad just bought some animals, then?"

"I guess you had to know Frankie, had to know Mom." He smiled to himself. "That's how I started falling in love with horses. Made me want to become a vet . . ."

Ash's smile was wistful, full of memory, full of love. But it quickly turned dark. "That was when we were young, before Pop . . ." Ash shook his head, cleared his throat. "Frankie died in the accident with my mom."

"I'm sorry," I said, holding back the urge to wrap my arms around him. I knew he didn't want that. "Do you miss them?" I asked.

"Every day," he answered, rubbing his stubbly chin. "It took me a long time not to feel like I was the one that should've died. That Frankie should've lived . . ."

"Survivor's guilt."

"I was older, supposed to protect him. Protect them. That's all I had been doing for years." He shook his head then, shook the memory away. "I was fourteen when they died. I just had a hard time processing it all. I went a little wild there a couple years ago."

We sat quietly for a while. Ash called trump. Spades. "Go big or sleep in the streets."

I laughed.

"What was your childhood like?" he asked.

"Oh, pretty normal," I told him. And it felt true to me. The loops hadn't kept me from a normal childhood for many years at least. Until, of course, they did. But I didn't tell Ash any of this, not yet.

I went to flip over the first card from the deck at the same time as Ash. Our hands grazed each other, and he surprised me, grabbing my hand for a moment, running his thumb across the back of my knuckles. I smiled at him. He smiled back. And there was nothing between us, keeping us apart, just for a moment.

But then the fire crackled and the moment was gone. I had secrets, baggage. He did too. He let go of my hand.

But I replayed it, that touch initiated by him, over and over in my mind as I fell asleep later that night. His hand holding mine, the dark lashes framing his eyes.

Me in my warm, toasty cabin. Ash in his tent by the fire.

I fell asleep wondering if maybe tomorrow would be the night that he didn't show up. He wouldn't think twice about forgetting this girl with the secrets and the bad, frizzy hair. And I wouldn't have gotten any answers out of him, and I wouldn't know how to begin looking for him. But that voice sounded surprisingly unconvincing in my head tonight as I thought about his hand grabbing mine. That pull between us.

Even so, this life we were weaving together in bits and pieces seemed fragile and fleeting, and would certainly come to an end. Didn't everything?

Nine

I'm in the boy's barn, but he is not there. The Victrola sits on an old wooden workbench. I touch the cold metal of the large, swirled cone. A stringed instrument sits next to the Victrola, a flat wooden frame with many strings. It looks related to a harp. I think it is called a dulcimer. I try to pluck a string, but I can't work my fingers precisely enough.

Over the workbench, a jersey hangs tacked on the wall. A baseball jersey, red and white, with the number nine sewn on the front. It is made of shiny polyester material. It looks odd, out of place in this barn, too modern beside the metal hand plows leaning up against the wall and the large wooden carriage in the rear corner.

I reach up to the jersey. It is silky and smooth under my touch. The colors whoosh into view, coming from my peripheral vision. Nine, I think. And I am gone.

Nineteen

I awoke suddenly in my library study carrel with my head on the desk in front of me, a small puddle of drool beside my mouth. I wiped it away on my sleeve and looked around. My ears rang with the whooshing, wind-tunnel sounds of my loop. It took several moments for my hearing to come back.

My vision blurred as I cleaned up my papers and put the microfiche away. My temples throbbed with the after-loop headache. I fetched my notebook from my backpack and jotted down a few notes. How could that modern-day jersey be there, in my boy's barn? And the significance of that number again. Nine.

I suddenly felt defeated. I had been gone and free from Ann Arbor for thirteen days, and what did I have to show for it?

I stomped home crabbily from another fruitless day at the library, another absurdly cryptic trip in the loop. I was utterly unable to make any headway in my mystery. In my life. In my control of these loops. I had been so excited that I had controlled one. One. But here I was.

And I was mad at myself for letting Ash take so much of my time, thoughts, and energy. I felt selfish. Because if he cared about me, even just as a friend, wasn't I merely setting him up for loss? It was all only a matter of time.

Ugh.

Time. I was racing the clock here. I needed to help my boy, figure this thing out, and for too many days, my notebook had nothing new written in it except ridiculous, poorly rendered portraits of the span of Ash's shoulders, the cuffs of his work jacket, his jawline in the firelight.

My boy was in the past, probably waiting patiently, being devastated by whatever he needed help with, and here I was, screwing around. For some reason, he was counting on me. He obviously couldn't lean on anyone else, couldn't depend on anyone around him.

And it was more than that. I was exhausted, wrung. This was killing me. The loops were killing me. Even if they were more infrequent lately, they were worse, harder. *Evolving.*

I jerked my backpack higher onto my back and stopped to catch my breath, the woods on the evergreen path suffocating me. I couldn't get my breath. I sat down then in the snow. I gasped, trying to draw enough oxygen into my lungs. My heart beat heavy, uneven in my chest. My head pounded; my vision blurred, burned.

I promised myself that I would spend the evening brainstorming new ways of coming at my problem.

When I walked up to the cabin, I saw that the door was cracked open. I immediately felt my hackles rise. Who was here? Who was looking for me?

But as I peeped inside and tiptoed around, I saw that nothing was out of place. Could I have left it unlocked? Could the wind have blown it open?

Then I saw Dala's box. She was gone.

"Dala!" I called. I clucked my tongue. Nothing.

I got out two saucers and poured a bit of milk in one, clicking the saucers together, her usual, most favorite, can't-purr-enough moment.

Dala didn't appear. I looked under the bed, inside the tub, behind the bathroom door. Everywhere. Then I flopped on the love seat, unsure what to do. I put my head in my hands, rubbed at my eyes. Was I really going to cry over this?

"Hey," Ash said, startling me. He stood at the still-open door.

"She's gone!"

And I immediately became furious, seething with anger at Ash. "You gave me that damn cat!" I yelled. "You gave her to me! Made me care about her! And now look! She's gone!"

"She is?" Ash's eyes scanned around the cabin. "Did the door blow open? That happens sometimes when it's not locked."

I stood up. "Don't you blame this on me!" I screamed, and my anger swelled. "She's out there, probably freezing! All alone!"

"She's a barn cat, Emery. She'll be fine."

"She's a runt! You said so yourself. And she's probably scared and not knowing what to do. And just feeling like she's in this all by herself!" I was poking Ash in the chest when I said this now, spitting my words at him. "You did this! Why did you have to show up here, anyway? With your stupid kitten and your stubble and your evasiveness and your impossible swagger!"

"Emery—"

"No, I have things to figure out! On my own!" I yelled at him.

He looked at me, although I could barely register his face through my blurry-eyed rage. "Get out of here!" I yelled, and pushed him with both hands as hard as I could, right in his chest. "She's out there all alone!" I pushed him again. He didn't budge. He just took it, his face drawn, stalwart. He reached his arms out for me, but I pushed them away.

"Just leave me alone!" I beat my fists on his chest then, and he let me. I hit him and I swore, every word in the book, and I bit my lip, biting back the tears, for my lost cat, for my lost little boy who needed me, for my lost hope . . . my lost chance for a normal life.

When I had exhausted myself, Ash gently smoothed my hair, and the last thing I saw before he turned to leave was the look on his face. It wasn't anger. It wasn't pity. It was the soft stare of empathy.

And in that moment, I was sorry, so sorry I had taken it all out on him, because I knew none of it was his fault. But as I opened my mouth to say the words, nothing came out. I just watched him walk out and shut the door quietly behind him.

I lay back on my bed, staring at the ceiling. I started dialing Gia's number about twelve times, but I never pushed Send. I didn't know if I was giving Dad something to track. But I had to talk to her.

Finally I called. Her phone rang only once. "Emery," she said, her voice low, relieved.

"Gia, is this safe?"

"I think so. No, I don't know."

"You quit texting me."

"Listen, I don't know what's safe. Emery, they are nuts looking for you. They had these dogs at the hospital, your house."

"Dogs?"

"You know, the kind that track scents. Loretta said they tracked you to the bus station."

"Jesus. Maybe I should just come home."

"Emery, are you crazy?"

"Yes." I felt homesick, defeated.

"I think you've had enough people telling you what to do. You've gotta make up your own mind."

"I know."

"You okay?"

"No," I said. "But I'm not coming home."

"You getting anywhere with all this?"

"Not really," I answered with a sigh. We were silent for a long moment.

"Remember the fifth-grade talent show, when I was doing that dance—"

"Your leotard split right up the back. Who could forget that? Thank God you were wearing underwear, Gia," I laughed.

"Yeah, too bad they were SpongeBob."

"Oh, jeez, I remember that kid—Rotten Ronald—he would never let you forget that."

"Emery, you ran up on stage and threw your sweater around my waist, started doing the dance with me, just acted like it was no big deal."

"Why are you telling me this, Gia?"

"I don't know. It just seemed like the time in the conversation when I was supposed to tell you some meaningful story, give you some awesome advice, and send you on your way. And I got nothing."

"Gia!" I laughed.

"At least I made you laugh."

"Thank you," I giggled.

"Plus, I was the one who made sure Ronald sat in all that paint in art class about a week later. I never fessed up about that."

"Gia!"

"What? I was ten."

I laughed hard then.

"Are you scared, Emery?"

"Yeah." We sat in silence for a few moments.

"I love you, Emery."

"Like a sister."

Sometime in the night, I heard a gentle knock at the door. At first I thought it was part of my dream. But then I slowly became aware of another noise that eventually roused me. It was a meow.

I quickly got out of bed and opened the cabin door. There, in a small wire pet carrier, sat Dala. She meowed pleadingly over and over when she saw me. "You're home!" I squealed, and I reached down and picked up the crate.

I brought Dala inside. I carried her to the bed, cuddled her, so glad to have her back. She purred and purred, and she did that little thing where she nuzzled her nose into my ear and then bit my hair a little. We sat on the bed for a while, playing. I scratched her belly, and she pretended to bite me, just enough to let me know she was playing. I held her like a baby for a while, petting her, in the crook of my arm, and she swatted at the curls of my hair hanging down. She seemed so happy to be back. She even ignored her milk dish for a while so that she could curl up in my lap and be petted.

But when she did go to her milk dish, I walked to the window. The tent was up now. I could feel the wind slipping through the cracks of the old window. It was getting cold. Very cold.

I picked up the pet carrier to move it, stow it under the bed, but when I did, I noticed a small folded piece of paper inside. I set the carrier down and opened its door. I took out the note, unfolded it. Ash's elegant print. "You're not alone, Emery. I'm here."

I shook my head against the many reasons why I shouldn't go out there, against the embarrassment of what a fool I had acted like earlier.

But I threw on my down coat, my Gia scarf, and my boots, and I went out to him. I knelt inside his tent and caught him for a moment, unexpectedly. He was lying quietly on his back, his hands folded over his chest. His lips were moving quietly.

"I'm sorry," I muttered, and backed out of the tent. He had been praying. I was instantly sure of it. I had heard the word *forgive*. *Oh God,* I thought. *I'm such an ass.*

"Emery," he called, and I heard him scuffling out of the tent.

"I'm sorry." I avoided his gaze. How stupid I was to just think it was okay to wander into his tent. How stupid I was to assume that we were . . . to assume anything. "I apologize for interrupting you . . . for everything earlier. I never—"

"Emery," he said again, and waited for me to look at his face. "You don't need to apologize." He smiled. "What did you want?" he asked.

"Thank you for finding Dala."

He nodded.

"Where was she?"

"Not to make you feel too bad, but it wasn't easy."

"Did you risk life and limb?" I smirked.

"Several times."

I blushed, kicked my feet in the snow.

"I had to climb an evergreen about twenty feet up to grab her out of there. Something must have scared her up there."

"Oh, Ash. I apologize."

"You were right," he said, his eyes lowering.

"No, I wasn't. Nothing I said was—"

"No, you were right. If I'm going to be here, then I'm *here,* you know?"

He looked up after a long moment, and I could see that a decision had been made. There was a look in his face, a defiant set in his jaw.

With some effort, I recalled why I had come out here in the first place.

"This is crazy, Ash," I told him. "You can't sleep outside. You'll freeze."

"I won't," he said simply.

"I see you checking on me through the window."

"I know."

He stared at me and he reached toward me for a moment, but then thought better of it.

"What?" I asked, breathless.

"I can't come in. I can't stay with you."

My head felt swimmy then. For a moment, I wondered if I might loop, but no, this was a different sensation. "But I . . ." What did he think I was inviting him for exactly? "I was just offering a place next to the fire so you wouldn't freeze," I replied. But it didn't sound true even to me.

"Of course," he said, his face reddening. He brushed a snowflake off the tip of my nose.

"Good night," he said. And he kissed me. Just a light brush of his lips against mine. His soapy scent filled my lungs, and I felt my vision going fuzzy along the edges.

It was too much. I couldn't stop it this time. My eyes fluttered.

No! I told myself. *No!* I told my body. *Not now!*

But my eyes rolled back, my body went rigid. Ammonia. The look of horror on Ash's face was the last thing I saw as he reached for me, and I was gone.

Nan

I'm in my Nan's backyard. She has her watercolors and her easel set up near her garden, which is in full bloom at the moment—big purple and white hydrangeas, yellow sundrops, pink and orange Oriental poppies. The colors are glorious, swimming with depth here in the loop.

Nan's gray hair is loosely tied up in a red bandana. She looks over to me and gives me a big smile. She looks like Mom.

I smile back.

I briefly wonder where my boy is. But as usual I'm glad to be here in my loop, and I'm happy to see Nan here, a first in the loop.

"Come," Nan says, and I walk toward her. She looks young, vibrant. She moves more quickly, deftly than she does in the home loop. She hugs me tightly for a moment. She feels real, substantial. She lets go of me and holds me by the shoulders, surveying me.

"Remember, sometimes it's better to get at things from around a corner than to come at them straight on."

I nod and smile. I remember when I had been in the home loop. I was nine or ten, and Nan had been teaching me how to paint. I had been copying one of Monet's water lilies. Nan had told me that it looked too real.

"Isn't that good?" I had asked. "To look real?"

"Truth is a funny thing" was all she had said.

Here in the loop, with Nan, now it makes perfect sense.

More than that, it seems to be very important.

Nan lets go of my shoulders then and carefully selects a brush for me out of her canvas apron. She hands it to me, and I set about mixing a perfect blue for the hydrangeas. I put my first strokes on the sturdy art paper, my fine motor skills sloppy and imperfect.

Nan clears her throat, and I look over to her. "Emery, some people have a hard time with things." She narrows her eyes. "Especially some things . . . truth, beauty . . . when all they've known is pain, hurt."

I nod. I think of Ash. Her eyes speak to me . . . of Ash . . . or is it of me? That's when I see the colors. They are coming, around her head, her face. "Not yet," I say, reaching for Nan.

She reaches back, and our fingers touch for an instant.

Twenty

My eyelids fluttered open. I registered the cabin, Ash. I was lying in his arms. I took a big gulp of air, my throat feeling raspy, dry.

"Emery," Ash whispered. He tucked a piece of my hair behind my ear. He looked scared, wide-eyed.

"I'm here," I whispered.

We stayed like that for a long time, me in his lap, his arms around me, my head against his chest, tilted up toward him. He traced the lines of every feature of my face with his fingertips. My eyes never left him. I reveled in the warmth of his body beside mine, the perfect fit of my body next to his, the natural and relaxed way he held me to him.

"Tell me," he said.

I sat up then, realizing we were on the floor, next to the

hearth. Ash seemed reluctant to let me go. He grabbed my hands, held them tightly. I stared into the fire, the waves of exhaustion pummeling me, my headache throbbing. I noticed Dala curled in a ball on my pillow. My vision tunneled, and I shut my eyes against it.

"Emery, just tell me already. You look so damn fragile right now. I need to know. I can't . . . I won't leave."

I considered the weight of this sentence. I opened my eyes and my vision steadied. I stared at our hands knotted between us, and Ash rubbed my knuckles with his thumbs, and somehow this calmed me. I didn't look up, though. I didn't know if I could see the look of horror or disbelief in his eyes and still continue. I couldn't. But I knew I had to tell him. The time had come.

"When I seize like that, when I leave . . ."

I closed my eyes and took a breath. I held it in for a long moment, weighing what hung in the balance, knowing in order to be completely honest about how I wound up here, how we wound up in this cabin, I had to tell him the truth. Yet I was also fully aware that he might just laugh in my face. He might just roll his eyes. Or worse, say that he believed me for months, like Gia, only to eventually flake out when I most needed him.

I took another deep breath. "Fuck it." I looked him square in the face and said, "I time-travel."

A spark from the fire jumped then and crackled, startling us both. I glanced at Ash briefly and saw a look of confusion on his face. A moment passed and he squeezed my hands tightly.

"Go on," he said.

I took a deep breath, and I didn't look at him. I just jumped in.

"I go to a different time, the past or the future, and then I come back here. I don't always go back to the same times, but there are a few times, a few people, that I seem to frequent a lot, especially lately . . . this little boy. Anyway, it's been happening since I can remember. It used to always be in my sleep, from a dormant state. Just recently, I started to initiate from a wakeful state, which makes things a lot more hazardous." I let out a shaky laugh.

But I continued quickly—I didn't want to lose my nerve. "I think of it as two lines, two parallel lines—two dimensions, really—running along beside each other ad infinitum." I ran my two fingers next to each other for a long distance on the fireplace hearth. "Whether these are different ends of one dimension, one time, just wrapped around, I don't know. But I go back and forth. I loop. That's what I call it."

"Loop?" he said.

"I might seize for, say, twenty minutes, but I know I've been gone for an entire afternoon. I think my other dimension exists with loops of time that meander away from the straight line, and then come back, meeting up at the same point with my home loop, with this dimension. So nobody misses me." I looked up at him then, just for a moment. "The way I explain it, to doctors, to myself, is always with a drawing like this. Just exactly how you drew the curls in my hair."

I took my hands from his and drew the two lines in the hearth, with one looping out to the side and then coming back to meet the other line at the same place. I watched Ash carefully then, watched him consider this, letting it sink in.

He nodded. I had told him. I had given up my secret.

"So you're saying you are mentally aware? Or really physically gone, in the other time."

"Physically, definitely."

"How can you be so sure?"

"I'm physically there. I just know I am."

"So it's not like a dream, or an out-of-body-experience, or . . ."

"In some ways it is. It's kind of slow-moving. My thoughts get cloudy there. But the physical part is not a question for me, although that is often what my team gets hooked on."

He gave me a look. "Team?"

"The doctors."

I continued, "See, I've never been able to replicate the book light. But I took a book light with me into the loop. This was probably four years ago. And I didn't bring it back. It's still there. This little boy has it. I tried to take other things, like his jump rope once. I tried, but I don't have that much control. But that is changing. That is changing lately. And I get information about future stuff sometimes. I'll know things when I come back." I didn't tell him about the key yet.

I wasn't exactly sure why. Something inside told me not to. *Slow down*, I reminded myself.

"What kinds of things do you learn about?"

"I have this song. I learned it, heard it in the loop long before it ever was out, on the radio. Long before it was ever thought up or written. And in one loop, I sprayed a whole bunch of perfume on me. And although they would never admit it, my team could smell it when I came back. I could tell. They couldn't quantify that, you know? But it was real." I watched his face carefully and added, "And I've met my father there, in the future."

"Really?" Ash asked, shaking his head. "You know, I have seen quite a few epileptic seizures at the farm. A stallion of ours had seizures a lot. They weren't the same as what is happening to you. I could tell that even after the first time. Your seizures are more savage." He continued, "Einstein believed in time travel. The possibility at least. Wormholes."

"Exactly. And there's a whole new school of thought that discounts the grandfather paradox and explains time travel as a possibility within theoretical physics."

"And the seizures?" Ash asked. "Medication doesn't do anything?"

"Not a thing, because they aren't really seizures." I was excited now, animated.

"Stop for just a second," he said. I felt myself instantly recoil. Was he going to doubt me?

He must've seen the frightened look on my face. He

grabbed my hand. "Back up just a bit. What is the grandfather paradox?"

I smiled, relieved, looking at his hand in mine. "It's the biggest theoretical argument against the possibility of time travel. Simply put, if you can travel in time, you can affect events that would change the present and the future, such as you could go back and kill your grandfather, making yourself cease to exist."

"So how is that solved?"

"Well, the new theorists say that the universe simply won't let you kill your grandfather, either physically stopping you somehow or just by the fact that you will go back in time and you will change your mind. Your sheer existence keeps the grandfather paradox from coming true. The universe steps in to make sure that you can't kill your grandfather."

"Do you believe this?"

"Absolutely. It puts words and explanations to so many things that happen when I go to the loop. I can't use my hands very well. I'm there physically, but I don't have the will that I usually do, the control. And I often get sidetracked. Early on, I figured that it would certainly be simple enough to prove my theories to Dad, to Dr. Chen, even Loretta. I would just find them in the loop and tell them. Or I could bring something back, or I could find someone there. . . ." I stared into the fire, my voice dropping to a whisper. "Am I scaring you?"

"Not a bit."

I let out a deep breath then. "But when I get to the loop, I kind of forget why all these things are so important. And I just *am*. I'm simply in the moment, and I'm happy to be."

"Doesn't sound so bad."

"No, it's not. But it's a bit infuriating when I get back." I turned his hand over in mine, seeing a long, skinny, crescent-moon scar on his palm that I hadn't noticed before. I traced it with my fingertips. Ash closed his hand then, took it back, but gave me a smile.

I got up and stretched out my muscles by the fire.

"Is it exhausting?" he asked.

"Yes."

I padded to the kitchen and poured myself a glass of water. "I imagine it's like an astronaut would feel after traveling in space."

"What does it do to you physically?" He looked at me like he didn't want to know, but had to know.

I was scared to answer. Completely truthfully, anyway. "Kicks my ass."

I settled back down in front of the hearth across from him and watched the firelight dance in his eyes. I rubbed at my temples, my eyes. I was exhausted. I quickly set down my glass of water so Ash wouldn't see my shaking hand.

"Well, it keeps oxygen from getting to my brain all the time. There's damage to my brain, like lots of small strokes. And I have damage to my optic nerve. I get double vision a lot afterward, headaches."

Ash rubbed his chin, took it all in. And he stared at me. "Emery, you have no idea how brave you are." He took my hands in his.

I smiled. I rolled these words around in my head. Not a freak, but brave.

We sat in silence in front of the fire, and I marveled at the electric thrill that shot through my body simply from having his hands in mine, simply from feeling the rough scrape of his palm against my own.

I knew that my secrets were a lot to unload on him, and I was sure his mind was reeling, and I was tired. Yet I was thrilled that I had told him, thrilled that he had believed me. Thrilled that he was still here, with me, holding my hands in his.

"Emery."

I turned and looked at him. He reached his hand out, cupping my cheek in his hand, his thumb stroking my cheek, and I found myself thinking, *So this is what it feels like.*

Neither of us broached the subject of Ash leaving for his tent. I didn't want him to leave, and I hoped that he didn't want to either. When the fire began to die, Ash got up, and I climbed into my bed. He tucked the red-and-white quilt snugly all around me. I did not expect anything more, because I knew there were still secrets between us. His confession was still coming, and it couldn't be forced.

But he surprised me and lay down on top of the covers right next to me. I turned on my side, and we were face to face. He stroked my hair. I fought sleep and studied the gorgeous planes of his face, the generous mouth, the deep hazel of his eyes, the perfect combination of chiseled jaw and dark stubble.

"Thank you, Ash, for believing me." I was exhausted, barely able to keep my eyes open.

"Thank you for trusting me with the truth." He leaned toward me, and the last thing I registered before I slipped off to sleep was the soft, gentle press of his lips against mine.

I woke deep in the night to hear Ash's slow breathing, with almost a light snore. He wasn't in the bed anymore, but sleeping on the floor in front of the fire, his coat pulled over him like a blanket. I turned my face into my pillow and breathed deeply. I could still smell him.

I sneaked out of my bed then and dragged the quilt with me. I curled up beside Ash on the floor, snuggling up next to him. For a while, I just wanted to lie there and look at him, feeling the warmth of the dying fire, smelling the scent of Ash's soap-clean skin.

"I lied earlier," I whispered. I heard him wake then, the rhythm of his breathing break.

"What is it?" he said.

"I lied."

"About what?" he whispered.

"Well, I didn't exactly lie, but when you asked me how this stuff affects me physically, I didn't tell you the whole truth."

"What is it?" he asked, and I could see his brow furrow, his eyes squint in that worried way.

"It's killing me, Ash."

"No, don't say that," he said, his voice raw.

"It's true," I continued. I wanted him to know everything. "I know it's killing me. The doctors knew it."

We lay there in silence for what seemed like a long while. "Don't say it," Ash said again. As if he could will it not to be true.

The look on his face was so pained, his mouth pinched, his brow dark. It moved me. The tears welled in my eyes, but I wiped them with the back of my hand. Ash cupped my face with his hand, pulling my chin to his face. He very slowly and deliberately kissed each of my eyes, my nose, his lips soft, warm, gentle. He wrapped his arms around me, pulling my body toward him, pressing me up against him. He kissed me again, and this was a new kiss. Different from before. This was a kiss that I could live in, retreat to for the rest of my life, measure all kisses against for all eternity. I responded with my lips, my whole body, desperate for more of him. It was like he had finally given in, let me have all of him.

But then he pulled back, looked me in the eye.

"I can't," he said, leaning his forehead onto mine. "I can't let you be—"

"It's okay," I said, suddenly desperately afraid that he would leave this cabin and never return. I put a bit more distance between our bodies, letting him know that I could resist, if I had to. "It's okay," I said. "This is enough."

Ash reached his hands out and grabbed mine. He held both of my hands between his large, roughened palms. "Go to sleep, Em," he said. "I'm here." Now that I was certain he was staying, my eyes gradually closed, and my breathing slowed and began to match his. Dala jumped down from the mantel then and curled up next to Ash's head.

He sighed deeply, I curled our intertwined hands next to my heart, and we slept undisturbed, on the cabin floor.

Twenty-One

When I woke up, Ash was already gone, and I surprised myself. The old me would have regretted telling him all my secrets, but I didn't. I felt lighter because he believed me.

Ash had left for the Wingings' before I even had the chance to make him breakfast. There was a sketch on the table, a gorgeous sketch of my hands. It had made me giggle and I held it to my heart. I pirouetted through the tiny cabin, knocking down one of the many Dala horses, making a mental note to pick up some Super Glue while I was in town that morning.

As I trekked my way out toward the square, I listened to the grinding crunch of snow beneath my boots. The snow had come last night, intermixed with rain and sleet, and the product was a glistening white forest with each surface covered in a zillion tiny, sparkling snowflake crystals. It was beautiful and still as I headed into the forest, onto the path worn by Ash earlier that morning.

I wanted to get something good to cook for dinner. I wanted to get some flowers for the cabin. I wanted to go to the Broken Egg, use their Wi-Fi, and check my email. I had told Ash that I wanted to see what crazy messages I was getting from Dad. I had asked Ash if he thought they could trace my Internet connection on my laptop or my email usage. "Maybe I should just use the library again," I said.

"Are they the FBI?" he had asked.

The look I gave him must've helped him understand that I was really in over my head. Dad was not the FBI, but I wouldn't put it past him.

In this beautiful morning walk, in this gorgeous December wonderland unfolding in front of me as I emerged from the forest, turning myself toward the square, I thought of Ash, how he had reacted to my secret, how he had accepted it, accepted me. I refused to give in to that tiny voice of insecurity, that tiny voice of doubt, that told me Ash was simply feeling sorry for me.

Look at yourself, Emery. Why you?

Last night, it had all seemed so real. He seemed so purposefully with me in every sense of the word. Almost.

But I didn't know. In the light of day, I caught a glimpse of my rumpled self in the diner's windows as I walked past and had to wonder. Why me?

I pulled his sketch of my hands out of my coat pocket. *No, this was real.*

I had spent a lot of my time in this life trying to determine what was real and what was not, and I was pretty good at figuring it out. Ash was real; what was between us was indefinable, undeniable. He had yet to share his secrets with me, whatever they might be, but I knew it would come.

If, for so long, so many things had felt like they were coming to an end for me . . . if for so long, I felt like I was floating, unattached to much, without meaning and purpose . . . now it felt like a beginning, something to peg myself to. Someone.

I had truly given in. I couldn't fight it anymore. What we were. What was happening between us.

I pulled open the door to Sam's Broken Egg, my laptop under my arm.

Daisy came right over with a pot of coffee. "Hi, doll," she said with a smile, smacking her gum. "You going to the Cranes' golden?" she asked.

"I think so," I told her. "I'm Emery."

"I've heard. What can I get you?"

"The Country Sampler," I answered.

I opened my laptop and clicked on my Internet icon. I had to see if they were onto me, if we needed to move on.

We. I had just thought in terms of the plural pronoun, *we*.

I smiled at that thought.

Daisy came back then with my order, and before I even realized it, I had eaten practically the whole thing, the biscuits, the grits, the bacon, and one of the two sausages. I hadn't eaten so much in a really long time. If Gia was here, she would have been pleased. She was always on me to eat more.

I quit stalling then and opened up my email. Fifty-three messages. Most were from Dad. I quickly scanned each of the earliest ones. They began with short messages. *Where are you?* Or, *What is going on, Emery?* Then, *Please get in touch with us, Emery.* Next, *Your team is worried.*

Your team. Not your dad. Your team.

It figured.

I skipped down to the last email from Dad, and it was longer, explaining that he was sorry he'd driven me to this, explaining that he would listen to me, blah, blah, blah. But it was like a wolf in sheep's clothing, and when I got to the end of the email, I realized I was right.

We have a new theory, Emery, one that needs to be protected. Don't make me involve the authorities. Dad.

A new theory. It needed to be protected. *I* didn't need protection. *It.* And then, of course, a threat.

And I knew he meant it, and I knew he didn't mean just the Greater Ann Arbor Area Police Department. He meant more than that. He had connections, and I felt scared.

I felt dark and unsure. And damn my father for his ominous emails and secrets and his inability to see beyond the science.

I never should have come here and checked my email.

"You looking for Ash?" Daisy had come back to refill my coffee.

"Um." I was still staring at my computer screen and didn't know how to answer. "Sam said he just saw Ash up at Crane Hardware." Daisy smiled a knowing smile.

I smiled back. I shut my laptop then and decided I would go surprise Ash before I continued on with the rest of my errands.

I found him in the back of the hardware store near the stacked bins of nuts and bolts, different-sized nails and screws. They were still in wooden bins; it felt very authentic, a bit of ordinary time travel.

His cowboy hat was bent over two bolts in his hand, scrutinizing the size. He was deep in thought over it, and I watched him for a beat, the beautiful span of his shoulders, tight against his work coat, his jaw locked in an expression of concentration. He turned then, saw me staring at him.

I recoiled for a second, embarrassed. And I saw the faintest hesitation in his body language, but then he smiled his crooked grin.

"Hey, Emery."

He came over to me, and we looked at each other. Ash grabbed my mittened hand for a moment and gave it a squeeze.

It settled me. "Just me, your everyday, ordinary, time-traveling cabin stealer."

"You want to come see something with me?" he asked.

"Yeah," I answered.

We paid at the counter, a handsome older gentleman manning the cash register who knew Ash by name and obviously liked him. "See you, son," he said as we walked out.

I noticed Ash wince at this, ever so slightly. But I didn't ask.

Ash led us out of the store, holding the door for me, of course. He headed back to Winging Stables. We walked silently. Halfway there, he grabbed my hand again, and I felt the warmth of his touch through my mitten, and right into the center of my being.

He walked us behind the oldest barn, gray paint peeling, old tractor parts thrown here and there around the edges of the building. But behind the building was a used blue-and-gray minivan, with what looked like a wheelchair lift visible in the open side door.

"I have to adjust the lift a bit. It wasn't made for an electric wheelchair like this boy has, so it's a bit narrow, and I'm going to widen it. But it will do."

He stepped back and crossed his arms on his chest. I was unsure what this was exactly. But I sensed it was something he was extremely proud of.

There was a certain line in how he stood, chest out, shoulders squared. He felt good about this.

It made me love him more.

"Are you doing this for someone? Helping them out?"

"Yes, a waitress down at the diner. Daisy. She has a handicapped son, no money."

"Ash—"

"It's just part of my penance, Emery."

I was getting closer. He was going to let me in.

He stepped closer to me, face to face, and I could feel his warm breath. "I want to tell you about it, Emery, so you will understand about . . . me."

We stood there for a long moment, behind the barn, in the freezing cold, but I was not aware of any of this. I was only aware of him, so close to me, hovering above me, me looking up, his head bent toward me. His breath was sweet, smelled like peppermint, and it drew me to him, hypnotized me, pulled me closer.

"I want to tell you everything. Later, Emery. Tonight. At night . . ." He was dangerously close now; the brim of his cowboy hat grazed my hair. "At night . . ." He closed his eyes then and continued. "At night, it's harder to talk yourself out of the truth. It's harder to run."

"Okay," I said breathlessly.

He broke the spell then, by clearing his throat, taking several steps back.

He walked me toward the square again. We said our good-byes, and I hurried on to my other errands. In the back of my mind, I knew that I would spend the rest of the day at the cabin, trying to decipher what it was that he was going to tell me.

Would it help me solve my mystery? Help me figure out what I should be gleaning from the loops?

Once I returned to Dala Cabin, the magical security blanket that was Ash had worn off. I was back to my old self, dissecting every last thing that he had said.

I knew he had something big to tell me, there was no question. Maybe it would explain the reasons that he was running from the past that he didn't want to talk about, the reason he didn't want to let me completely in.

Maybe it had something to do with the silver key.

I mixed the batter for my rosettes and started to heat the oil. Dinner might have to be plain pasta, for I needed an oven and not just a hot plate to be the Julia Child of the UP, but I could still make my beautiful, favorite dessert, my little snowflake-shaped cookies. I had found the rosette iron at the little Swedish shop near the VFW.

As I dipped the iron in the batter and placed it into the hot oil, my mind traced over my conversation with Ash. I was unsure how I fit into this confession that Ash had to give me tonight.

His penance, that was what he had called his project for Daisy. And hadn't I overheard the two blue-haired ladies in the booth next to me at the diner talking about how they thought there was a Good Samaritan around Esperanza these days, paying people's parking tickets, taking groceries to the widow down by the bait shop, buying a bicycle for the one Winging girl?

Was this all Ash? The bike was. The van was. I knew that. Was he also responsible for everything else? I was sure it had to be him. What was it that he was trying to atone for?

My heart ached for him, for whatever it was that he was carrying around with him. For whatever debt he felt he was repaying.

I placed the first rosette on the paper towels I had laid out and dipped the iron in the batter again. I clumsily dropped the iron in the pan, and the hot oil splattered, burning the palm of my left hand.

"Ouch! Shit!" I quickly ran my hand under the cold kitchen sink water, and a thought jumped into my head. It flashed across my mind in big neon letters, and it leveled me.

Of course! I felt like I had been socked in the stomach, and I pulled out a kitchen chair and sat down, reminding myself to take deep breaths.

I looked at the vase full of Christmas roses on the table and laughed. I laughed at myself and how silly I had been. I caught a glimpse of myself in my reflection in the east window. I had put on my favorite cream sweater dress, tights, fancy leather boots, and I put my hair in a messy pile on top of my head. I had smeared on a bit of blush, some glittery lip gloss. I had pulled out all the stops. I felt foolish—ridiculous. Angry at myself for being so naive, so ready to believe I could be something special to anyone who didn't wear a white lab coat.

I had been locked up for too long, lived a life of nothing for too long, and as soon as I was free for a moment, here I was—a fool.

Ash knocked at the door then, one serious knock, then another. Dala looked up from her place on the hearth. Meowed once as if to tell me to answer the knock.

I opened the door and knew that I was flushed, probably crazy-looking. I bit my lip and tried to regain my composure. He was absolutely breathtakingly gorgeous with his wind-chapped cheeks and his five-o'clock shadow. He took one look at me, and a hand went to his heart. "Wow."

He took a step in, but I could tell he sensed something was wrong. "The hot plate," he said, motioning toward the boiling, sputtering oil. "Let me get it."

I watched him walk into the kitchen, drop his coat on the back of one of the chairs.

I could hardly make myself say it. "Am I part of your penance, Ash?"

"What?" He spun away from the hot plate. He looked at me, stricken. "What?"

"Is that why you're here with me? Is that what this is? You're just helping out a . . . a . . . freak?" I spit that last word out and turned away from him, folding my arms across my chest in anger, in embarrassment.

"Why would you say that?" he answered, turning me toward him. "No," he answered evenly. "Of course not."

"I'm fine, you know. I can be on my own, Ash. I was fine,

until you—" My voice broke then and I stopped, not trusting myself to go on. I didn't want to cry.

"No, Emery. Don't say that. You know it's not true." His voice was even and low. He was standing over me now, his head bent toward mine. "Don't say it."

"But you *are* holding back. And you should. I mean, look at what I am. I'm not able to think about the future. It's best. I shouldn't hope."

"Don't say that. Don't ever say that."

"I had given up hope before I came here."

"Listen, Emery, so had I. And you are not charity to me."

"Then what is it, Ash?"

He pushed a stray curl from my eyes then, tucked it behind my ear. "Don't you see that this is real, right here, right now, you and me?"

"Then why the distance?"

"I'm right here." He moved even closer, our faces only an inch apart.

"You know what I mean. We keep dancing around this . . . us. What are we doing together? Why can't we be together?" I said, lowering my gaze for a moment. I had never been with a guy, barely kissed any, but now I knew what it felt like to want to.

He was silent, and when I looked up, his eyes were soft, pleading with me. We both stood there, neither moving. If it wasn't me imagining this, if this was real, what was it that was stopping him?

"You don't want me like I want you," I whispered.

"Emery. Don't say that. Don't even think that. I'm not who you think I am."

"I know you." I touched the freshly healed scar on his brow. As we touched, he pulled me into his arms. And he kissed me. His lips pressed firmly onto mine, then gently, ever so gently. His mouth kissed my lips, my cheeks, my neck, and he pulled my body closer to his, one hand on the small of my back, one hand in my hair.

I was melting, melting into him, pulled from the very core of my being, together, me against him, him against me, and we gave in to that force between us, each part of us molding into one another. And I kissed him back, tasting his lips, his tongue.

He picked me up, swept my legs out from under me with one arm, and walked me over to the bed, laying me down gently. He tenderly hovered above me, kissing my collarbone, my jawline.

"I know you, Ash, the real you," I whispered.

His body became taut. He stopped kissing me. He stood up, running his hand through his hair. He pinched the bridge of his nose and paced for a second. "No, you don't" was all he said. Then he grabbed his hat and his jacket and walked out, leaving me confused and angry and alone.

I threw on my coat and scarf and took off after him. Out into the frigid, snowy, quiet night. I saw him standing on the rocky shore of the lake, his body silhouetted by the lighthouse beam every few seconds. His shoulders were hunched, his hands balled into fists at his sides.

The white waves crashed into the rocks, and as I approached him, I could feel the freezing cold drops of the lake water splash me in the face, on my hands.

The lighthouse continued its rhythmic work. The light shone on Ash's face every few seconds. I watched him as he clenched and unclenched his jaw. I wanted nothing more than to reach out to him and have him accept me. Accept us.

He didn't turn and face me. "I know what's right and what's wrong."

"You're not making sense," I pleaded.

"You can't get involved with me. I. Can't. Do. This."

"It's too late for that," I said.

"We can't be together."

"We *are* together, Ash, whether you stay here with me or not."

"Emery, you don't know what I've done, what I'm running from, what I've—"

"So tell me! I told you everything. Like I'm such a barrel of fun over here, for God's sake. Look at me, Ash! I'm having loops that involve your drawing of your mom, loops right at Next Hill. . . . Don't I deserve to be let in?" I fingered the key in my pocket then.

"I'm a danger to you," he said. "A danger to the Wingings. I never should have—"

"Ash, please—"

"I can't let you get hurt because of me."

"Ash—"

"I've stayed too long, and it will catch up to me and then you, if—"

"I don't care! Tell me what you're talking about."

He turned then, and I could see it in his face: his decision had been made. He shook his head. This was it.

I panicked and withdrew the key from my pocket. I didn't know what it meant to him. I didn't know what it might do.

But I had to try. I had to try.

I held the solitary silver key up with two fingers, right in between us, and I watched as the lighthouse beam captured its metallic surface in its funnel of light. "Tell me what you need to tell me," I said sternly. "What does this mean?"

Ash actually shuddered—his entire body shook at the sight of the key. He turned from me, grabbing the key away from me yet not looking at it. "Where did you get that?" he asked with such disdain, with such repulsion.

In that instant, I would've given anything—*anything*—to take it back.

"That is precisely, exactly, why I have to leave Esperanza," Ash said, his voice low, barely a whisper.

He walked away from the lake, and I let him go. Because I had no other choice. I sat down on those rocks there on the Lake Michigan shore and wept because I had nothing else left to do.

Twenty-Two

Ash had left. He was gone, and he stayed gone.

The next night, as the little cabin began to darken after the light of day, I looked for him out the west window, hoping against hope that he would show up with his tent, his sleeping bag, and just make camp in the clearing.

That was all I was asking for. He didn't have to run to me and grab me in his arms. He didn't have to declare his undying love.

I just wanted him near.

Even Dala seemed worried. She paced in front of the door at dusk, just when Ash would usually show up for dinner.

We waited, Dala and me. Playing with a long string of yarn from my Gia scarf, giving Dala endless hours of entertainment. I painted Dala, asleep in her favorite position on the mantel. I sketched her paws, clawing, working at the air in her sleep. We played with the red satin mouse. We wasted time. We were sure he was coming back.

But he didn't come back.

On the second day, I forced myself to leave the cabin. I showered, dressed, and made my way into town, all the while trying to figure out what that damn silver key could mean to Ash. How it could have forced such a terrible reaction.

Did it open a lock? Was it a house key? A key for a locker?

I really had no idea.

I walked to the bus station and bought a ticket to the town of Charlevoix. I had planned this trip several days ago. I was going to the Northern Michigan Historical Society, to see if there was any information that could help me out about the church. But I knew I was not going to enjoy it. I had thought that Ash and I would take this trip together. That we might visit the nearby art museum. Make it into a getaway, like the two sisters had suggested. But now it was just me.

The gray, itchy seat on the bus was uncomfortable, and I had to sit next to a teenage couple with too many piercings who were making out noisily next to me. It was disgusting. They smelled like clove cigarettes and body odor.

My phone buzzed at the start of the trip, and I found a text message from Gia. *NSA?*

I thought about this. What did *NSA* mean? What did it stand for? All I could come up with was National Security Agency.

Could that be it? Were they really in on this? After me? My insides turned cold just thinking about it. Did that mean Dad had told them . . . what? That I could time-travel? Was that a national threat?

A soon-to-be-cultivated military strategy? I let out a deep sigh. I texted her back, asking her what she meant exactly. Maybe Gia was just being a drama queen. This seemed a little nuts. But I knew it had to mean something big for Gia to chance getting in touch with me.

I kept checking my phone. But nothing. No response from Gia.

I curled myself as close to the window as I could and tried just to zone out.

Slurp, smack, slurp from the couple next to me.

I kept picturing Ash's face out on the shore when I'd shown him the key. He looked stricken, like he'd seen a ghost.

It struck me deep in my center, skewered me. How had that key done that? And what was he running from? What was going to catch up with him?

The ride felt like it lasted forever, but it was only a bit over an hour. The Historical Society was in the downtown area of Charlevoix, next to the minor-league baseball stadium, not far from the bus station, but I took a cab. I didn't want to get too exhausted. I didn't want to take any chances. If I could keep from looping, I was going to.

I felt sort of naked, exposed, out in the real world, away from the isolation of Esperanza, my cabin, Ash, what I had begun to think of as my home. I began to peer at everyone around me, strangers on the street, wondering if any of them could possibly know my secret.

The Historical Society was really just an open warehouse space, with several large wooden tables, a few study carrels, and rows and rows of metal bookcases. There were sections of old, dusty hardcovers; boxes of microfiche; collections of area yearbooks; stacks of yellowed newspapers; and lots of other odds and ends, including an assortment of traditional, vintage Swedish costumes for the local Swedish Days Festival that was held each summer.

I wondered if I would still be here, in the UP, when summer came around. Or if I'd even be alive.

The young woman working at the society was named Sylvia Glad, and she was every bit her name. She spent more than an hour uncovering blueprints for me, church building plans, old church newsletters, and other documents. I pored over the papers, the books, the photographs. It was tedious work and exhausting.

In the end, we found nothing.

"Can I ask exactly why you're interested in this church?" she said, her green eyes smiling at me.

"You can ask," I told her, giving a sigh. "But it's a very

long and difficult story." Just thinking about where to start, where to begin with the spiral of near craziness to tell this tale was enough to wear me out. "I'm sorry," I told her. "I don't mean to be rude."

"Oh no," she said, shaking her head and folding up the last of the northern Michigan maps that we'd been looking at. "It's just that you seem so heartbroken. I wish I could help."

"Thanks," I told her. *Heartbroken. And she didn't even know the half of it.* "You've been a big help."

I didn't know what else to do. I didn't know how to go about trying to find Ash. I didn't know what to do about the church, about my mystery in the loop.

"Thank you," I told Sylvia, "but I think I'm done in for today."

"We'll be here, should you want to come back," she answered.

I grabbed a hot dog and a Coke from a nearby deli and waited at the bus station for the next bus back to Esperanza.

I sat on the wooden bench in the small waiting room, my backpack at my feet, and I slouched down and ate my hot dog, sipped my Coke. I kicked at the dirty and sticky tiled floor. I was drained, exhausted. But the food and drink helped to perk me up a bit.

It was then that I noticed a man dressed in a dark suit, leaning against the wall, near the vending machines. A woman with a small child waited on the bench across from me, reading picture books. They didn't seem to give this man any notice. Neither did the clerk behind the ticket window. He sort of blended into the background. Yet, when I took the time to turn and glance at him, he seemed to be staring at me.

I got goose bumps on my arms. But then I talked myself down a bit. I mean, it was just a guy. A slightly suspicious-looking guy.

Charlevoix was a fairly big town. Could Dad be monitoring each of the larger suburban public transportation depots? Did he know I was in the area? Did the NSA? I considered this. It seemed far-fetched. But this guy was wearing dark sunglasses. And it was really overcast today. At the moment, it was sleeting outside, gray and gloomy.

I could feel my heartbeat pick up a bit. *Calm down,* I told myself. *They're just sunglasses.*

My bus pulled in, number eighteen, and I stood up, my knees knocking a little. I boarded the bus, watching my ticket shake as I handed it over to the driver.

My stomach lurched right into my throat when I saw the dark-suit guy get onto the bus behind me.

I was trapped. Found. Caught. Freaked.

I couldn't really explain how I was suddenly so sure he was following me. I just was.

I moved to the very last seat, and I put in my iPod headphones, slouched down very low, and tried to look nonchalant, tried to look unsuspecting.

I watched Dark Suit walk down the aisle of the bus, his sunglasses off now. And he looked straight at me. There was no denying it. For a moment, I thought he was going to come right back and pull me up out of my seat by my ear and take me back to Dad, but he didn't. He just sat down, three seats ahead of me.

I noticed he had a small Bluetooth in his ear now. And he was talking into it.

As the bus got going and we started up Route 31, I calmed my breathing, tried desperately to get a grip. Could this guy really be here for me?

I thought about what Gia had said. CIA haircuts. I didn't know what a CIA or an NSA haircut looked like, but I was willing to bet it looked something like this guy's. I thought about her text. I took my cell phone out of my pocket. Still no response. That had to mean something. I decided I would ditch it, leave the phone here on the bus.

How was I going to get away from this guy? I flew over the possibilities in my mind. And I made a decision. I had come too far just to give in and be caught, just to be a helpless victim again. I calmly thought out exactly what I needed to do, and I made a plan.

I hunkered down low in my seat, kicked my feet across the empty seats next to me, and feigned sleep. Inside, my stomach swirled, my heartbeat pounded, my palms sweated. But I had to make this look believable.

After what seemed like a decade, the bus slowed to a

stop near Good Hart, and I figured that this town was as good as any other. I kept myself still and resisted the urge to steal a glance, as the bus brakes squeaked and ground to a halt.

At the very last moment, after the five standing passengers had already left, I hopped up from my faux slumber and quickly, quietly took three large steps toward the back automatic door, sliding down the steps and out the door, onto the sidewalk.

I immediately took off running when I hit the sidewalk. I turned my head for just a second once I found my gait, to see if Dark Suit had seen me leave, to see if he was after me, to see if he'd noticed.

It was difficult to tell as I glanced over my shoulder at the bus windows. Maybe it had been my imagination. But the breath quickened in my throat when I saw the silhouette of a figure, a figure that looked a lot like the dark-suit guy, standing up, looking out the back window as the bus took off. I kept going down the sidewalk at a good clip then and turned into a small coffee shop. I immediately sat down, getting my bearings, looking over my shoulder the whole time. Did that really just happen? Was that guy really after me? Or was I simply becoming a paranoid nut?

I wiped the sweat from my brow and shook my head. What had just happened?

It was easier to tell myself that it was nothing—my imagination, the projection of my own fears—now that I was no longer in Dark Suit's presence. But what was the truth? I didn't know.

And if Dad had sent him, if this man was after me, did he know I was going to Esperanza now? Was my hideaway spoiled? I wanted to get in touch with Gia, to make sure she was fine, but I didn't want to risk it, and I didn't want to put her in the middle of it all any more than I already had.

I used the coffee shop telephone to call a cab. It would be expensive, definitely. But I had money.

I didn't have much else. But I did have money.

When I arrived back in Esperanza, I was shaken, disoriented, still unsure if I could believe what had most likely happened.

I stopped in at Betsy's, hoping that Jeannette would know something. I leaned on the glass counter, feeling the exhaustion wash over me. I gripped the edge of the counter with both hands and fought the urge to just rest my head on the cool glass for a moment. I blinked my eyes, felt the thrum and buzz of the loop beginning to swirl behind my eyes.

"Hi, Jeannette," I said, trying to sound cheerful, trying to sound normal.

I wanted to hear something, anything, about Ash. But no one had seen him. Not a soul. He had just disappeared.

"I never thought he was here for good," Jeannette said.

"Why's that?" I said, knowing I was doing a lousy job at covering my heartbreak. I pushed back the thrum, fought against it.

She seemed to consider this for a moment. "He showed up here several months ago, Emery. I hadn't seen him since he was a baby. His mom, Dolly, she and I had been great friends. But his dad . . . There's a lot of history there. Dolly and I broke contact over that man. But when I saw Ash's face, standing at my doorstep, I knew instantly who he was. He looks just like her." Her eyes held a far-off expression. She shook her head, went back to rolling dough for her famous pasties.

"He's had it tough" was all she'd say. I could tell she felt as if she had said too much. Inside, I was panicking, frantic. I didn't know what to do with myself, didn't know how to go about trying to find Ash.

I couldn't even think of leaving Esperanza without knowing where he was.

Jeannette pushed a pink-frosted donut over the counter to me. "You'll still come to the anniversary party, won't you?"

"Sure," I said, pushing against a new swell of the loop, resisting it. "Is there something you need help with, anything?"

"You could watch the kids for me so Jimmy and I could get everything ready. The kids wouldn't be underfoot then."

"Consider it done," I said. I swallowed hard, steadied myself, holding on to the pastry display case. I had won; the thrum abated. For now.

I arrived at the Wingings' later that night, still looking over my shoulder constantly yet trying to talk myself out of the worst-case scenario.

I let Lily Winging paint my nails while I babysat. Lily chatted nonstop about Ash, how she had a picture of him up in her room, what his favorite color was, how he had taken her fly-fishing. I plastered a smile onto my face and watched the clock above the TV slowly tick, finding it difficult to keep my spirits up.

I checked that all the doors were locked in the house, the vision of the dark-suit guy in the back of my mind at all times. My ears pricked up at the slightest sounds. I expected, what? Sirens? I shook my head, tried to tell myself it was all my imagination, paranoia.

After my nails were a fabulous shade of purple, I found Garrett and Cody in the kitchen spraying a can of whipped cream into each other's mouths, and I just let them finish it off. I didn't have it in me to do much else.

I sat with the kids in the family room and watched an episode of *Scooby-Doo*, braiding Lily's hair for her, and my eyes kept finding their way over to the computer that sat on a desk in the corner.

"Lily?" I asked. "You don't think your parents would mind if I used the computer? Checked my email?"

Lily shook her head and turned back to her Magic Tree House book. I tied her braid with a pink ribbon and got up. I sat down at the monitor and wiggled the mouse, taking a deep breath.

When I logged in to my email, I saw that there were lots of messages from Dad, none from Gia. I counted the ones from Dad—twenty-nine messages since the last time I checked. I opened a few at random, and they were mainly accusatory in tone. The farther down I went, the more desperate, the more violent, they began to sound.

I know where you are, Emery, read one from three days ago. *I will find you. We will get you back here.*

Earlier, at Dala Cabin, I had constantly been checking out the window, expecting Dark Suit to appear from nowhere, cart me back to Dad. I had talked myself out of it for a while, but now, after this email, I knew there was no talking myself out of it. I couldn't quite wrap my head around it, but Dad was near. Coming. I sighed deeply. I realized then that I had to stop hoping and waiting for Dad to turn into the future version of Dad, the kind Dad of my loops who would never, ever do this to me.

I couldn't wait any longer.

And that was when I noticed the most recent email, from yesterday. In the subject line was one word: *apology.*

Dear Emery,

You're right to avoid me, to run. I won't ever be able to let you go.

But you have to understand you are my baby girl. We can beat this.

Two lines of text, and it hit me in my core. It was horrible and honest and real. Dad knew he would never be able to let me lead a normal life, he would always need me in the lab. For scientific reasons, for parental reasons.

He understood why I had to run. He just couldn't *let* me.

And that was the problem, the essence, of what was between us, because I too understood why he couldn't let me go. I just had to go.

As I sat there in the Wingings' family room, surrounded by the familiar theme song to *Scooby-Doo,* I realized that this conundrum was probably at the center of all the worst problems in life, all the real problems. The ones that you could solve for yourself, but in turn, you couldn't solve for others. Or if you solved them for others, for the ones you loved, you couldn't solve them for yourself.

"Are you okay, Emery?" Cody asked. He had come over from the TV then and had his hand on my shoulder.

I quickly closed up my email and tried to raise the corners of my mouth, tried to find a smile.

"Yes! Oh, I'm fine," I told him, giving his belly a tickle, but he looked at me for a moment, and then he jumped into my lap and kissed me on the cheek.

I felt this kindness, this moment, deep down, and it took all I had to bury a sob inside me. I pushed back the emotion that the email from Dad had brought to the surface—the betrayal, the guilt, the sting of the reality coming down on me from all sides.

I glanced at the time. Seven o'clock. I slipped into the

bathroom, changed quickly into my only good dress, the cream sweater dress from my last night with Ash, which only made me feel worse, as if that was possible. I swiped on some lip gloss, pulled my hair into a quick knot.

"We should go!" I told the kids when I was finished, trying to sound chipper. I then helped the kids into their fancy shoes, their dress coats, and we walked over to the round barn together, Cody holding my hand the whole time. Dress shoes or no dress shoes, Garrett, of course, jumped into three piles of snow in the two hundred yards that we had to walk, but I couldn't blame him. The snow looked fluffy and smooth, like cotton candy.

"You look so pretty, Emery," Lily told me as we walked up to the barn.

"So do you," I told her, giving her hand a squeeze.

The barn had been transformed. The whole place was covered in winter white—white Christmas lights and tulle bunting hung from the rafters. White chairs and tables sat upon a newly laid, white-tiled dance floor. White lacy tablecloths and golden Christmas-tree centerpieces sat upon the tables, with white and gold balloons forming a canopy over the dance floor. There was even a five-piece band setting up their instruments on a raised platform, a makeshift stage. The party was no small feat. I even found myself smiling a bit as the kids ran up to their parents, giving them hugs and kisses.

My eyes scanned the barn, desperately hoping for a glimpse of that certain line of Ash's shoulders. I saw Daisy, the others from the diner, that odd Mr. McGarry, the ladies from Betsy's, everyone from the town, really. But no Ash.

"Thank you," Jeannette told me as I gave her a hug. Her hair was expertly done, a few well-placed bobby pins keeping it from her face. She looked radiant.

"Congratulations," I told them. "You have pulled off a beautiful party here."

Jeannette leaned close in toward me, whispered in my ear. I didn't hear her exactly. I heard the word *dad,* and then it sounded something like "phone call for Ash."

"Oh" was all I could manage. But before I could ask any questions or really process that, Jeannette was pulled away by what must have been Mrs. Crane, a thin, waiflike old lady with beautiful blue eyes and a mass of pearls at her neck.

Who called for Ash? My head swirled. I certainly could have misheard. Had my dad called? My heartbeat quickened. Part of me wanted to grab Jeannette and shake her, force her to repeat what she'd said, tell me the whole story.

But I didn't.

As I looked around at this party, the Winging family, all hugging and kissing hellos to their guests, their friends, I felt a hollow spot in my chest, an aching there. I felt empty. It was hard for me to care about anything at this point.

Maybe I should just march into the Wingings' house and call Dad. Let him come and get me, take me back to the hospital, plug me back in, get it over with. If the fiasco on the bus had really happened, then Dad would be here shortly.

What did it all matter without Ash, anyway? The end was coming soon, one way or another. I could feel it.

It was difficult—no, impossible—to regain that sense of a new beginning, of a newfound freedom from just a few weeks ago, when I had stepped off that bus into this little blip of a town.

My eyes scanned over these people around me, all happily chitchatting and hugging, greeting each other in their Sunday best. Many of the children were dressed in their Christmas clothes—lots of greens and reds, velvet dresses, Santa sweaters. They had their own way of life here, with their *ehs* at the end of sentences, their six-month-long winters, and their slow, leisurely pace. But they seemed happy, engaged in life. A couple of weeks ago, I was inspired by these yoopers, but now I was like an outsider looking in.

I watched as Garrett and Cody picked ice cubes out of the punch bowl with their fingers. I found Mr. Crane in the crowd, realizing he was the man who owned the hardware store. I watched him as he glimpsed Mrs. Crane and her pearls from across the room. The look in his eyes, the tilt of his head, the way he gazed at her . . . My breath caught in my throat.

Their history, their happiness. Their love. I would never have this. I swallowed hard against the lump in my throat and told myself to stop the pity party. It would do no good.

I stayed on the outskirts of the festivities for a while, ate some cheese and shrimp, discussed bowling shoes at length with Mr. McGarry. Despite everything, I was hoping Ash would show. I couldn't quit scanning the crowd.

At dinner, I sat with the Wingings. The food was fabulous. Double-baked potatoes and filet mignon, made by Sam's Broken Egg, and a dessert of the most gorgeous individual rolled-fondant cakes, with tiny holly berry decorations—Jeannette had truly outdone herself.

I went to the bar for a Coke, and it was then that Mr. Crane stood up to give a toast. I didn't hear that much of it. Truth be told, I was biting back tears from the get-go. It wasn't until she handed me a napkin that I realized Daisy was standing next to me.

"He's here," she told me.

"Who?" I asked, but my heart skipped a beat.

"Your Ash. He's here," she said, annoyed and entertained at the same time. She gestured toward the far entrance of the barn.

And there he was, looking nothing short of otherworldly himself. My Ash. He wore a dark pair of jeans and corduroy jacket. Even from this distance, I could see that his jaw was set and clenched. But I didn't care. He was *here*.

Garrett and Cody Winging were already all over him, pulling on his arms, dancing around him.

"Well, go get him, you dummy," Daisy offered.

I started to move toward him, and he saw me. He did

that thing again, where he put a hand over his heart, and he stopped dead in his tracks, gave me a smile.

The band had started up, and they were playing a familiar country tune. I hugged him in greeting, and he picked me up a bit, twirled me. I nuzzled his neck, breathing in his scent, relishing his skin against mine.

"You're back!" I said, pulling away a smidge, and I drank in the sight of him.

"I'm sorry," he said. "Just know that."

We stayed like that, embracing, and it gradually turned into a dance. I clung to him. He grabbed my right hand and brought it to his heart, and we danced slowly, my head resting on his shoulder. As other couples filled up the dance floor, we stayed at the edges, on the fringe. In our own world.

"I don't want to be someone who hurts anybody, Emery," he whispered in my ear. "Especially not you." His voice was low, music to my body, sending a shiver down my spine.

"Ash, I—"

"No, let me get this out. I tried to stay away from you. I tried to keep myself and my troubles away from you. . . ."

"But?" I looked up.

"But I can't stay away from you." He looked hard in my eyes. "If you only knew how I fought this, us . . . how I tried not to let us matter . . ." He let his voice trail off, and I held him close to me. "It's like, I would have myself all steeled against it, talked myself into running to the East Coast or something, anything to keep myself out of your hair. And then you would just slay me with . . ." He let his voice drift off again.

"With what?" I asked, enrapt.

"With kindness, Em." He touched his brow. "Your courage. Your laugh. Your belief that there is still good in this world, even when things are so broken." He smiled at me then. "How you believed in me, Emery." He kissed my lips. "And then there's your terrible Scrabble playing, yet your absolutely ridiculous confidence in the process." I smiled. Ash pressed his lips to my cheek, my neck, softly.

I closed my eyes, savored it, savored him, next to me, with me. Here.

"I had to come back. At least to tell you why I couldn't stay. So you wouldn't think it was you. I couldn't live with that."

"Thank you for coming back," I answered, feeling the frantic grip of fear in my belly, knowing that he could run off again, could spill his secrets and leave me here. But I knew that sometimes you had to let things happen, work themselves out. You had to come at things from around a corner.

He was here. In my arms. I smiled up at him. "So . . . you're back."

"So I reckon I've got some explaining to do. Want to get out of here?"

He grabbed my hand then and led us toward the door, snatching up our coats on the way out.

We walked back to the cabin in silence, but he held my

hand, our bodies in sync each step of the way. And when we were almost there, he let go of my hand, put his arm around my shoulders, and pulled me close to him. I wrapped my arms around his waist as we walked, and it was easy, natural to walk this way, locked together. I took this as a good sign. I was so happy to have him back. There was a part of me that really thought that he had been lost to me forever, that I would never have this chance, this one more chance.

When we got to the cabin, he led me right to the love seat and sat me down. He immediately started pacing the floor in front of me.

He paced for what seemed like forever, running his hands through his hair, rubbing at his chin.

"For starters, I killed my father."

"No," I said, shaking my head, but Ash looked at me hard, and I knew instinctively that this was a test, and I would pass. I didn't know what I had been expecting him to tell me, but it wasn't this. "Tell me it all," I said. "Start at the beginning."

He fell to his knees then beside the couch, with a heavy sigh. I reached out and stroked his cheek, but he grabbed my hand and gently pushed it away.

"Pop wasn't always bad. He wasn't always a monster."

I watched him look at me, but past me, his eyes, his thoughts, traveling back. "When we were little, he was okay. He would take us fly-fishing. All the time. I try to remember him like that. Me and Frankie and him in our waders. Pop making funny faces at us, trying to make us laugh. Us trying to be quiet, to not scare the fish away."

Ash looked down then, put his head in his hands for a moment. "I mean, he always had his moments. He would turn. But as the years went by, he drank more and more. It ruined him. Completely. He beat my mom. Beat her on and off since I was probably nine or ten. I remember this one time, he beat her so badly she bled from her left ear for three days. I kept going back and forth, whether I would chance calling the doctor when Pop was at work, or maybe the cops. Whether or not to chance him beating the piss out of me when he got home and got drunk again."

He stopped for a moment, and I could see the little boy that he was underneath. I could see him reliving all of this, behind his eyes.

"It was around that same time when he beat her so hard, it punctured her lung. She was pregnant, not with Frankie, with . . . She never . . . She made some excuses for him at the hospital. No one ever pushed. No one could ever believe that Pop . . . He was just so damn good at hiding it, and I suppose he had a lot of friends. The sheriff was his friend. And Mom never wanted to give him up. I reckon she was waiting for the old Pop to come back, that same old smile, the guy we loved. I guess I was waiting too, for a while. . . ."

Ash pinched the bridge of his nose then. "I could tell you a million stories about him, Emery, each one worse than the last. By the time I was probably twelve, the real Pop, the one who taught us how to fish, the one who taught us how to hammer a nail, ride a horse, he was gone. Replaced by the drink. By this monster. Mom could rarely leave the house, she was so bruised."

"Oh, Ash," I said. "I'm so sorry."

"It doesn't matter. None of it matters. But there's more. I'm also responsible for my brother's and my mom's death."

I sat quietly, struggling with all this. My Ash? Responsible for these deaths? Taking someone's life? I found this hard to swallow, hard to believe.

He looked up and challenged me. "Do you still want to hear the rest?"

I nodded, unable to fathom the lifetime of horror and pain that Ash had to confront on a daily basis.

We have the choice to be more than our DNA, I remembered Dad telling me.

"I was fourteen, it was in April. A couple of friends of mine, we lifted some fireworks out of my friend Pauly's garage, and we were shooting them off on the baseball fields. We broke into the sprinklers, had them all going. Typical kid thing to do."

Ash stopped himself then and shook his head, visibly sick from the memory. "Somebody called the cops. We got in trouble. They called our parents, and the cops made examples out of us."

"My mom comes to pick me up at the police station, brings Frankie. I don't know why, probably because he wouldn't shut up, wouldn't want to be left behind. Probably she didn't want Pop going after him. Anyway, it happens very fast. One moment we're driving home, the next I hear that terrible scrape of metal on metal, hear the glass shattering. And the next thing I know, I wake up in the ambulance."

"You were with them?" My hand went to my mouth.

Ash nodded, swallowed hard. "The drunk driver died. Mom died. Frankie died. I had a concussion, a gash on my scalp. Sixteen stitches, that was it. That was the extent of my injuries. I survived."

"Ash." I reached for him, but he shook his head. I finished, "You've got to know that it wasn't your fault, really, Ash."

"I know, Emery. I know. My head knows that. But in here . . ." He pounded on his chest. "In here, I'm not so sure.

"Last April, the anniversary of their deaths, about seven hundred beatings from Pop later—'cause once Mom is gone, there's just me—anyway, I realize that I'm as big as he is now. And I stand up to him. I clock him one right in the jaw, catch him square. He's drunk, of course, telling me over and over how it was all my fault. I mean, he beat her senseless, bloody, for years and years, but I'm forever the one who killed her, *killed them*, you know?

"Anyway, the old man can't handle that I hit him back, because, I don't know, for years, I just didn't fight back. I didn't want to be *him*, you know? I just took it. I guess I thought I deserved it."

His chin quivered at this sentence, and it took everything in me not to reach out to him, not to pull him close to me. But I knew he wanted to finish, so I let him go on. He needed to go on.

"So the old man is pissed out of his mind, and he comes at me like an animal. We're on the back porch. He's like I've never seen him before. Worse. And before I know it, I'm on the ground and he's on top of me, and he's got a knife, a kitchen knife, and I grab it from him, right in the palm of my hand." And he held up his hand, the scar I remember. His hand was shaking violently.

"We scuffled. He kept telling me that he had warned me—'cause after they died, he would always tell me that once I had suffered enough, he would just kill me too. That's what he told me, when he was drunkest. Anyway, it all happened so fast." He stopped then, and looked at me, square in the face. "I stabbed him. I left him there, dying. I left him there, Emery. Just ran. I killed him."

"Ash, oh God, Ash." I reached out then, and he laid his head in my lap, heaved a sigh so heavy with heartbreak. I stroked his head. "I'm so sorry, Ash." So this was the weight on Ash's shoulders, on his heart. It hurt me for him. It was difficult to reconcile these atrocities, this crime, with the Ash I knew. But I realized this was a gray area, a horrible, nightmarish gray area. *It must have been self-defense in some way,* I told myself. "Ash, you had no other choice." It was almost a question.

Ash cleared his throat. "The worst thing is I was glad when I did it. To finally be rid of him. And . . ." He pulled himself away from me at that moment and bowed his head low.

"I wanted him to die, Emery."

I took my hand away from his cheek, just for a second so I could climb down on the floor beside him and hold him. But when I took my hand away, in that moment, in that flash of a second, Ash looked up at me. And I could see the fear in his eyes, the fear that I would be repulsed by his ultimate confession, his ugly truth, his story.

When he saw me climb onto the floor next to him and open my arms to him, his face softened, he let out a sigh. I stroked his hair, kissed the hollow of his throat.

"The moment after, I just ran. Left the farm, left Pop, left school, left my dog. Stopped a few other places, finally wound up here. But I'm sure they're after me. The cops'll find me."

"Ash, I don't care. And you can explain—"

He closed his eyes and shook his head. "I can't let you be with a monster, Emery. I can't let you be with someone who could do this. I can't let you be with me."

"Ash, you are not a monster! And you must know on some level that I can't leave you. You must know that this is something that is beyond my control."

"Emery, don't say that."

"Ash, I'm so sorry you have had to carry this."

"You have to get away from me, Emery. What if . . . I

mean, he was *my dad*. What if . . . what if *I'm* him, Emery? What if it's in me?"

"Ash, you are not him. You never could be."

He nodded then, ever so slightly, his head in my arms. Dala, as if on cue, knowing Ash needed her, jumped down from the mantel. She sidled up to Ash, licked his hand three times, and curled up in his lap.

"How did you get the key?" he asked quietly, petting the cat.

"In my loop."

He considered this. "Really?" Ash sat up then, turned to me. "When I looked at it more carefully, it's not *the* key, although it's close."

"What's *the* key?" I asked, ignoring Dala's insistent meows as she climbed into my lap, biting at the buttons of my sweater.

"After the accident, my father put the key to my mom's totaled car on a string and gave it to me. Told me I had to wear it around my neck always. As a reminder for what I had done. What I had caused. He beat me bloody, knocked out three of my bottom teeth the first time he caught me not wearing it, knocked my mouth right into this old Victrola, one of my mom's antiques."

That was when I felt my body tense with no warning. I tried to push back the thrum from behind my eyes, but it was too intense. Violent. Hard. My eyelids fluttered. Then I was gone.

My Boy

I feel and hear the familiar whooshing sounds in my ears, in my head, and I smell the ammonia, strong, so strong. And then I'm there, in the loop.

I'm with my friend, my little boy, whom I haven't seen in such a long time. Things look so bright now.

I remember completely that I need to be back with Ash. I need to be with him, but here I am with him again, as a boy.

This is him.

I realize that's why Ash seemed so familiar to me when I first met him. I know him from my loop.

He is my little boy. Wow.

Once I realize this, it all seems so simple, so obvious, nearly poetic. The line of his brow, the crooked smile.

I feel the need to go back, want to give my new wisp of control a try again, but I'm torn. As always, once I'm here, I can never quite feel the urgency of all the regular, worldly worries.

And I do desperately want to spend some time with this Ash, this smaller, baby-faced Ash.

We sit in an old schoolhouse building, a gymnasium maybe, a cafeteria. Yellowish orange light casts through the high-set windows. I can see the dust particles floating in the streams of sunshine that fall across the wooden plank floor.

He sits cross-legged across from me. Dala sits in his lap. I'm surprised, pleased to see Dala here. I brought her, *I think for a second, but here in the loop, it doesn't seem like such a big deal.*

Boy Ash looks up from the cat and smiles at me. The same crooked smile that I love in the other time, my real time. I smile back.

"Can you dance?" he says.

"I can," I answer enthusiastically, as if it's a perfectly normal conversation, a perfectly normal request, and, well, for this time, for this loop, it feels like it is.

So I stand up then and stretch. I feel good . . . energetic. My boy puts some music on, although I don't see him get up. Beethoven's Fifth plays over the loudspeakers of the gym. And I begin to dance. First, I warm up with the normal stuff—pliés, relevés, chassés—but soon I'm jumping and jetéing, and really getting into it.

It feels great. And Ash, the boy Ash, he clasps and holds his hands under his chin, watching, grinning, occasionally clapping at a particularly skilled combination.

I don't usually have this much coordination here, *I remind myself. I try to snap my fingers then, and I can't. Things are better, but I'm still clumsy, not really myself.*

I try again to bring my thumb and middle finger together, to press them together, pushing them against each other to hear that inevitable snap! *But I can't do it. I can't make my movements fine enough. My hands move like they are in mittens, like they are some kind of malformed claws.*

This is odd, *I think, and it is then that I start to see the rainbow of colors around Boy Ash's face, not just in my peripheral vision but around him, a bit like a Catholic saint halo from the old Greek or Russian Orthodox paintings, a bit like a burst of light or a firecracker right behind his head.*

"I'm going," I say.

"I know," he answers.

"Ash," I say.

"Ash," he says with a smile, as if to say "yes."

And I'm sucked back, the whooshing sound filling my ears again, my eyes, my brain.

Twenty-Three

I awoke slowly in Ash's arms. I first became aware of his humming. He hummed the theme to *SpongeBob SquarePants,* and I felt it first, then heard it. And then I felt his hand on my cheek, my forehead, a finger tracing my lips.

He sat with me draped across his lap, my head cradled next to his chest. I could hear the beat of his heart, and it sounded fast. It sounded worried.

And that was when I realized that it wasn't his. It was mine. And I needed air. I needed air. I—

And I had to take a gulp of air because coming back had been more difficult than I had expected, more difficult than usual. My eyes popped open.

"You're okay," he said. But he sounded alarmed. "You

weren't breathing for a second. I was almost going to start CPR."

We were sitting on the floor right in front of the fireplace. "I'm okay?"

"You're okay," he answered, but he got up and filled a glass of water and brought it back for me, and I could see his hand shaking a bit. His jaw was clenched tight. "Drink," he ordered. "Let me take your pulse."

I let him. "It's getting worse. But you were there, as a boy," I said.

He ignored me. He was rubbing his chin, thinking, counting the pulses in my wrist. "I don't know how to tell you this," Ash began, his voice quivering a bit. "I don't even know what to make of this, Emery, but unless I'm losing it, unless I'm really . . . just . . ." He dropped my wrist then, obviously satisfied that I was okay for the moment.

"What?" I said, standing up, taking a few wobbly steps to the kitchen table, Ash at my elbow. "What is it?" I tried to keep my cool. "What happened?"

Ash walked to the west window, looked out at the dark night. He shook his head, like he was trying to clear it. He took a few steps back toward me. And he steadied himself with a hand on the table, rubbing his stubble with the other hand. "Emery, you left."

"I left?"

He nodded. The color had drained from his face.

"I always leave, Ash."

"No, Emery. You really left. I was holding you, waiting for the loop to be done. You had stopped seizing. You were still, and then you disappeared. You disappeared, for Christ's sake!"

"What?"

"You just dissipated, like faded into static or something. I could feel you getting less and less concrete, and then you were gone. It only lasted a moment or two. But I'm not crazy, Emery. You were gone. I'm not crazy."

"I was gone?" I couldn't quite take this in, and that was saying something. I, who had had years of digesting time travel, could not quite digest this hiccup. This was different, unexpected—but not totally unbelievable.

"I was gone," I repeated, and then I recalled how I had danced, really danced in the loop, how I had had control of my limbs, my entire body, my *hands* a bit even. I had really, actually, physically been there.

"The cat. Oh my God, Dala. She came with me. Where did—" I stood up on wobbly legs and clicked my tongue, but I knew.

"She left with you," Ash said.

"She didn't come back," I said, plopping back down at the table. "I didn't bring her back. Is she okay? Do you think that she's—"

"Emery, I'm sure she's fine."

"But my poor little kitten. I—"

"Emery, you've got to focus on the bigger picture. Don't

worry about the cat. You nearly died." Ash's voice broke over that last word, and it brought me back to the gravity of this situation.

"How did I come back?" I asked, hungry for this new knowledge, how this fit in with all the other pieces, what it could mean for my control, what it could mean for this feeling I had. We were getting closer. I knew it. We were getting closer to . . . the truth. The end?

"You came back just as you had gone. I could feel the weight of you before I could actually see you, and then you weren't quite solid right away, and then . . . then you were here." Ash flopped into a kitchen chair and put his face in his hands, shaking his head. "Of course, whether your heart stopped or not, I don't know. But you came back and you didn't breathe! I counted three seconds, three slow seconds, and you didn't breathe!" He was yelling now. He was frantic.

I didn't know what to say. The tears welled in my eyes. I didn't want to do this to him. And Dala, poor Dala. But Boy Ash would take care of her. He would.

Ash continued. "It's not that I didn't believe you before, Emery. I did."

"I know," I said, reaching toward him, placing a hand in his hair. He looked up and grabbed my hand. He placed it onto his heart. It was racing.

"It's just that I didn't expect it. I didn't expect—"

"You didn't expect me to disappear like a ghost?" I laughed, trying to lighten the moment.

"No, that's not it," he said. "I didn't expect to feel so utterly helpless, so devastated at the thought of you not coming back. I was scared, Em. I was scared that this was it for us. That you were gone."

"I'm not gone," I told him, and he pulled me into his lap. "I'm right here, and we will have lots of time, Ash. We are going to figure this out."

"It wasn't just that I thought you were gone from me; it was the thought that this was it for us, and I never took the chance to tell you what you mean to me." He avoided my eyes then, and I saw tears forming in his as he blinked, looking down at our intertwined hands.

I placed one shaky hand on his chin and lifted his eyes up to mine.

"I'm fine," I said. I held his beautiful hazel gaze. And, in true Ash form, he did not give in, he did not cry. He held it together for me. He placed a hand on my neck then, and he kissed me softly, tenderly on the lips. I placed my hand on his stubbly cheek and leaned my head into his chest.

"I know how you feel about me, Ash. You don't have to tell me. You show me every day." I took a deep breath, slowed my breathing down, tried to calm my body. "It's the same way I feel about you."

He seemed to consider this for a moment. "We have to leave Dala Cabin," he said into the quiet of the room, staring into the dying embers of the fire. "We have to run."

"I know," I said, and sighed, thinking of my adventure on

the bus. "When you were gone, I might . . . maybe . . . have been followed while I was in Charlevoix."

Ash's face turned dark. "By who?"

"A man." I watched his jaw clench. "I'm sure he was sent by Dad. But I may have just imagined the whole thing. I was upset—"

"We'll have to leave. Tomorrow."

I didn't want to leave Dala Cabin. This had been our home. Our haven. But I knew it was for the best.

Through the thin shades on the east window, the sweep of the lighthouse beam shone through the window, and Ash got up from the table then, picking me up with him.

He laid me gently on the bed, and I kept my arms around his neck. I pulled him down close to me, and I kissed him.

But he stopped, taking both my hands in his. He sat down next to me on the bed. "We can wait," he said.

I nodded and met his eyes. "Okay," I answered, relieved. I had had enough firsts for tonight.

"It's a minor detail. But no more pretending, no more chivalry." He kicked off his boots then, stripped down to his long johns. I smiled at him. He climbed in next to me, and he threw the quilt over both of us.

It had been a long day, and all the pretense that had stood between us had fallen away. There was no need for it now. He pulled me close to him, wrapped me into his body, and held me there, his body warm. It felt like home.

He hummed a tune for a few seconds, the theme song to *SpongeBob,* and I chuckled.

"So I'm there, as a boy?"

"Yes," I said.

He seemed to consider this. "I reckon that I would remember meeting you, knowing the force that was Emery Land, whether I was five or fifty," he said. "I don't remember it."

"And why would you have given me the key, do you think?"

"I don't know," he answered. He stroked my hair, nuzzled my neck. "Tomorrow we'll make a plan and pack."

"Tomorrow." I hummed a little bit more of his song, and then I listened as Ash's breathing grew slow and deep.

The beam of the lighthouse came every few seconds, the rhythm of his breathing, the ticking of the old-fashioned windup bedside clock, and then the shining light. The presence, then quick absence, of the light played tricks on my eyes, and I could see Ash clearly in the beam in an instant, sleeping soundly, a faint smile curled onto his lips. Then, as the light disappeared, so did all visual traces of him. Only blackness was left. I knew it was just my eyes, that he was still there, but I scooted closer to him, held on more tightly. I fell into the pattern of his breathing. I buried my face in his collarbone, kissed his neck.

We were together. I felt that flutter, deep in my center, deep in my being. For a moment, only a moment, I felt that unmistakable certainty, that unabashed optimistic sense that, yes, everything could and would turn out okay.

As I drifted off to sleep, there was something in the far reaches of my mind, something to do with Jeannette that I had meant to tell Ash. But it was gone, floating just outside my consciousness.

It would wait until tomorrow.

Twenty-Four

I felt all kinds of nostalgic as we packed up our few things in Dala Cabin. I didn't want to leave. With each item that I stuffed into my duffel, I kept asking myself, *If this is the beginning with Ash, then why do I feel this ridiculous sense of dread?*

I watched him as he made the bed, his mouth turning up at the corners, just a fraction. He was humming again. It was good to see him happy in spite of his conscience, his burden.

I thought of my own father then. Flawed? Yes. A monster like Ash's was? No.

My episodes were more violent now, but I was also gaining some control. Things were going to turn out all right. With that, I could even envision talking some sense into my dad.

Then why did my stomach feel as though it was twisted into a permanent loop?

I wondered how close Dad was to finding me. I wondered again about the guy on the bus. It all just seemed so crazy, now that I was back here, back where I felt safe.

"Let's go have breakfast," Ash said as he pulled on his boots. "And we'll talk to Jimmy. We'll tell him as little as possible. Then we can look at the bus schedules. Maybe trains. Figure out where to go."

I smiled. I busied myself with packing, distracting myself. I chose my favorite yellow Swedish horse. Certainly, Roy, the real estate guy, wouldn't mind if I took one as a souvenir.

I folded up the last of Ash's flannels and tucked his razor in my duffel too, and then I sat down for a moment, surveying the tiny room to see what I had left. It looked pretty clear, as if we had never been here. As if these last couple of weeks had been inconsequential. I laughed at the thought.

I threw on my coat and hat, scarf, mittens, for it had gotten very cold, with a windchill well below zero, and I brought my laptop with me in my backpack. We trekked outside, and I shuddered as the wind hit me. I pulled the scarf higher on my face.

We made our way toward Sam's diner. I had to email Gia, to tell her I was fine, to tell her not to worry. It was the only way—the only safe way. Or was it? I couldn't decide if I should email her. Or maybe send a note via snail mail. Or do nothing. But I wanted her to know.

It was difficult to make the trek through the woods. The snow had gotten deeper. It had developed an icy crust, but not one that was thick enough to support my weight. With every step, I fell in, and it took all my energy to pull myself out each time and continue on. Ash helped, but my limbs were rubbery, worn out, when we finally reached the diner. I unwrapped myself and plopped into a booth at Sam's.

I saw in my peripheral vision that Daisy was walking over toward us, and I felt my eyelids flutter. *No!* I thought. *No.*

"Are you okay?" I heard Ash's voice from what seemed like very far away.

I gritted my teeth and fought it. I wrapped my mind against the pull, the whooshing sound. *No,* I repeated. *No.*

I calmed my breathing and clenched my fists. And I slowly gained ground. *No,* I repeated.

And then I was back.

"Are you all right?" Daisy asked, standing over me, looking half horrified, half annoyed.

"I am," I answered. "Can I have coffee?" Ash reached his hand over the table then and squeezed my hand.

"Coffee for me too," he said, not taking his eyes off me.

"Sure." Daisy gave me the once-over and left us alone.

I put my head in my hands then and breathed in and out slowly. I was okay. I could do this.

"Are you sure you're all right?"

I nodded slowly and slipped my laptop out of my backpack.

Daisy returned with our coffee, and she said, "You know, there were some guys in here earlier asking about you, actually."

My eyes flew up to Ash's. "Who?" he asked.

"They were asking about both of you," Daisy said.

"What did they look like?" Ash whispered.

"I don't know," Daisy said, looking from one of us to the other. "What's going on?"

Suddenly I remembered what Jeannette had said last night at the party. Someone had called about Ash. For Ash? It didn't matter *who* had called. Something was happening. Someone was onto Ash. Onto us.

"What did you tell them?" I asked.

"I told them I didn't know you."

"You did?" I asked. "Thank God."

"I didn't know what was going on, but it didn't seem right." Daisy looked at us questioningly.

Ash was already standing up, throwing on his coat. "Thank you, Daisy. Thank you. But we have to leave."

"Were they wearing suits?" I asked.

"Yeah, blue, maybe black suits."

I felt the thrum behind my eyes then, the swell and push against my temples. I stood up and steadied myself. "We have to go. Thank you, Daisy. It's fine."

Ash was already swinging open the door to the diner, and I was right behind him. My mind kept going. Could this really be happening?

"Let's go to the Wingings' first," Ash said, scanning the street ahead of us. Everyone was suspicion personified, the black sedan parked by the hardware store, the man attaching his jumper cables to his truck near the bus bench, the kids throwing snowballs in front of the library. My senses were heightened, too much to take in.

I ran alongside Ash, slipping every third or fourth step on the ice, his hand gripping my mitten, pulling me along. "Please, please," I whispered, pushing back the thrum, the pressure behind my eyes.

When we got to the stables, we ran into Jimmy Winging coming out of the gray barn.

I watched as Ash tried to act casual, calm himself. "Jimmy, did anyone come around this morning looking for me?"

"No, don't think so," Jimmy answered, giving Ash a long stare.

"Thanks, sir. I hate to ask this, but is there any way we could borrow your Jeep, sir?"

"Mind telling me what's going on?"

"I can't, Jimmy."

"If you tell me more, I can probably help you with more than just the Jeep, son."

"Sir, please, I wouldn't ask if . . ."

Jimmy took the keys from his jacket and handed them to Ash.

We silently got into the Jeep, and Ash took off toward the cabin. "We'll grab our stuff. Then we'll just keep going."

It took us only three or four minutes to get to the cabin, but it felt like forever.

Ash drove the truck as close as he could get to the cabin. There didn't seem to be anyone around. No tire marks. No sign of anybody.

We both quickly went inside. We grabbed our bags and threw them into the back of the Jeep. I heard in the distance the unmistakable sound of tires grinding on snow and ice.

"Ash!" I cried. "Someone's coming."

"I know."

He pulled me to him, his body tense against mine. "Take the Jeep, just go. I'll stay and—"

"Don't even say that. I can't leave you. We are not splitting up."

"Let me deal with them, whoever it is. Please, Emery. I'll meet you at the Saugatuck exit on 31 south."

"No! I'm not leaving you!" I screamed.

"You have to, Emery. Please!"

The tires sounded louder now. And I had an idea.

I could see the car coming now, closer. It was a black Mercedes. A familiar black Mercedes. My dad. I shook my head.

He was coming after me. I couldn't believe it. I didn't want to believe it.

The reality of betrayal pierced me in the gut, nearly bowled me over. But it steeled me too. I knew what I had to do.

"It's my father," I whispered. "Ash, just trust me. Let me do this. Let me say what I have to say. Just go in the cabin."

"Emery, I don't know—"

"Please!" The tone in my voice was crazy, loony, desperate. So Ash turned then, reluctantly, but he went into the cabin, leaving the door open behind him.

I waved as Dad pulled up. There were several people in the car with him. In the passenger seat sat the dark-suit guy.

"Dad," I said as he got out of the driver's side.

"Emery!" he said, and stepped forward as if he was going to hug me. I stepped back instinctively. Dad winced but accepted this and kept his distance. Then he smiled, a wide, plastic-looking smile.

The anger pulsed in my veins. Did he really think he could do this to me so easily? Like this was some warm, happy homecoming?

Dad looked me up and down. "It's gotten worse," he said.

"Yes," I answered. Dad looked so drawn, pale, old, behind that fake smile. And I felt my anger soften a tiny bit.

But not much.

"Dad, I don't want to go," I told him calmly.

"You know you have to come back with me." His eyes

were hard, forceful, not pleading. And the tip of his nose was red, like it always was in the cold weather.

Despite everything, there was some small part of me inside that was glad to see him. I had missed my father. And I had the smallest, tiniest bit of remorse concerning what I was about to do to him, especially when I thought about him in ten years, twenty years. My future dad.

But seeing him here, seeing Dad show up here in my town, my haven, with his thugs and his happy facade, I knew that I would never go back to him, to his rules, to his prison, to his cold and calculating lab. I couldn't wait for my future dad any longer.

I put my head in my hands then, for a long moment. Just for show. I couldn't give in too easily.

"Is there any other way? Any other option?" I feigned.

"You know there isn't."

"I don't want to go back to that life," I told him, looking up again.

Dad took a step closer to me then, leveled his eyes to mine. "That life," Dad scoffed. "Well, have you thought about *death*, Emery? Have you spent time thinking about what that might be like?" He took a step back then, as if he had been too forceful. As if he knew he had scared me back into submission.

He was wrong. But I was going to play along.

I covered my face with my hands for a moment. "Just let me go in, get my stuff. Give me two minutes?"

"Of course." Dad looked a bit stunned that I had given in so quickly.

I walked slowly toward Dala Cabin, pushing back the thrum, the buzz, the swell behind my eyes, trying desperately to make my gait look like someone who had just submitted, given up her free will, her life . . . not someone running for, reaching for, straining toward that last scrap of freedom.

I closed the door to the cabin behind me. "Listen to me, Ash. Go open the window. Leave it open, like I climbed through it."

Ash looked at me incredulously. "What?"

"Just do it!" I hissed, tearing off my gloves, my coat. I didn't know why I felt like our chances were better if I could feel him under my skin, but I just did.

Ash opened the window. "Take off your coat," I said.

He did as I said, took off his coat, his hat, gloves. I pulled him toward the hearth then. "You listen to me, now." I grabbed his hand. "Hold on to me. And I'll hold on to you."

"What are you doing?" he asked, bewildered. "You're not going back with him?"

"I'll never go back," I told him.

I turned his face toward me. I spoke directly in his face. My eyelids fluttered. "I'm taking you with me. The loop. I won't let go. You don't let go. We have to try."

"What?" Ash asked. But even as he said it, he was wrapping his arms around me.

I heard a car door slam. I was certain they were getting ready to knock the door down. "Don't let go," I said.

"I won't."

Ash took in a big breath, and then he nodded slowly.

"Emery—"

"Shhh," I told him. "Hold on to me." I let the feeling come then. I wrapped my arms around Ash like the world depended on it, because mine did. And I let the feeling come. I willed it. My eyelids fluttered. My eyes rolled back, my body stiffened, and before I was gone, before I left, before I looped, I thought I felt his body stiffen against mine.

With Me

The whoosh fills my ears, my eyes, and I'm there standing on the bank of the stream. The boy is there too, and he jumps up and down, clapping.

He points up at Ash and smiles. He drops his picnic basket, which opens, and Dala jumps out, spies a yellow butterfly, and takes off toward it.

Ash is standing next to me, and he tries desperately to shield his eyes, yet he can hardly move.

I, on the other hand, feel just fine and lean over toward Ash, grabbing his hand in mine, intertwining our fingers. "We're here," I say.

The boy leads us up Next Hill, near the stream. I help Ash, pull him along, as he's very clumsy, moving like he's made of stone.

We walk slowly, plodding up the hill. His face holds a grimace, his eyes squinting against the bright sunshine.

"Look at the key," the boy says. And he points toward the stream. Ash shakes his head. He can't do it. He holds his head in his hands, like it hurts.

I walk down to the stream and bend over, gliding the tips of my fingers across the surface of the water, feeling its cool, calming motion. I wait there for a long time. Calmly. Yet I know I'm waiting for something.

I busy myself trying to snap my fingers, but I can't. I'm getting better here. My fingers meet more easily than the last time I tried in the loop, but I can't make them snap, can't make my movements fine enough.

A water strider catches my eye as it comes flitting by on the surface of the water. I watch the stream then, the calm plane of the water resettling after the wake of the bug disappears. After a while, I see the familiar shadow shapes moving on the surface of the water, just out of reach at the edges of my vision. I'm not surprised.

The inky shadows move and form, then unform, in and out. I want to look away. I could shift my eyes just a bit, a centimeter, and the images would be gone. I don't like the way these shadows feel near me.

They feel unnatural to me, yet I can't look away. I know I must keep looking.

The goose bumps rise on my arms again, and I focus on the water as hard as I can. I see swirling grays and blacks. I feel a slippery, snaky sensation in my stomach.

It's then I see a collision in the surface of the water, two vehicles crashing together. Then the shadows converge, swirl. It is gone.

I hear my boy behind me. "Tell him to go home," he says.

A sadness catches in my throat, and I feel my eyelids flutter. I take one quick glance at Ash, and he is staring, transfixed at the boy version of himself, all the color drained from his face.

I feel my body stiffen, and I know I need to get to Ash. I move myself forward, walking as quickly as possible, and I throw my arms around him.

My eyelids flutter. The thrum. The colors and then . . .

Nothing.

Blackness.

Twenty-Five

I felt a hard surface beneath my head, beneath my body. I realized that I was lying down. I slowly regained consciousness, bit by bit, and then . . . *I need air. I'm drowning, choking, suffocating.*

I heard Ash's voice from far away. "One, two," he said. I felt weight on my chest. I felt a slight rise in my lungs. "Three!" he screamed.

My eyes flashed open. My hands flew to my throat. I sat up and gasped, coughed, gulped for air.

"Thank God! Thank God," Ash screamed. He put his arms around me and yelled, "Thank God! Oh, Em," he said, placing his ear next to my chest, listening to my heartbeat, listening for my breaths.

My throat was ragged, rough, my vision blurry and disorienting.

"Oh, Em," he said again. "Thank you, God."

"You saved me," I whispered, my voice gravelly. "You saved me."

"You saved me, Emery. How did you take me with you?"

"It's evolving." I shrugged.

"And you're getting more control."

"Yes."

"Emery, I had to perform CPR. My God, Emery, I had to do CPR for at least five minutes."

I nodded.

"I can't believe you're okay. I can't believe you're back. You *are* okay? You're okay?" He took my pulse again, pulled me to him.

"I'm fine," I whispered, but I was weak, barely conscious.

"Emery, I don't quite know how to tell you this."

"What is it, Ash? Do we need to leave now? Are they here?" I tried to stand up, and my legs buckled. Ash caught me.

"I'm pretty sure they're gone. Look outside. It's a lot later. We'll leave soon, though. In a minute." The door was open, the windows too, and the sky much darker. The cabin itself was a wreck. Had Dad done this? But Ash didn't seem to care about any of it. He watched me, only me, half carrying me to the love seat.

"What is it?" I asked.

"You . . . you're not time-traveling."

"I'm not? How can you say that, Ash? After you came with me. You saw it. You experienced it!" I was flustered. Angry. Hurt. Betrayed.

"It's not a different time you're going to."

"What do you mean?"

"That little boy. It's not me, Emery."

I looked at him for a long moment. It was almost as if I could feel the ideas and concepts and theories sliding and switching around in my brain, accommodating, assimilating.

He took a deep breath. "It's my brother."

"But he died with your mom in the accident."

He nodded, staring at me, waiting for it to sink in. My eyes widened. "Really? You're sure it's him?"

"Positive."

"It's not time-traveling," I said, mulling this over. "You think it's—"

And he said it. "I think it's heaven."

Twenty-Six

We went outside and quickly discovered the Jeep tires were slashed. I tried to picture Dad tossing the cabin, taking a knife to the tires. And it was surprisingly easy. That plastic smile on his face.

We grabbed our stuff from the back of the Jeep and left Dala Cabin quickly and quietly. We barely spoke. We slipped silently on foot into the forest, the wind ripping, roaring around us, through the evergreens. A severe, frighteningly heavy snowfall had begun while we were in the loop. And although I could feel the cold in my bones, I was so glad for this storm, so glad for its cover, for its slim-to-no visibility, because we had no idea how close Dad was, where his thugs were.

Ash grabbed my hand and pulled me off the path, into the thick of the pines. I followed him wordlessly.

I imagined at every turn that we would run smack into Dad or one of his dark-suited accomplices, but I just kept my head down against the wind and put one foot in front of the other, trusting in Ash, trying desperately to keep up. I was worn, exhausted from the loop, but I concentrated on my breathing, my footsteps.

We emerged from the woods near Winging Stables. I held my arm up against the onslaught of heavy, slushy snow falling now. It was really coming down out here, beyond the shelter of the trees. Ash led us toward Jimmy's truck, and we slipped inside.

Ash checked under the floor mats, and there were no keys. Ash flipped a panel off the dashboard, and he was in the process of hot-wiring the truck when Jimmy's stocking-hatted head appeared out of the swirling snow at the driver's-side window. I gasped, and Ash threw his arm around me in protection.

Jimmy's face registered with us, and Ash unrolled the window.

Jimmy pushed his hand through the window and handed Ash the keys.

Ash looked at him solemnly and took them.

"They came here looking," Jimmy said. "I sent them on a goose chase to the bus station. I didn't know anything . . . I hoped. I wanted to buy you some time."

"I will repay you, sir, somehow," Ash said. "The Jeep, they slashed the tires and—"

"Don't you worry about that. Just go. I hope I bought you a few hours. I'm here for you, son. I don't know what kind of trouble you're in, but I'm here for you. And, Ash, do you know your father called yesterday? Left a message with Jeannette."

Ash's jaw clenched. He nodded. "Thank you," he told him. "We have to leave."

We took off, driving slowly, carefully, holding our breath with each passing car.

"Jeannette told me about that phone call. I didn't quite hear her. I should've told you. Who do you think really called you?" I asked Ash.

"Probably the cops," he answered flatly.

We drove through town, the snow hurling down from above, big heavy flakes now, but with the wind, it looked like it was coming from above, from below, from the east, the west. It was everywhere.

We were on the outskirts of town when we saw three police cars with their flashing lights on driving quickly in the direction of the cabin.

Ash and I exchanged a dark look. Neither of us spoke.

After we reached the highway, Ash broke the silence. "They must be searching the town, the forest. They probably thought that we doubled back on them, that you crawled out the window and into the forest."

"Who knows what they think?" I said.

I dared to breathe easy only after we had crossed the Mackinac Bridge and left the UP far behind.

I was shaken by the depth of the search that would be going on for us. Dad. I tilted my head on the headrest and tried to keep my breathing even, slow.

We drove for a long time, hours. We put mile after snow-covered mile between us and what had just happened. Between us and our hideaway, our cabin, our safe place.

The afternoon turned to evening, and we were in Illinois, the highway slushy and gray from the beaten and battered snow. We stopped only for gas and coffee.

I had told Ash what Frankie said—to go home. Ash had heard him too. So that was what we were doing, hoping that Dad would not know enough about Ash to follow us there, hoping that the police would not expect Ash to show up there. But Frankie wanted us to go home. We had to.

"It's not every day that you get orders from heaven, Emery," Ash had said.

I agreed with Ash. I did, in that we had to do what Frankie said, no matter where Frankie was. But heaven? No way. No fucking way. I leaned my forehead against the car window and went over everything in my mind, every last loop I could remember, each person I had encountered there. Could it really be something other than time travel? Could I really have been so impossibly wrong for so long?

I turned my head farther toward the window, struggling

to keep myself from crying. I mean, was I dying and coming back each loop? Just going back and forth in some semi-alive state? Was each loop bringing me closer to really dying? Permanently dying? No. I couldn't face these questions right now. It was too much.

We drove past rolling snow-covered farms, one after another. They were idyllic in their white blankets of snow, each looking much the same as the last, most with Christmas trees twinkling in the windows. But I knew that I would recognize Ash's farm immediately. I had been there many times before.

I was still reeling. However, there was a small part of me that was happy to be on this road trip with Ash, glad to be together. Even as we sat here, on the edge of reason, on the edge of reality. It was silly of me, but honestly, I just loved being next to him. I couldn't get enough of that feeling.

And I was scared of what it would do to me to have to live without him, now that I had understood and experienced the alternative.

I sat in the passenger seat, watching Ash drive. His profile was strong, but the way his mouth set when he was deep in thought gave him a softness that wasn't there when he was aware of himself. He was quite possibly the most beautiful person I had ever met in real life, the five-o'clock shadow on his jaw, the disheveled wave to his thick strap of hair, the goodness in his eyes.

It broke my heart to know that he couldn't forgive

himself. I couldn't do that for him. I couldn't take that on for him. If I could, I would. If I had learned anything from the odd little life that I had lived, especially in the last few years, it was that you had to be kind to yourself. Sometimes no one else was.

Ash caught me staring at him. He placed a hand on my knee and squeezed. "We're okay," he told me, the old tightness setting in his jaw again.

"I love you," I told him, not realizing I was going to say it. It just came out. "I mean, we haven't said it, but I know—"

"Emery," he said, smiling this Cheshire cat grin.

But I had more I wanted to say. "I love you, Ash. And that you can't forgive yourself over the accident, over your father, it's terrible."

He rubbed at his stubble. "Emery, I don't want to—"

"I know. But for me, I need to talk about it."

He didn't argue with me. So I began quickly. "I need you to hear me about this. You know that it was self-defense. I'm not saying that it isn't awful, Ash. But what I'm saying is just the way you told me the story. The way you looked, what you said. I think you know that you didn't do it on purpose."

His jaw clenched. He nodded. "Maybe."

"Explain it."

"I still killed him."

"That's not it, Ash. Tell me what it is."

Ash was shaking his head then, and in a moment, he

slammed on the brakes and violently turned the wheel to the right, parking us on the shoulder of Interstate 39.

"The truth is, Emery, after he rolled onto that fucking knife, after his blood was all over the boards of our back porch, all over me, I stood up from the whole mess, and I just looked at him. I could've called the cops. I could've run for help. I didn't. All the pain and the scars, the look in my mom's eyes after he beat her. I just stood there thinking of all that, Em."

His eyes got this faraway look, and I knew that he was traveling in time, right back to the scene. He had probably replayed it in his mind thousands of times, measuring the degree of his guilt, wishing, praying for a second chance.

"I looked that bastard in the eyes as he realized exactly what was happening to him, as he dug the knife out of his throat, and I spit in his face."

Ash's voice broke on his last few words, and I heard him choke back a sob. I grabbed his hand then. "Oh, Ash."

"I left him for dead, Emery. He called out to me—'Son,' he said—and I left. I was glad he died, Emery. Glad that the earth was rid of him. And I think, I think . . . if he hadn't rolled over onto that knife . . . I'm pretty sure I would've done it anyway myself."

I leaned over and held his face in my hands.

"I'm a monster, Emery."

"You are not a monster. You are—"

"A monster, who should never trust himself around anyone ever again. I caused my mom's and Frankie's deaths, and I killed my own father."

"That's not true."

We sat there on the side of the road, cars and semis whizzing past us. And we were quiet with one another. I stroked his hair, his cheek, his lips. I held his hands in mine.

"Ash, I—"

"Emery, it doesn't matter what you say. I was there. I know me. I saw me in the moment. I knew me in the moment." He looked away, staring straight ahead.

I could feel it behind my eyes, beginning. In fact, I realized then that I was starting to always be aware of it, there, just behind my eyes, a buzzing always present, waiting for an opportunity. "Ash, you can't do this to yourself." I reached for him, but he flinched away.

"I used to always wish I could go back, just another chance to go back in time, to try to do . . . better. But, Emery, I don't know. If I was there again, in that moment. That's the worst thing, the worst truth, that I still *understand* me."

I couldn't stop it then. I gritted my teeth and tried to push it back, but it came, and my eyes fluttered, my body tensed. My breathing became ragged.

"Emery!" Ash grabbed me by the shoulders. "Don't go, Em. Stop it. Fight it." He spoke evenly right into my face, but I could hear the terror in his voice. Was it because he was afraid that this time, or the next time, or the time after that . . . I wouldn't come back?

I stared directly at Ash's face, and I fought it. I pushed against the buzzing. I concentrated on Ash's face, his deep-set eyes, that one crooked tooth. I felt my body relax just a bit.

My breathing slowly came back to normal. "It's okay," I told him. "I'm okay. I'm staying here."

Ash took my pulse then, he watched me for a few minutes, and I buckled myself back up. "We'd better get going, Ash."

He started up the car again and checked the mirrors, signaling our entrance back onto the freeway.

We drove for a long time, and the snow let up, leaving a clear night sky, deep blue-black in color, with the stars shining brightly. I watched Ash as he drove, the way the moon lit up his silhouette, the straight line of his nose, the wavy curve of his forelock. The soft pull of worry at his brow.

"What kinds of things did you bring back from the loop that convinced you and your dad that it was time travel?"

"Oh, Dad was never convinced."

"Really?"

"Dad knew—had scientific proof—that my brain activity was more than normal, was . . . evolved. But he didn't ever believe me. The team keeps coming back to telepathy, precognition of some sort. But I have always known it's more than that. It's outside of me. It isn't just an ability of mine; it is a physical transference."

Ash seemed to chew on this information for a bit.

"What is it?"

"Why can't you accept that it's heaven, Em?"

I sat still for quite a long time then.

"The afterlife," he repeated. He reached out and grabbed my hand.

"You think so?" I swallowed hard.

"Don't you? It all fits. I mean, the whooshing, the brighter feeling, Frankie. You said yourself that for the longest time you were not having symptoms of cardiac arrest, and that was what your team thought of as the most important, most impressive key. Maybe they would think now since you're having—"

"My team." I let out a laugh. "I don't want to give them any credit that they could even consider the truth of any of this. Plus, Ash, I'm going there physically now. You went with me. Explain that."

"Listen, I can't explain it all, Emery. But I think that's what it is. Don't you? I mean, if we are accepting time travel here, wormholes, loops"—he shot me a glance—"then why can't we consider heaven?"

"What about my dad in the loops?" I asked. "In the future?"

"I'm not sure," he said. "But maybe . . . it's not him."

"I think it could be my grandfather," I whispered, confessing. "He died when I was very young."

Ash just nodded.

"What about my song, though? How do I know about that?"

"I've thought about that. I don't know. Maybe . . . maybe you have to alter your version of heaven a little, Em. Maybe it's not all white clouds and angels and robes. But maybe it is . . . sort of a well of all things good . . . all creation . . . all ideas. . . ."

I wanted to have an argument against that. I opened my mouth to say something, but I couldn't think of anything, so I just said, "I've never even believed in heaven."

"I have. I mean, is it so hard to think that there's a life after death, that there's more beyond this? You can accept time travel, but you can't even consider some sort of heaven? I mean, unconditional love, forgiveness, a better place, a bigger plan? Especially after you and me . . . after us?"

I looked at him and squinted. He had to have known what I was thinking, about his father, his guilt, his refusal to forgive himself. "I don't know, Ash. You tell me. Is it?"

He didn't say anything then. His face changed, hardened, and he gave his attention to the road.

This made me mad. He could call me on my gaps in logic, but I couldn't do the same? And if it was heaven, what did that mean for me? I blinked back tears. "I can consider heaven, Ash, okay? I am considering it. It's just . . ." I sniffled then, unable to control the emotion in my voice. "I mean, is it so easy for you to think that I'm dying?"

Ash blanched, then recoiled. His mouth fell open. "Emery."
I realized then that he hadn't thought of it this way. "Em—"

"No," I said. "If it's heaven, then I'm definitely dying. I mean, look at me—"

"No, don't you dare say that, Emery. I can't even consider that." He squeezed my hand hard, and his face twisted up with emotion. He spoke fast like he had to explain this all away. "You're getting control of it. You're crossing the bridge between here and the afterlife. You're not . . . dying. You go back and forth. You slide from one place to the other."

I nodded, squeezed his hand back. "Okay," I agreed, because the look on his face when I suggested otherwise, it was horrible. He looked gutted. Devastated. I couldn't handle it. So I agreed with him. Glossed over it. Because that was what he needed to hear, and I wanted to believe him. I wanted to believe his idea of it. That it didn't mean certain death for me.

Ash held my eyes for a moment, and it was like we agreed not to go there, agreed to ignore the possibility of death. I told him, "It all sounds so crazy when you say it out loud—time traveler, a visitor to heaven. Who's to say one could be true but the other couldn't, right?" I forced a little laugh.

"A time-traveling angel?" he joked, bringing my hand to his lips, kissing it. He gave me a smile and then turned back to the road. I watched the silhouette of his Adam's apple move as he swallowed hard. And I turned my face again toward my window, and I too swallowed against the tears.

Twenty-Seven

Ash drove the Wingings' truck down the long gravel path that wound toward his home. A white aluminum fence lined what must have been a more than mile-long drive. A handmade sign hung at the entrance. It read A-OK RANCH, welcoming us.

"I made that in woodshop in seventh grade," Ash offered.

"That's Next Hill," I said, pointing behind the red barn, past the two small outbuildings. The time was well past midnight, but the stars and moon shone brightly in the dark winter sky, giving a romantic glow to the property.

"Uh-huh," Ash answered, raised his eyebrows. "You've really been here."

"With my boy . . . Frankie."

When Ash parked in front of the house, I jumped out immediately, excitedly. "I've been here!" I cried, motioning toward the red barn, then toward the blue-and-yellow farm-house.

I surveyed the landscape, taking in the farm, everything I had seen before on my many trips to the loop.

Ash took a few steps into my view, and I watched him as his eyes swept over this place. I had been so excited to be here, to see Ash's boyhood home, to prove that this was the place in my loops, that I had forgotten, for an instant, what this place meant to Ash, the crimes that it hid, the pain that accompanied every memory.

Ash stood tall, his shoulders square against the farm laid out in front of us. He slowly turned toward the house, a wary smile on his lips. There were too many memories here, too many ghosts, too many painful pasts.

"There's no FOR SALE sign," he said quietly.

He walked slowly up to the house and stopped on the welcome mat. It was old and ragged.

"I'd have thought that everything would've been auctioned off already, sold," he said. "This was ours." He scuffed his boot on the mat. WIPE YOUR PAWS, it said.

"What was your dog's name?"

"Southpaw," Ash answered. "A German shepherd. I hope he found a good home." Ash's brow knit in concern, guilt.

"Do you want to go in?" I asked.

Ash nodded and clenched his jaw. He turned the key in the lock. He grabbed my elbow and we stepped in.

The grandfather clock in the foyer struck loudly and nearly knocked the wind out of both of us.

"Whoa!" I said, and Ash grabbed my hand then. I cuddled myself into him. The clock finished, chiming for 2:00 a.m.

We walked in silence to the kitchen. It looked like a house someone still lived in. Ash tried the lights, the water. They worked, but we kept the place mostly dark, hoping not to draw attention to ourselves, although the nearest neighbor wasn't for miles.

"Someone must be staying here," Ash said, staring at the dishes in the sink, the newspaper folded on the kitchen table. "Hello?" Ash called out. We stood silently, listening. But no one answered, only the hollow echo of Ash's voice.

"Who could it be?" I asked.

"Maybe my dad's brother, or one of the men who used to work the land with Pop. I don't know."

We stood in the kitchen for a moment. Ash gave me a hard look. "It's like it could've happened yesterday."

"You don't think that it . . ." I let my voice trail off, reconsidering.

"What?" Ash asked.

"Nothing," I said, shaking my head. I noticed that Ash was staring at a knife block on the kitchen counter. Six steak knives were exactly where they should be, but a wide slot at the top was empty. The butcher knife. Gone.

"We should leave," he said, his eyes still on that empty slot. "I want to leave this house. We can spend the night in the barn. I'm sure whoever is staying here won't be out there in this weather, but they could come home any minute. Who knows?"

I watched his gaze slide over to the French doors behind the kitchen table. These opened up to large back porch, to where he and his father had . . . fought.

I squeezed his hand, and he broke his stare, shook his head. He walked cautiously through the first floor and I followed.

My eyes took in everything—the quilt on the back of the sofa, the beautiful oak floors, the photos on the walls, a knickknack shelf full of antique pocket watches. It all looked so normal, wholesome. It was hard to imagine the horrors that Ash and his brother, his mom, had had to endure here.

Ash was taut, silent. And when I saw the rigidity in how he carried himself, the at-the-ready stance of his muscles, I could instantly see what this place meant to him, what terrors it truly held. Yet it was his home.

Nothing was ever so black-and-white. I thought of my own father then.

"It even still smells like him here," Ash said. "Beer, sawdust." He walked toward the family room and sat down on the sofa then, and I kneeled down next to him.

"I'm sorry." I laid my head on his knee.

He absentmindedly played with the curls of my hair.

"Is Frankie happy?" he asked.

"Very," I answered. His posture softened.

He pulled me into his lap.

"I can't figure out how we're going to get through this, Em. I keep going over it and over it in my mind. I keep playing out all these different scenarios, and I don't know . . ."

"We'll talk to the authorities, get them to see what happened—"

"I don't even mean that. We're going to figure this thing out with you. We're going to be okay. We're going to . . . I don't know . . . grow old together. Raise our children with a German shepherd, and a white fence, and—"

He kissed me then, softly, earnestly, his hands on either side of my face.

I wanted to believe what he was saying. I wanted to believe that the cards weren't stacked against us. I wanted to believe that we lived in a world where we could just will things to happen the way they damn well should.

"We should go," he said, getting up from the couch.

I followed behind him closely.

"In the loop, Frankie told me something," I began, not wanting to upset Ash. But I knew I had to get to the bottom of it.

"What?" he asked, turning to me.

"Well, he told me to look at the key." Ash's face paled,

and I shook my head. "I'm sorry. I know it's hard, but I think there's something he wants us to know. And then it was like he showed me the accident, the two vehicles."

"Oh God, Emery, I can't." Ash shook his head. "I can't."

"Please, Ash. Just talk to me about it."

Ash put his hands on his head, and he took a deep breath, and he reached into his pocket and pulled out the key.

"It's not the same key. It's not the one from Mom's car, the one Pop made me wear. This one is more square at the top, like Pop's key to the truck. My mom always drove the station wagon. My dad drove the truck."

"So it's not *the* key," I offered. "But what could Frankie want us to know?"

"There are clippings of the accident," Ash said quietly. "They're in my parents' room, the closet. You can look at them if you have to. I can't. Not tonight. Not here in this house."

Ash walked toward the front door then. "I'm going to pull the truck behind the barn, get some blankets and flashlights. I'll be close. But hurry up. You never know when someone might show up."

I watched him out the window for a few moments. His gait was slow, his shoulders sagging. He was carrying such a weight.

I had to keep searching. I had to figure out what exactly Frankie wanted me to know.

I went up the stairs toward the bedrooms. There were

pictures, photographs on the wall leading up the stairs, a German shepherd looking like he was grinning, a smiling blond woman with Ash's eyes, a young Ash holding a small baby. My stomach lurched at the sudden understanding of just how much loss Ash had endured.

I had to look through those clippings. There had to be someone, an officer, a witness, the name of someone I could contact for more information. This couldn't be a dead end here.

This house could not be a dead end.

I flipped on the closet light of the master bedroom and stood and stared at the contents of the closet. A large, stand-alone jewelry box sat in the back of the closet, a dark wood with fancy clawed feet. A collection of antique brooches sat on top. I picked up a turquoise brooch and felt the smooth surface between my fingers. I set it down gently. On one side of the closet hung men's clothes: work shirts, jeans, dark colors. On the other side hung women's clothes: lots of pastels, yellows and greens, the prettiest pink polka-dot shirt. This struck me as so sad. I don't know why, but these details, this reality of Ash's parents, and how Ash and his father had never packed up Ash's mom's stuff. It hit me deep in my core.

I found several old boxes of photos on the shelf above the men's clothes. I sifted through a box with bank statements, utility bills. A crate full of old *Sports Illustrated* magazines. But behind that I found a shirt box. And that was it. Several yellowed clippings about the accident. I sat on the floor of the closet, cross-legged, and read them over and over.

There didn't seem to be anything new. Nothing suspicious. Nothing jumping out at me. Alvin Miller. A fellow Bloomington farmer, driving drunk. He was killed in the accident as well.

Once I had practically committed the details to memory, I rubbed at the kink in the back of my neck and decided I'd better go. Ash was probably getting worried, nervous. But I wanted to look at a few boyhood pictures of Ash first.

I couldn't help myself, but I tried to keep an ear out for any noises, any cars driving up the gravel road.

I sat on the bed in Ash's boyhood room and pushed my face into his pillow. I ran my fingers along his high school yearbook, his baseball trophies. I found a book of his sketches on his desk. I was awash in all things Ash, and I loved it.

I picked up a silver-framed photo on the nightstand next to Ash's bed. It was a younger, teenage Ash and little Frankie. I saw then that the boy in my loops was definitely Frankie. I noticed the subtle differences, his sticking-out ears, his smile to the wrong side. Frankie.

I put the photo down and quickly retraced my steps in the upstairs rooms, making sure I hadn't left anything out of place. In the master closet, I realized I hadn't put the shirt box back. When I placed it behind the crate of magazines, a different box caught my eye. It was marked "Wedding."

I took this box down quickly and opened it. I pulled

out a white and cream satin album with a picture on the cover—Ash's mom and dad, their wedding day.

They were beautiful. And happy-looking, and full of dreams for the future, surely. Had they known the heartache that was in store for them? Had she known his potential then? I felt a bit guilty looking through the album, like it was none of my business, but I had to.

Ash had his dad's build and coloring, but his looks favored his mom—the same eyes, the same line to his nose, the same crooked smile. But his mom had a beauty mark below her left eye. It stopped me for a moment when I noticed it, yet I couldn't place exactly why.

I flipped the page to a portrait of the bride and groom in front of the altar and let out a gasp.

It was *the* church. The altar, with the kaleidoscope stained glass behind them.

"Holy shit." I couldn't believe it. "Holy shit," I repeated. All my searching. Here it was. I stared at the colors, the abstract pattern.

I flipped the pages of the wedding album quickly, looking for something, anything, that might stand out, might lead me to what Frankie wanted me to find. I passed the smiling faces of Ash's parents again and again. Ash's parents dancing. Ash's parents cutting the cake. Ash's parents sitting on an old stone bench outside their church. Nothing jumped out at me. What was I looking for?

Sweat broke out on my brow now. I felt so close. I skimmed

through the photos, studying them more slowly. Over and over. But it wasn't until I was about to give up, about to search the rest of the closet, when I found what I was looking for.

As I stared at the last photo in the album, I noticed that the backing on the inside back cover seemed worn, ragged, ripped at the bottom. And my eye caught an old, tattered corner of paper sticking out from behind the backing. I tugged at that piece of paper and saw that someone had deliberately slit the backing with something, a knife or scissors. A piece of paper was hidden under there. I pulled it out quickly, carefully. It was a heavy, thick sheet of stationery. I opened it and could see immediately that it was a letter, written in blue ink, in a clumsy scrawl.

My Dearest Dolly, it began.

I felt my throat tighten then. I wiped the sweat from my brow, my heart picking up its pace. I flipped to the end of the letter and saw that it was signed *Your Joe.* Ash's dad had written this.

I felt like an eavesdropper, a criminal, a sneak. But I knew I would read it. I had to read it. I owed that to Frankie . . . and to Ash.

I've missed you. And I'm sorry. I can't begin to apologize to you. You know everything where you are, Dolly.

You know everything. You know Alvin wasn't driving his truck that night. You know that it was me, Dolly, that Alvin was riding shotgun.

You know that I let him take the fall. I didn't know he was dead when I ran off. I didn't care, I guess. I just moved his body over to the driver's seat, and I took off into Houbolt Woods there. I was sober enough to save myself, not a scratch on me.

And I tell myself that I didn't know it was you that I hit, but where you are, Dolly, you know the truth.

How I can live with what I did, I don't know. But you know I'm not the heathen that I've behaved like. Not deep inside. It's too late for me, I reckon.

I am glad for the sour pain I feel during the few times I let myself get really sober. Like now.

I deserve it. I deserve much worse.

I'm sorry. I'm so sorry, Dolly.

The letter continued for a few more lines, but the writing was smudged, blurry.

I reread the letter several times and tried to make out those last few lines. I couldn't tell what they said. But I could recognize Frankie's name. Something about "our son Frankie."

I couldn't believe it. My mouth hung open.

My heart pounded in my chest, and I could feel the buzzing forming behind my eyes. I clenched my teeth then and willed myself to calm down, to push it back.

I plopped on the floor of the closet then for a long moment, cross-legged, and placed the letter on the floor next to me with two fingers. I didn't want to touch it. I didn't want to read it again. I didn't want to see it.

He forced Ash to think it was his fault for so many years.

I hated this man. I hated this excuse for a man, even if he laid his remorse out in a letter for all to see. Because it was a coward's apology. A demon's apology.

Even if, in his heart of hearts, he truly meant it, I hated him for what he had done to Ash. Even if that letter showed a sliver of the real Joseph Clarke, I hated him. It wasn't enough that he beat his wife senseless for years? Or that he was the drunk driver? He had to blame his only living son and push his guilt onto him for years?

Could Ash really have spent the last six years of his life not knowing the truth?

I put my face in my hands then and shook my head, my heart breaking for Ash. What would this do to him?

Twenty-Eight

The snowdrifts pushed up against the west side of the barn, probably three or four feet deep, and the wind was cold, wet. But it was warmer here. Warmer than the UP, but that wasn't saying much. I walked slowly over to the wooden sliding door of the barn, the letter in my hand.

When I slid the door open, I saw a faint, warm glow of a lantern coming from the far side of the barn. It wasn't much light, but I could see enough. I could see the shapes of things, impressions. The barn was an empty and unused shell, a large rectangular building with horse stalls on the left side and a hayloft in the rear, a ladder leading up to it from the east corner. The same barn I had met Frankie in.

My eyes adjusted more to the dim light as I took a few

steps inside. The hayloft at the other end of the barn looked cushy and full of fragrant hay. And the rickety wooden walls gave more protection from the whirling cold wind than I'd thought they would.

I could see stacks of burlap sacks, old farming equipment, and a small snowblower, all abandoned near the empty horse stalls. On the right-hand wall, a collection of antique-looking garden tools hung from a pegboard: rakes and shovels, diggers and a sickle, a pair of small axes. Surely part of Dolly's collection. And there, on that same wooden workbench, sat the Victrola, the dulcimer. And tacked above that workbench was the jersey. It was dusty, dirty with cobwebs, the number *nine* not as shiny as in the loop, but still calling out to me like a beacon.

I stood nervously inside the door of the red barn and shifted my weight from one foot to the other. I made out Ash's figure in the hayloft. I walked toward him, the single sheet of stationery a heavy weight in my hand, and on my heart.

Ash gripped a small flashlight between his teeth, and he was laying out a flannel blanket over the hay on the floor of the loft.

"What did Frankie call you?"

Ash stopped what he was doing, took the flashlight from his teeth. He regarded me with a smile, his eyes far away. "Nine or Niner. Everybody called me that. My baseball number."

And, in the end, that was all I needed. It all made sense. I made my peace with it all.

I stood staring into space, accepting how wrong I had gotten everything. But I was here. I was doing what Frankie wanted me to do.

"What is it?" Ash asked, knitting his brow. When I didn't answer, he quickly backed down the slim ladder leading from the barn floor to the loft.

"I found this," I said. And I just handed him the letter. I had no words that could possibly soften the impact.

It didn't take long for him to read his father's confession. I watched the look of bewilderment flash across his face, and then his eyes went back to the beginning. He read it over several times.

"Where did you find this?" he asked, his voice low, quiet. His eyes never left the letter.

"In your parents' wedding album."

"My father was the driver?"

Ash's hand that held the letter began to shake. I saw his face flush with anger. "How did I never know this?"

"I don't know, Ash, but this isn't—"

"That bastard killed them himself. *He* was the driver!" Ash brought his hands to his head in exasperation. "All these years, Emery!" His voice echoed off the empty walls of the barn.

I looked at Ash, the depth of hurt and confusion and loss in his face, in his eyes.

"And the key," Ash said, digging the key from Frankie out of his pocket. "This key is just like the one from my dad's truck. And Alvin Miller drove the same kind of truck. Same make, same model, just a blue one, not red." Ash shook his head in disbelief.

"Frankie wanted you to know the truth," I said.

But it was like Ash couldn't hear me.

"Pop was here in that house, force-feeding me this bullshit about how I had killed them, how *I* had killed them!"

"I know." I tried to put my arms around him, but he was furious, pacing the barn floor.

"Look at the key . . . huh."

We were quiet together in the barn then, Ash with all his ghosts, all his demons. Me standing, watching him. Ash paced, shaking his head in disbelief. Every muscle in his body looked tense, his jaw, his neck, his hands—everything clenched, at the ready.

So many years—*years*—of anguish, heartache for him.

I thought again of those French doors. The scene of the crime. So many crimes there in that house.

I didn't know what to do for him. When he finally stood still, I reached for him, and I held him. I felt his tired, wiry limbs relax and give in against me. He rested his head on top of mine.

"I'm sorry," I repeated.

"I think I need a minute," he said, letting go of me.

"No, please stay," I said.

"I'll keep close. I need to walk. Clear my head."

Reluctantly, I let him leave. With his ghosts.

I watched him walk out of the barn door, into the night, into his past. I hoped that he would find peace in this somehow, at least open the door to it, open his mind.

Twenty-Nine

My heart twisted in my chest for Ash and what he was wrapping his mind around out in the cold, but I knew I was doing what I was supposed to be doing.

I climbed up to the hayloft and found a second flashlight. I stuck it in my back pocket and turned the lantern to its lowest setting, hoping to keep our hideout a secret. I finished the chore that Ash had begun, arranging us a makeshift bed.

He had brought two pillows from the house, and I fluffed them, placed them next to each other. And then I unfolded a few more blankets, laid them out for us to sleep under. I noticed that the yellow quilt looked handmade. I kneeled in the sweet-smelling hay and took the flashlight out of my pocket. I shined the light onto the seams of the quilt, and sure enough, it was all hand-sewn, a patchwork quilt with many different materials, mostly yellows and oranges, calicoes and ginghams, plaids and florals.

I wondered to myself if Ash's mom had made this beautiful piece of handiwork. As I kicked off my boots and changed into my blue flannel pajamas covered in ducks, I decided that she must have.

I quickly snuggled underneath the blankets and thought about how it would've been nice to meet her, to know her, to talk with her.

I looked up through the peaked barn roof above me. It was low, closer to me than a normal ceiling. I peered through the wooden slats of the roof. I could see the stars, clearly, brightly shining in the dark winter sky. Tiny bursts of light twinkling through the dreary gray slats. I lay there for a long moment and looked at the stars. And I hoped against hope.

I sat up for a second and reached for my backpack then, and I took out the yellow Dala horse for good luck. I looked around, searching for somewhere, some ledge, in the hayloft where I could place it. A little piece of our haven, our cabin. I realized then that there was something written on the underside of that horse that I'd never noticed. I turned it over and shone the flashlight on it. In tiny red writing, it read, "A life without love is like a year without summer. —Swedish proverb." Smiling, I placed the Dala horse under my pillow.

I snuggled into the cozy bed and tried to set my worrying aside. I tried to recapture that feeling that I usually had in the loop, that feeling of only the here and now, that feeling that nothing much else mattered. I was here with Ash, now. I smiled to myself and cuddled under the warm blankets and the soft downy yellow quilt.

I was exhausted, but my mind was reeling. The day had been too long. Too much had happened. Too much was still in front of us. What were we going to do?

I was lying in bed biting my nails when I heard Ash's boots on the ladder to the hayloft. He didn't say a word. I heard him shuck off his boots. Then I could feel the heat of his body instantly, as he lifted up the comforter and climbed in next to me. His hands encircled my waist, and he pulled me toward him.

And when I began to kiss him, really kiss him, and melt my body into his, he responded hungrily, and he did not push me away.

I awoke the next day in the early-morning hours, with only the faintest bit of light filtering into the barn. A note sat on the pillow beside me. *Out back* was all it said.

I dressed quickly. I could hear Ash behind the barn. It sounded like he was chopping wood.

I heard a new noise then, tires on gravel, and my stomach turned. A million thoughts flew through my mind. I shoved my feet into my boots and nearly fell down the ladder, running toward the sliding barn door.

I quickly grabbed the handle and pulled the door open a tiny bit, peering out at the drive. There was a car parked in the driveway, a nondescript green sedan. I couldn't see much, but then a figure came into my view. Someone walked up the steps to the house. It looked like a woman, maybe a young girl, my age. She rang the doorbell, waited a few moments, and then she looked through the window of the door on her tiptoes.

Ash intercepted her then, on the porch. And I could see them talking. They were only a few hundred feet away. He listened, nodded.

But there was something familiar about this figure. I opened the door to the barn a bit more and stepped out, sheltering my eyes from the rising morning sun blaring off the snowdrifts.

The girl turned around then on the porch, and I saw her. Gia. The same sparkly, cat's-eye glasses, the same bright smile, but her hair was short, a pixie, and her eyes were round with worry.

"Gia!" I cried. "How did you? When? Dad's not—!"

"Emery," she said, and she ran over to me and squeezed me. I responded, knowing instantly something was wrong, terribly wrong.

"Oh, Jesus, Emery. It's bad. I couldn't risk getting in touch over the phone. I came to warn you."

"I know what we're up against," I told her.

"No, you don't," Gia said.

"What are you talking about?" I said.

"This." Gia pulled her messenger bag off her shoulder.

She walked toward her car then, which I realized must have been a rental, and she emptied the contents of her bag on the hood. She looked at the items and then looked at me solemnly.

"Your dad," she said.

On the hood of the car lay a cell phone, an envelope thick with cash, and a small plastic case, holding what looked like two syringes of amber-colored liquid.

"My father gave you this?"

"I was with him in Esperanza. Them. He wanted me to come with them to find you. So I just played along. What could I do? I figured I'd try to help you out, tip you off somehow. I was at the bus station when . . . well, however you got away."

"Is he on his way?"

"No. After you two got away, he gave me this. Told me to wait for you in Ann Arbor. See if you showed up there. He gave me this stuff. He paid me, Emery. And he gave me the shots—the drugs. 'Just in case she initiates a problem,' he said. He told me that it would be 'best for everyone invested in this' if you would come happily, of your own accord, with your friend. He wanted you to come back and not know what he was capable of. Unless . . . unless you wouldn't come quietly."

My mouth hung open in disbelief. Even after everything that had happened, I still couldn't believe it had come to this.

"I'm so sorry," Gia said.

I didn't know what to say. I couldn't think of anything.

"So how did you know to come here? Now?" Ash asked.

"I told Dr. Land that I was going back to Ann Arbor. He rented me a car, sent me on my way. He was off to check Charlevoix. I think the guy at the library told him something about that. But I stayed yesterday in Esperanza, and I asked around. I remembered that lady at the bakery, and she remembered me. She liked me, believed me. I could tell she was protecting you. But I eventually convinced her I was on your side. She gave me your name, Ash, a little information. I worked out what I could, found your address. I'm just so glad that luck was on our side. That you were here."

Ash let out a bitter laugh then. "Luck," he said under his breath.

"There's something else," Gia said quietly, wringing her hands in front of her.

"What?" I said, unsure if I could take any more.

"Your Nan," she said quietly. "She passed away, Emery."

"Nan?" I whispered, bringing my hand to my mouth. I instantly thought of the loop, my Nan. . . . I couldn't believe— But yes, yes, I could believe it, couldn't I? I had seen her with my own eyes. I had met her there.

"Nan," I whispered, thinking of Mom, knowing they were together now. "My Nan."

"Maybe we could go back together . . . for the funeral. Talk to someone, anyone. Get my parents to take us to the police or—"

"Gia," I said quietly, "I can't go back there."

I watched something register on her face then, acceptance, defeat maybe. "Okay," she said after a long moment. "I believe you. I get it," she said.

"Thank you," I told her. I hugged Gia then. "Thank you for warning me, coming here."

I stared long and hard at the syringes on the hood of the car. Dad would never be able to let me go. He would never be that future dad. That dad didn't exist, and it broke my heart.

"Your father will find you soon," she said, shoving the syringes and stuff back in her bag. "You've got a day at most, I bet. If that. Especially if I don't answer his calls."

I noticed for the first time that Ash held a tiny evergreen tree in one hand, a Christmas tree, and I sensed that this was something he'd wanted to surprise me with. But I also realized that our time was done here. Things had turned.

"And don't use your email. Or use Wi-Fi," Gia said quickly. "I think that's how he tracked you to Esperanza."

"I haven't used it here," I said. "Thank you." I grabbed her hand and squeezed it.

"Should we go to the cops here? What do you think?" Gia asked, breathless.

"No, we can't," I said.

Gia looked from Ash's face to mine. "Is there more to

this story? Are there more reasons you're running?" Gia asked finally.

I looked at Gia. She seemed small, scared. My gaze flitted to Ash.

Ash simply nodded at Gia. "Yes."

"You can fill me in later," Gia offered. "But you need to figure out what you're going to do before they show up here. I mean, he's calling it a matter of national security, Emery. He's saying *you* are a matter of national security—"

"NSA," I whispered, hardly believing it, thinking of yesterday, the scene at Dala Cabin.

"Emery," Gia said, "they have a new theory. They are very serious about finding you. It's some kind of big—"

"We know," Ash offered without looking up. "We know what it is."

Gia let out a sigh. "They wouldn't tell me, of course, but it sounded big."

We three looked at each other.

"Near-death experiences," I whispered.

Gia looked stricken.

Ash cleared his throat. "And there are a lot of people who would go to great lengths to protect a . . . specimen . . . a secret that could prove an afterlife."

The seriousness of the situation sank in.

How long had Dad suspected this? How long had the team not told me? I thought of how my dad had asked me outside Dala Cabin if I had thought about death. Had he been testing me? Seeing whether I had figured it out?

"Do you want to go back?" Ash whispered. "Maybe they can do something. They—"

"No," I answered. I had come this far. And I was getting control. I was not going back, leaving Ash and permitting a section of my skull to be surgically removed.

We stood in silence, unsure of our next move.

Suddenly Ash's posture stiffened. He dropped the evergreen tree next to him and grabbed my arm.

He pointed into the distance, off toward the highway, shielding his eyes from the sun. "There," he said, pointing down the winding path to where we first turned into the lane for the A-OK Ranch.

"Who the hell is that?" he said through clenched teeth.

I peered past the early-morning sun. "A red truck. It's coming up the road. You think it's the person who's living in your house?"

"That's my father's truck," Ash said. "Let's get in the barn."

I grabbed Gia's hand, and Ash pulled us both into the barn, sliding the door behind us. He stood still and quiet, peering through the slats of the barn door, and I could see his chest rising and falling quickly, too quickly, his fists clenched at his sides.

"Who do you think it is?" I whispered, still holding on desperately to Gia's hand and Ash's arm. "Your uncle?"

"Emery, I might be losing my mind, but I swear that it looks like my father driving that truck."

I pushed him out of the way then and looked through the slats of the door. The truck came hammering down the lane, too fast, the back tires fishtailing, the driver obviously recklessly, crazily drunk. Ash leaned over, above me, and watched as well.

"No," Ash said. "It can't be."

"Maybe he made it. Maybe he lived." I felt the buzzing, the thrum, my constant companion, beginning to swell behind my eyes.

The truck screeched to a halt right behind Gia's rental car, and I watched as a large, lumbering man unfolded himself from the driver's seat. The same man from the wedding album, just bigger, thicker. With years of hard work and anger and violence woven thickly into those muscles. He turned his head toward the barn for a second, and I saw his face. He had the same dark hair as Ash, peppered with gray, but that was where the resemblance ended.

"My God," Ash whispered. "Emery, that's him. Alive and in the flesh."

"It's him," I said. My skin crawled, the look in his eyes was so dull, so animal. My eyelids fluttered then, but I pushed it back, clenched my fists.

"I left him for dead, Emery." Ash turned from the door then, and his hands went to his head. "How can this be possible?"

Gia looked out the slats through the door and turned to us, taking a few steps back from us, looking from one of our faces to the other. "He's drunk." She looked stricken. But she didn't ask any questions.

And I was silently glad for it. It was too much to think about explaining this right now.

"I just can't believe it," Ash said. He shook his head and paced.

I watched through the slats as Ash's father walked one time around the green sedan, scanned the property, and then started up the front porch. He walked the slow, labored walk of a drunk, tripping over one of the porch steps. He turned the key in the front door and let himself in.

"That bastard killed my mom and brother," Ash said through gritted teeth. He repeated it, louder, to Gia and me. And then he repeated it again, practically yelling it. His words bounced off the barn walls, echoing and hanging there in the empty space around us.

"Ash, calm down," I told him.

"No, I will not!" Ash walked to the door, banged his fist on it. "I have to talk to him, Emery. He has to hear me out. I will never be free of this if I don't." Ash stopped then, regaining his composure, turning toward me squarely.

"I have to do this. And then I'll finally be free of him."

"Do what?" I squawked. My heart leaped in my throat then.

"Just talk to him."

"I understand," I said quickly. "But not now. Not now, when you're upset. You're angry. He's obviously drunk. You're in shock over everything. You can't—"

"Now," Ash said. "I have to, Emery. I'll never be free of this if I don't."

"No," I told him. "This is crazy. You can't just walk right in there. I won't let you! This is crazy!"

Ash quickly grabbed me to him, held me close. "This is nuts," he said, putting his face in my hair. He breathed in deeply. "We'll leave after I talk to him. Start fresh, anywhere you want. Just stay here with Gia. I'm calm. See? I just have to talk to him."

"No," I said, feeling my heart beat hard. "You can't leave me. Not now. Not like this."

"Gia," Ash said, turning toward her. "Stay with Emery. You may have to revive her if she loops."

"Like CPR?" Gia asked, visibly swallowing.

"Yes." Ash nodded. "Can you do that?"

Gia nodded, her eyes wide.

"Do you have a cell phone?" Ash asked.

"Yes," she answered.

"If I'm not back in ten minutes, call the police."

"No way!" I screamed, and I pulled Ash toward me. I pulled him by his arms toward me, locking my hands around his wrists for everything I was worth. I would physically keep him here if I had to.

"Be reasonable, Ash," I said, trying to sound calm, smiling

at him. But something about my face must've given me away. I bit back the thrum behind my eyes.

Ash kissed my lips lightly. "Fight that flutter, okay?"

I laughed at the silliness of that saying, but only in an attempt to lighten the darkness I saw in Ash's face. "Ash, you don't *need* to see him. You'll never get what you need from him—forgiveness or closure or—"

"I have to face him, Emery, just one last time."

"No, you don't."

"I have to show him that I'm not him, that I—"

"You aren't him, Ash. That's why you don't need him."

He tilted his head to the left a little. He looked at me, but past me. He thought on this.

"Just walk away, Ash. We can start fresh."

"Just you and me," he answered, a faraway look in his eyes. I let his wrists go then, and he rubbed at his stubble. He pinched the bridge of his nose, turning from me. His shoulders sagged, and his head dropped into his hands.

"He's my father."

"I know he is," I whispered. "But you are so much more than his son."

Ash sighed deeply. "I can be free of him now." It was almost a question.

"I think you can." He turned back to me then, and I reached out for him. His long limbs folded into me, his head resting on top of mine.

We stood like that, together for a long moment, the

early-morning sun slanting through the barn roof, covering us with its golden light. I listened to Ash's breathing as it slowed. I felt his heart beat next to my ear.

"I saw my grandmother in the loop the other day," I said, still reeling from the news of her death, from Gia showing up, from everything.

"You did?"

"The first time ever in a loop."

He pulled back, looked in my eyes. "I don't . . . I don't know why. . . . Maybe, Emery, the reason you could always go back and forth so easily for so long, maybe it's because you're not just of this place. . . . Maybe you are . . . I don't know . . . *more.*"

"Or maybe, simply, these loops were meant to bring us together, Ash. I was sent here so you could save me."

"Or you were sent to save me, Emery."

I considered all these beautiful, intricate events and otherworldly coincidences that had played out to bring us together, to bring us here, to this now. Somehow they made sense, perfect sense.

"I love you, Ash," I told him. "But let's not talk like this. It all sounds so serious, so final."

"And we're just beginning," he said.

"Let's pack up our stuff," I said.

"Let's get out of here."

I walked toward the ladder, the loft. I motioned for Gia to come with me, and we climbed up. Ash looked through some cabinets on the east wall of the barn, collecting things for our trip.

"Where will you go?" Gia asked, helping me fold up the yellow comforter in the loft. I wanted to bring it with us.

"I don't know," I said, knowing the *where* did not matter. I grabbed the Dala horse from under my pillow and put it in my backpack. I looked around at the loft. We didn't have much to bring with us, but that was okay.

"Emery," Gia said, reaching her hand out and resting it on my arm.

"I'm okay," I said, shaking my head, blinking the tears back.

A movement caught my eye through the slats of the barn wall. I took a few steps toward the wall and peered out. I could see the back door of the house from here, and I could see someone coming around the house, walking purposefully toward the barn. It was Ash's father.

Something horrible and ferocious slunk up my spine then.

"Gia, call the police," I said, stumbling backward, hurrying down the ladder. "Stay up here and don't come down until they're here."

"What?"

"Call the police!" I hissed at her. "Call the police now!"

"Emery, I don't—"

"Just do it!" I yelled at her.

"Ash!" I screamed as I jumped the last few rungs down

to the barn floor. "It's him!" I felt the thrumming, the buzzing behind my eyes, and the edges of my vision began to fade black as I ran the first few steps toward Ash. I felt the loop about to overtake me. My body stiffened.

I smelled the ammonia. But I gritted my teeth and clenched my fists, closed my eyes against it. "No!" I screamed. "Ash!"

I bit it back, with every ounce of energy in me. I fought that swell, the buzzing. I pushed it back, pushed against it with my mind, with my body.

I opened my eyes, and I saw Ash. He stood in the middle of the barn, one hand reaching out to me, but he faced the barn door, at the ready, his muscles tense.

"Ash, it's him!"

The barn door slid wide open, the winter sun pouring into the dark space, blinding me for a second, and then I saw a dark figure, his father in shadow. His gun came into full view first. He carried a shotgun, wavering in front of him. Then a few steps more into the barn, and I saw his body, his stance. He moved forward in a drunken shuffle.

"My God," I whispered.

The pressure behind my eyes came back suddenly, ferociously. It was a deafening roar in the space behind my eyes. I held my muscles tensely, grinding my teeth, biting back the urge to just give in, let it swallow me. I couldn't go! Not now! NO!

I took a few steps toward Ash then, and I watched Ash's back. He had his arms out, as if he was protecting me. He was an imposing figure, standing there, erect, threatening, but I wanted to reach out, touch him, grab him, tear him out of there.

"Go back, Em," Ash said, never taking his eyes off his father.

My eyelids fluttered. I pushed my mind against it, but I was so tired, I was so spent.

"I wasn't expecting you," his father said, slurring his words. "I was expecting trouble, but not you, Asher."

"Let's just talk, Pop."

"Seems like last time you were here, you tried to kill me." I noticed a shiny red scar on the thick fold of his neck then. "Shouldn't the cops have found you already?"

Ash held his body taut, his fists clenched. He grabbed something out of his back pocket. He took a step toward his father then, and threw something on the floor of the barn. The letter. It landed near Ash's father's feet.

Ash's voice was low, scary. "You killed them, you son of a bitch. You and your drinking. You killed them over and over every day with the beatings and the drink. And then you really killed them. Behind the wheel, and you made me think it was my fault. For years!"

Ash's father took a few steps forward then, a sloppy, drunken gait, kicking at the letter. The shotgun wavered menacingly. "Son," he said, "ain't no one gonna believe you." There was such venom in his words, such force. It scared me. I had to do something, and do something now.

"We called the cops!" I screamed, running forward, forcing myself in front of Ash, placing myself directly in the space between the two men. "They'll be here any minute." I kept my eyes on Ash's father. He swayed from one foot to the other, and I could tell that he was more drunk than I had given him credit for. I could smell the alcohol even from five feet away.

"I don't know who you are, miss. But you shouldn't have done that," he said quietly, and then he reached out for me, slowly, lazily, keeping one hand on his gun.

Ash reacted like an animal. "Don't you touch her!" he growled, pulling me behind him, shielding me with his body. "I'm not going to kill you, Pop. I'm not going to exact my revenge. I'm not going to become *you*." Ash spoke through gritted teeth, keeping one arm wrapped around me behind him. "But don't you make me defend her, because I will, Pop. I will."

"Let's leave, Ash."

"I loved her . . . Dolly," Ash's father said. "But don't make me go to jail." He didn't lower the gun, but something about his expression changed. His eyes softened.

That was when the siren blared in the distance. I didn't know if it was that or the German shepherd running through the open barn door, or maybe the combination of the two. But what happened next was a blur, a nightmarish blur.

A loud crack—a deafeningly loud crack—erupted, and I flew backward, with Ash pushing me, throwing me, out of the way. I stumbled over the floor of the barn, landing flat on my back. I lay there, the wind knocked out of me, gasping, flailing for air, the edges of my vision going black, fuzzy. I screamed Ash's name, but I heard no sound. After what seemed like the longest of moments, I finally was able to scramble to my feet.

And I could see Ash's father sitting on the ground. He was mouthing words, but I couldn't hear them. I was deaf from the crack of the shotgun. But he was crying and pulling a limp, rag-doll Ash into his lap, the dog whimpering and hovering above them.

"No!" I screamed. "No! Ash!"

Two uniformed police officers rushed toward us then, guns out. "Help us!" I yelled, pointing at Ash's father. I struggled to get to Ash. The officers took the gun from Ash's father, and they pulled him away from Ash.

I moved slowly, so slowly. I had to get there!

"My son! I didn't mean to—" I could hear Ash's father bawling, my hearing coming back.

"Ash!" I screamed. I was on my hands and knees, pushing the dog away from him. Southpaw was licking his face, whimpering.

I saw blood, several thick scarlet drops of blood shining atop the dirty barn floor.

"No!" I pushed the dog away with all my might, and then I saw Ash's face. "Ash!" I screamed. "No!"

I leaned over him, the light of the early-morning winter

sun shining directly upon him. He turned his head a fraction of an inch. And he looked in my eyes.

He smiled.

My heart broke.

I saw the blood soaking his chest, the ragged remains of his shirt where the shot had caught him.

"Ash!" I screamed, and laid my head on his chest, heaving, crying, sobbing. "Nooo!" I pleaded. "Don't move!" I felt his face; it was cold. "Let me get a blanket—"

He grabbed my arm and pulled me back, practically on top of him.

"Emery, stop," he whispered, pleading with his eyes.

So I just kneeled next to him, and I didn't take my eyes from him. "No!" I whispered. "Please, no!"

I was semi-aware of a cop applying pressure to Ash's chest, ripping his shirt from his body, desperately trying to stop the bleeding. "Get the ambulance! The paramedics!" he screamed to his partner.

But I didn't take my eyes off Ash.

"Did you think this would happen? Did you—"

"Emery, please. No, no," he wheezed.

"Let me get something for the blood, maybe, just—"

"Emery, stay," he whispered.

I broke then. I gave in. I sobbed. I let him pull me to him, and I leaned in closely so I could hear him.

"It's okay, Emery," he said. He reached up one shaking hand to touch my lips.

I sobbed. "Ash! It wasn't supposed to be this way. It wasn't supposed to—"

"Yes . . . it was," he said. "It always was."

"I love you, Ash." I sensed he was going. I knew it. I kissed his lips.

"Love seems like such a small word right now, for you, Emery," he whispered. "You deserve big words."

"Don't go!" I pleaded, sobbing.

"It's okay, Em. You"—he touched my cheek then—"you, Emery, know where I'm going."

"Don't leave!" I screamed.

But it was too late. He took one last shallow breath, and then he exhaled, and . . . stillness.

Thirty

I heard the sirens wailing in the distance. I heard Gia's sobs behind me. The policeman began to administer CPR, but I knew.

"Gia," I whispered, not taking my eyes from Ash's face. "Just in case, tell my dad I forgive him, okay?"

"Emery, what?"

"Just tell him! Tell him I forgive him. Promise me!"

"Okay, okay," she sobbed. "I promise."

"And you know I love you, Gia. Like a sister."

I let it come then. I willed it to come.

I let it wash over me, the buzzing, the whooshing, and I didn't fight it one bit, one iota. It came, pushing, swelling behind my eyes. And I let it.

It felt the same as always, but then I felt a searing pain in my chest as I heard the whooshing, and I smelled the ammonia.

And there I was.

Ever since the beginning, all these things, these loops, the gods, the fates, his family . . . love had been leading me to Ash.

It was always that small and that grand of a plan.

Home

Here I am.

I'm standing in Dala Cabin. I look around me. The little wooden horses, their colors, are a bit more brilliant. In place of the logs, the fireplace has a small bunch of hydrangeas and wild lavender in an old-fashioned glass soda bottle. On the mantel, Dala sleeps curled up, a little ball of fluff. The windows are glistening clean, and I can see that it isn't winter. It is summer outside, all green and growing and alive.

I turn, and the door to the cabin opens. It is Ash.

Of course it is.

"Are you here?" he asks, smiling, looking whole and real and gorgeous, and even better than—no, just exactly like—real life.

"I'm here," I say.

"I knew you would be. Is it for good? Are you—"

"I don't know," I say. "I'm not seeing the halo or anything yet."

As usual, when I'm here, these things don't matter that much. The here and now, it matters. Ash matters. Ash and me together matters.

We take a few steps toward each other, and his smile is brilliant. I open my arms, and we fall into each other. He smells like soap and hay. His body feels warm, feels real, feels like . . . home.

"Your middle name is Destin," he says, and hugs me tighter.

"Yes. Who told you?" I ask.

"Your grandfather. It's French for 'fate,'" he says. I nod. Like always, he seems to have a grasp on it all, everything under control.

"I love you, Emery," he says, and he kisses my lips softly.

"I know," I say. And that's when I try it. I look down at my right hand, and just like that, without any problem, I snap my fingers.

Acknowledgments

I want to send heartfelt gratitude to the following people:

Caryn Wiseman, for believing in my writing, for showing me how to make a good story into the best it can be, and for unwavering support. This is a gift so rare.

Suzy Capozzi and her team at Random House, for loving Emery and Ash as much as I do. For believing in this story, for giving me this chance, for your impeccable editorial advice, there really are no words.

Eva, Heather, and Mom, my first readers and cheerleaders, for your inspiration and understanding, your time and friendship.

Greg, for everything, always.

About the Author

Gina Linko has a graduate degree in creative writing from DePaul University and lives outside Chicago with her husband and three children. She teaches college writing part-time, but her real passion is sitting down to an empty screen and asking herself, "What if . . . ?"